Leif stopped at the bridge. Oren, Ephraim and young Forrest hunkered around the fire pit, the flames lighting up their faces in the dark, and it hit him—they were his responsibility now, his family. And Zola, Zola was his wife. He wanted her in every way a man wanted a wife—in every way. The question; when, if ever, would Zola accept him in every way as her husband? And could he keep them all safe?

Pretty Pride

by

Dorothy A. Bell

Pretty Pride

Cover Art by *Tina Lynn Stout*

The Wild Rose Press, Inc.
PO Box 708
Adams Basin, NY 14410-0708
Visit us at www.thewildrosepress.com

Publishing History
First Edition, 2023
Trade Paperback ISBN 978-1-5092-4969-5
Digital ISBN 978-1-5092-4970-1

Published in the United States of America

Chapter One

1887

In the small tack room, her brother Forrest stuffed his clothes into the clean flour sack she'd saved for an apron. Zola set the empty feed bucket to the side of the open tack-room door. "What do you think you're doing?"

"What's it look like I'm doin'? I'm gettin' out of here. I'm goin' into town. I'll ask Ephraim if he needs a hand at the stable. Oren's always got more work than he can handle. I'll pick up the slack. I can help—do odd jobs for folks. Sleeping at the stable in town won't be any worse than sleeping here. I can earn enough money to pay for you to have a room at the boarding house. I know I can. I'll take care of you, Zoe. You can count on me."

Zola had to reach up to put her hand on his thin shoulder. At thirteen, Forrest had shot up faster than a weed in spring. He'd outgrown his clothes, his shoes. His straight brown hair, grown way past his too-big-for-his-head ears, straggled down over his dark brows, getting in his brown eyes. This morning she'd noticed he'd sprouted a few pale brown whiskers on his chin.

They weren't starving. They had fruit, vegetables, and meat, but Forrest needed what Zola couldn't provide. He needed his father and mother. She needed her parents, too. At twenty, she was all too aware of her inadequacies and their precarious position.

"Papa and Mama would want you to finish school, Forrest. You work hard enough here on the homestead."

Forrest squeezed her hand and gave it a flip to get it off his shoulder. "This ain't—*isn't,* our homestead anymore. We have no place here. We don't belong. And I'm gettin' out before that bastard Amos Emory moves in."

"We don't know Mr. Emory will be the new owner," she said and folded her hands at her waist to still the grinding, fear-fueled ache in her gut. "Besides, I promised the bank president, Mr. Shaw, we'd stay on for a while, take care of the place. We may not own this land anymore, but it will always be our home. This property will always be known as the Pretty homestead, no matter who occupies the house.

"It's not so bad living here in the barn. I mean, the roof doesn't leak, and we have heat and plenty of food. We'll go on as we always have, taking care of the stock, seeing to the gardens and the fields."

Face red, furious, Forrest tossed a pair of very holey socks across the room toward the pot-bellied stove in the back corner, then he rounded on her. "It's gonna be hell, and you know it. Emory's gonna get this place for pennies. The whole damn town knows it. Shaw, the crooked shyster, is gonna let him do it. This auction thing is a farce. Emory is gonna use you, Zoe. You think I don't know what he's after, but I do. I know. I'm not stupid. I've seen how he looks at you. He drools, Zoe, he actually drools, the slimy slug. What I don't get is why you're so all fired determined to stay on here? You could go into town right now, this morning, and get work at the mercantile or the emporium, do mending for folks, sewing, something—anything would be better than staying here and letting that—that maggot paw you, break you. I won't let it happen. I'll kill the bastard."

All the starch went out of her. Zola sighed and sat down on her brother's cot. Shoulders slumped, head down, she folded a pair of his threadbare trousers and set them aside on the bed. "Sit down, Forrest."

"No, I'm done talking. I'm done listening. I'm plain done with the whole damn mess."

She took his hand and gazed into his angry face, a boyish face, a face that reminded her of their mother. Tears clogged her throat. She swallowed the hard, cold lump. "Please, we don't have a lot of time. We've taken care of the stock, but you need to clean up, and so do I if we're to be presentable for the auction."

"Auction be damned."

"Forrest, you will stop cursing."

"Well, you shouldn't have promised Mr. Shaw you'd stand up at the auction. The whole town's gonna be there, watching. Bad enough you promised we'd stay on. Why? Why'd you do it, Zoe?"

She inhaled and let her breath out very slowly. The time had come to confess. She hadn't really understood her refusal to leave herself until last night. But this morning, she had to come clean, say it aloud, not only for her brother's benefit but to put her feelings into words to justify her determination not to abandon their home. Not yet, maybe not ever, if she could gather enough evidence. "We both believe Mr. Emory was instrumental in Papa's death. Sheriff Daniels wouldn't look into it, but you and I know Papa did not die an easy death. And Mama, going the way she did, I think Mr. Emory had a hand in that too. And now he's after the homestead, and he's after me. I read something once, '*Keep your friends close, but keep your enemies closer,'* that's what I'm going to do. If we leave now, we may never know who killed Papa or why. I have to know. I have to see justice served."

Letting go of his hand, she finished folding the clothes he'd stuffed in the duffel bag, leaving them in a pile on his cot. Coming to her feet, she wrapped an arm around him and patted his chest. "Come on, get cleaned up. We don't have a lot of time. The auction starts at one, and we have a long walk into town."

****

Auction
September 3, 1878
Pretty Valley Pioneer Savings and Loan
Prettydale, Oregon

On the podium, set up on the steps before the Pioneer Savings and Loan, the auctioneer cleared his throat and ran a bony finger around the inside edge of his highly starched collar. Removing a pair of wire-rimmed spectacles from his inside coat pocket, he placed the stems over his ears, adjusted them on his nose, and pushed them up to read the leaflet before him. "On the block today is the Pretty homestead," he said in a loud and commanding voice.

Facing the podium, the crowd in the street quieted.

The auctioneer scanned the crowd, nodded his approval before he continued. "Pretty homestead property: two thousand, seven-hundred twenty-five acres timber, six hundred ten acres high meadow, seventy-five and a quarter acres fertile land suitable for cultivation. Exclusive water rights to Pretty Creek, with permission for a pond. Dwellings: one new hay barn, one new stock barn, chicken coop, one pig sty, one domestic two-story farm house in good repair—unfurnished. Farm equipment: plow, sower, and reaper, one flat bottom sled, one wagon. Livestock: two milch cows, a dozen laying hens, one rooster, two sows, one boar, a team of plow horses, one fifteen-year-old mare broke to saddle."

The auctioneer took a deep breath, cleared his throat again, and without looking up, he waved the sheriff to nudge forward a young woman and a gangly boy who'd been standing in the shadows behind him. The young woman, a gray shawl covering her head and shoulders, gaze never landing on anyone in the crowd, arm around the boy at her side, stood chin up. The boy jerked aside to break free. She stepped back and pushed him to stand with her next to the podium.

"The bid," the auctioneer said, voice cracking, his pale countenance infused with splotches of red. "The bid for the homestead includes one domestic, a female. She can work a plow, bale hay, feed chickens, and butcher, and she's an excellent cook. One farm hand, a boy. He's a hard worker, honest, can read and write and do sums. They require no care. They have private quarters in the stock barn."

The auctioneer swallowed hard. His Adam's apple ratcheted up, then down. He coughed, and fumbled with the leaflet and the other papers in front of him.

"What the hell?" Leif Kenyon said aloud to himself. He studied the auction handbill and re-read the listing.

The man next to him, a short, stocky fellow sporting a bushy, black, curly beard and dressed for the weather in threadbare overalls, and frayed corduroy coat, leaned his way to fill him in. "Kids of the deceased: Zola Pretty and her little brother Forrest. Old man Shaw, the president of the bank, out of the kindness of his heart, and being a good Christian, gave the Pretty kids their choice of gettin' kicked out into the cold, or stay on and work. The girl chose the latter, looks like."

The crisp autumn air had a bite to it. Leif estimated there were about twenty or thirty gathered, a mixed group of loggers, farmers and their wives. No children. Everyone wore their warmest outer garments, wool coats, scarves, hats, and gloves.

The girl visibly shivered in the cold with nothing but a shawl to keep her warm. And the boy had to be freezing, too. He'd outgrown his trousers by a couple of inches. The sleeves of his canvas coat came nearly to his bony elbows. Leif frowned, scanned the crowd, and wondered what the hell kind of tragedy had brought this about.

"We'll start the bidding at six hundred twenty-five dollars." The auctioneer's voice returned Leif to the purpose of his presence here in this little mountain community.

Whispers from the crowd followed the auctioneer's opening figure. A ruddy-complexioned, pig-eyed, pot-bellied, scowling man stepped forward, removed his hat, and scratched his balding head.

The auctioneer nodded. "We have a bid of six twenty-five. Do I hear six-fifty?"

"Doesn't say anything about those two kids in here," Leif said to no one in particular and waved his auction handbill in the direction of the pathetic pair standing next to the auctioneer.

"Good, good," said the auctioneer, sounding relieved and excited. "We have six fifty. Can you give me seven, seven? Who will give me seven?"

The pot-bellied man snarled and whipped his hat off

his head.

"Seven, I have seven," the auctioneer said, his voice dead-pan.

Silence followed. No one moved or said a word.

"Now folks, the homestead is big. The timber alone is worth three, four times seven hundred dollars. Give me seven-fifty."

"You biddin'?" asked the citizen next to Leif, voice hushed.

"What?" He'd been studying the girl. She was kind of short. Unable to get a good look at her, he couldn't guess her age. She had freckles, which stood out clearly against her pale cheeks and pink nose.

"You waved your paper and made a bid of six-fifty," the citizen next to him said. "Old blackhearted Emory ain't best pleased. He's givin' you the evil eye. Bet he thought he'd steal the Pretty place and get himself a ready-made bed partner to boot."

"I didn't bid. I was pointing at the girl and her brother," Leif said and waved the handbill in the air.

"We've got a bid of seven-fifty," said the auctioneer, pointing his gavel in Leif's direction.

The pig-eyed grump whipped off his hat and hollered, "Eight hundred, damn it."

The citizen next to Leif said to him under his breath, a breath that smelled of tobacco, "Ole' Emory, bare-fisted, knocked out a steer, he did. Smacked him in the jaw, broke it. Killed him dead. He ate that steer. There's a rumor he's had three wives. All of 'em dead, gone. None of 'em lived longer than a year after they hitched up. He has a mean, black soul, does Amos Emory. I'd think twice before I go against him. Best back out now."

About to make a final call, the auctioneer raised his

gavel.

Something snapped Leif into action. He waved the paper in his hand. "Twelve hundred dollars."

"Twelve hundred going once, going twice to the brawny Swede in the back," said the auctioneer. Laughing, he smacked down his gavel. And the crowd cheered.

Twelve hundred dollars? Leif had hoped to pay less than a thousand for the property. He had a total of fifteen hundred dollars on him, but some of that he'd allotted for supplies and necessities. He always had a twenty-dollar gold piece in the bottom of his left boot. He had a bank draft for five hundred dollars in the brim of his hat, but he didn't intend on touching it unless he absolutely had to.

He'd visited the homestead the day before yesterday and surveyed the timbered land. The house looked sound enough—it would need a white-wash and a new roof in a year or two. The outbuildings appeared neat and in good repair. The livestock, healthy. The stockyard fences could use some new rails. The timber, consisting of blue spruce, cedar, and Douglas fir had Leif salivating, eager to set up his mill and get started.

Pretty Creek, fed by a small lake near the crest of the Cascades, ran all year round. The exclusive rights to the creek came as an excellent bonus. The road to the homestead, not more than three or four miles from town, needed grading. All in all, he thought it a prime investment and a bargain if he could get it for a thousand. Two hundred over his bargain price didn't worry him overmuch. Actually, he'd expected more competition.

But the girl and the kid? A confirmed bachelor, he didn't know what to do with them. The girl, from what little he could see, wasn't a kid. Her brother, by the mulish expression on his face, looked to be a handful, surly and obstinate. Then again, who could blame him? The humiliation had to be overwhelming.

Leif made his way forward. The crowd parted for him. The pig-eyed, pot-bellied, belligerent bidder blocked his progress and slapped one of his meaty paws to Leif's chest. The other paw he balled into a fist and thrust it in the auctioneer's face. "God damn you, Shamus Prine, you didn't give me a chance to counter the bid."

The auctioneer, a sneer on his lips, huffed and said, "The bidding is closed, Amos."

Leaning over the podium, Mr. Prine looked Leif in the eye and asked, "You do have the twelve hundred in cash, sir?"

"I do," Leif said loud enough for all to hear. He opened his coat to reveal his money belt.

Perspiring, Mr. Prine gave him a nod of approval.

"All I got on me is eight hundred, and you know'd it. I could get the cash as soon as the bank opens Monday, Prine," said Mr. Emory.

"Amos, this auction has been posted for a month. It is as it says in the ad a cash-only auction, no checks or promissory notes."

Mr. Emory gave the podium a push and set it to rocking back and forth.

Mr. Prine caught it before it toppled over.

"Nobody around here 'cept me's got that kind of cash on hand," Emory shouted and waved his hand out over the crowd of gawkers. "Never figured on no outsider. Those kids...the girl, they done this. They brought this...this rube in. Bet he's some relation." Hand raised to strike, Mr. Emory lunged at the girl.

Leif grabbed Mr. Emory's wrist and wrestled it down to his side. Bending down, he got in the man's face. "I found the notice of this auction in the Oregonian. The Central Oregon Crier picked it up. I've been keeping an eye out for timber property."

Sputtering, red in the face, Emory called him a son of a bitch.

"Mr. Emory, Amos," said Mr. Prine, stepping out from behind his podium, "I'd like to proceed with the business. Excuse us, please." He waved Leif to follow him inside the bank.

Chapter Two

Through a veil of very hot and humiliating tears, Zola stepped away from the podium, the quarreling bidders, the crowd of interested onlookers, and made her way to the alley between the bank and the mercantile. She pressed her back to the cold, hard stone of the bank wall, closed her eyes, and let the tears flow.

Forrest followed her. Muttering to himself, he kicked at the loose dirt, busted bricks, and stones. "That's the fella...he's the one who came snooping around the other day. I'm sure of it," he said and picked up a brick and chucked it, hitting an empty crate at the end of the alley. He shuffled his way back to her, stood next to her, put his back to the wall, and slid down on his haunches, head in his hands.

"Yes, I believe it is the same man," Zola said. Ruthlessly, she swiped the tears from her cheeks with the back of her wrist.

They'd watched the tall, broad-shouldered stranger from the hayloft, staying in the shadows, thinking he was from the bank or one of Emory's men. He inspected the house, peering in all the windows, testing the porch floor and posts. He entered the barn, opening and closing stall gates and tool boxes. He'd gone out to the corral to check on the gates and posts, and the breeze took his hat, tossed it into the dust freeing a head of thick, wavy, tawny hair. Retrieving his hat, he'd faced the barn, and she got a good look at him and thought him handsome in a plundering Viking sort of way.

Forrest sniffed and wiped his nose on the back of his coat sleeve. "Well, one good thing, he routed Emory good and proper. I guess we should be grateful to him for that."

"True. Yes, we should be grateful," Zola said, feeling far from grateful about anything.

"I want to go home, Zoe," Forrest said, coming to his feet.

Zola stiffened her spine and tugged her shawl closer about her. "Yes, home, let's go home. There's nothing more to be done here."

"When do you s'pose he'll move in?" Forrest asked, looking up and down the street when they reached the head of the alley.

Zola tugged her shawl around her shoulders and neck. "I don't know. We have plenty to do. Garden is waiting. Potatoes to dig up, apples to pick, beans to dry."

****

Inside the bank, Leif signed the last of the documents and handed Mr. Prine his pen.

"When do you propose to take full possession? We'll have to file this deed with the state. It could take a month, but you can take possession any time," said Mr. Prine, tucking Leif's document copies into an envelope.

"A week or two, I should imagine," Leif said offhand. "It would be helpful to know a bit more about the Pretty family misfortunes."

Mr. Prine sat forward in his chair, thin, well-manicured fingers laced together. "Well, as I explained, and as the documents to the title state, Mr. Pretty acquired the original portion through the Land Donation

Claim Act of 1850. When he took a bride, she claimed her three hundred twenty acres. He also took advantage of the Homestead Act and added the timber property. Then, over the years, Mr. Pretty filed claims on the mountain behind the homestead and wisely acquired exclusive rights to the creek."

"Yes, yes, I understand all that, but how did the bank get hold of this property if it was doing so well and with so many obvious resources for income?"

Mr. Prine sat back in his chair, a contemplative, shuttered expression on his face. He pressed his thin lips together and combed his mustache with his fingers. "Confidentially, I don't fully understand it myself. Three years ago, almost to the day, Mrs. Pretty, Eleanor, took to her bed, and three months later, around Christmas time, she passed. Next thing, the stock barn caught fire right after a big storm, must've been around March or April of last year. Some thought a lightning strike. We'd had a couple of big storms about that time. The big barn burned to the ground, taking with it a large portion of the feed barn. Then came the summer, and some kind of poisonous weed killed off a hundred head of Pretty's cattle. Mr. Pretty, Abner, put up the timber as collateral to rebuild the barns and restock, so he couldn't cut any of it until he paid off the note. The barn got built, but again the livestock perished, what with one thing and another. He hired a crew to eradicate the poison weed. His neighbors were fearful it would spread to their fields. Mr. Emory, the nearest neighbor, being among the loudest.

"With little income, Mr. Pretty borrowed more money to pay for harvesters. He collapsed, died, this last spring, must've been late May or early June. The bank had to take what little profit he garnered from his harvests and put it toward the loans. Miss Zola sold off everything that wasn't nailed down in an attempt to reduce the loan but by September she'd missed three months of payments. Mr. Pretty had only been paying on the interest, not the principal, which made the homestead a total of six months in arrears. We had no recourse but to repossess and put it up for auction."

Leif took a few moments to digest it all. "What's this Emory want besides land?" he asked.

Mr. Prine rose abruptly and stood before his window looking out onto the main street, hands clasped behind his back. "Lately, he let it slip a couple of times there might be gold in Pretty Creek. And there's talk of the Northern Pacific line connecting the valley up with the Central Oregon Southern Pacific. There's a really good pass that follows Pretty Creek and the Pretty homestead property."

Mr. Prine turned around and met Leif's interested gaze. "And...he wants Miss Pretty. He's been bothering her. She's been holding him off. He's sore as a bear with a bad tooth today. He had dreams of joining the two properties, building a dynasty."

Leif, mouth open, chuckled before saying, "I can understand the railroad, but gold? Is there any proof of gold in Pretty Creek?"

Thumbs hooked in the fob pockets of his satin vest, Mr. Prine shook his head. "None that anyone has ever heard of. South of here, along Price Creek, they've found some. But I'm going to warn you now, Amos Emory isn't going to leave this alone. I shouldn't say it, but I must warn you, he's a dangerous man.

"Miss Pretty is adamant he spread the poison weed

around on purpose. And personally, I wouldn't put it past him. She also firmly believes Mr. Emory is responsible for her father's collapse. She claims her father was beaten to death. No one was allowed to see the body. Sheriff Daniels denied her claim. Again, I wouldn't put it past Emory. And as for the sheriff, Daniels, he's good friends with Mr. Emory."

Lips drawn up to the side, Leif considered the warning. "I'll want to hire someone right away to look after the place until I return. Now I've seen Mr. Emory in action, I think it best not to leave the place in the hands of a defenseless young girl and a boy. Can you recommend someone reliable, a trustworthy man who would be interested in the position of foreman?"

****

Emerging from the alley, Zola put her arm around her brother's shoulder. The gig pulled up in front of them, the horse nearly running them down.

"Get in," Amos Emory said, voice a snarling order. He lumbered out of his conveyance and lunged for her.

Head bowed, shoulders hunched, Forrest rammed him in the belly, fists flying. "Get your dirty hands off my sister. She ain't goin' nowhere with you."

Mr. Emory shoved Forrest to the ground.

Slapping at Mr. Emory's arm, Zola bent over to help Forrest up. Mr. Emory wrapped his arm around her waist and picked her up off her feet. "Let go of me."

****

Exiting the bank, Leif heard the scream. A gig blocked the entrance to the alley. The source of the commotion appeared to be the Pretty kid, arms flailing, balled fists pounding on Mr. Emory's back.

Mr. Emory could do little to deflect the kid's strikes,

he had his hands full of one kicking, scratching, biting, redheaded female wildcat. Leif came up behind the man and put him in a hammerlock. "Put her down," he said quietly, calmly, dead serious.

Mr. Emory hesitated to comply. Leif increased the pressure against his Adam's apple. "Put her down. Put down my property...*now*."

The Wildcat, taking advantage of Mr. Emory's immobilized state, chomped down hard on his meaty thumb, drawing blood. Her attacker yowled in protest and dropped her. She landed on her hands and knees in the dirt of the street.

Leif tossed Emory aside and sent him headfirst into the street. The fancy bay horse shied, and the wheels of the gig rolled over Mr. Emory's arm. Leif ignored the man's howl of pain and turned to help the girl. "Miss Pretty, are you hurt?"

"No, no thank you, I'm fine," she said, and brushed a long, lush strawberry coil of hair from her flushed face. Taking her arm, her feet getting tangled up in the skirt of her dress, Leif helped her awkwardly to a teetering, somewhat unsteady upright position.

Emory had righted himself and grabbed Leif by the arm. "Mind your own business," he said, huffing, puffing, but unable to move Leif out of his way.

Leif let go of Miss Pretty. Towering over the man, he wrapped one hand around Emory's throat. "Miss Pretty and her brother are my business. Leave now, or I'll press charges of assault and attempted abduction."

Emory slapped his hand away, laughing in his face. "Oh, that's a good one, that is. Out of the way? I'll see Miss Pretty gets home."

Leif opened his coat and revealed his sheriff's

badge. "I don't know who represents the law here, but I'm sure someone inside the bank will know."

Emory sputtered, opened his big mouth, appeared to think better of it, threw up his scratched and bleeding hands, and backed away. "I'm goin'. I'm goin'. But I'm not done. You got no idea what kinda trouble you got with these two. And you got no idea who you're dealing with. No idea."

"Oh, I think I do. Now get." Leif waited for the gig to move off before addressing Miss Pretty and her brother.

"Are you sure you're not hurt?" he asked her, placing his hand beneath her elbow.

"Thank you, I'm fine, really. We need to be on our way. Forrest, let's go. Thank you for your assistance," she said. Her arm around the boy's shoulder, they started to walk away.

"Wait, we need to talk. I'm glad to have caught you two." Lief couldn't see her face with her back to him, but her head went up, and she froze in place.

The boy took another step, but she put her hand on the boy's arm to hold him back. Chin up, she slowly turned to face him. "If we're to get home before sundown, we need to be on our way."

"Look, I'm hungry," Leif said. "You both must be hungry too. It's cold out here, even in the sun."

She wasn't a beauty, not with those freckles. But her mouth, those lush, full, rose pink, fleshy lips, reminded Leif of a not fully opened rose blossom. Her shawl hung off her arms exposing a neat, well-endowed figure. Her horrible brown dress followed the curves of her full bosoms, her tiny waist, and rounded hips—maybe a little tummy. And then her glorious red hair. It did leave a man to wonder where else he might discover such a thick patch of curls. He calculated she might be in her early twenties, her brother around twelve or thirteen years of age.

Miss Pretty, cheeks flaming, brown eyes spitting fire, set her jaw. "Yes, we are hungry and cold," she said. "You may have bought our home, but you did not buy our minds or our will. We can feed ourselves once we're home." Her pert, patrician, pink-with-cold nose in the air, she walked away.

"I could order you to stay," he said to her back.

She spun around. "Is that what you're doing? Are you ordering us?"

He shook his head. "No, I'd rather we start our...our partnership on a friendlier footing. You tell me your concerns, and I'll tell you mine. Until an hour ago, I had no idea you and your brother were included in the sale. We need to talk."

"Partnership? A few moments ago, I was your property?" she said, those luscious lips drawn up into a sarcastic sneer.

He shrugged his shoulders and acknowledged the hit. "Needed to use a word Mr. Emory would understand. If you and your brother are going to be living on...on land I now own, I'm going to feel responsible for your safety. I'm sorry it has to be this way. But we don't have a choice."

Some of the starch went out of her, and her shoulders sagged. The boy turned his head and gazed off into the distance, boyish cheeks wet with tears, lips trembling. Miss Pretty put her hand on her brother's arm. Eyes downcast, she said, "Yes, I suppose it would be best to set the ground rules right off." She brought up her gaze and glared at him. "We have no money to buy a meal. There's a quiet place to sit at the livery. We could talk in private there."

Leif heaved a big sigh. He took her arm and turned her firmly in the direction of the hotel. "I can see right off there's one area where we're gonna have big problems, Miss Pretty. Come along, Master Pretty, I'm buying you and your sister a meal, and we're going to talk."

Chapter Three

The Abbot sisters, seated near the atrium, lingered over their Saturday afternoon tea.

Oh, drat it anyway. Of course they're still here. Zola ducked her head.

The moment they entered the dining room, those two old heads turned in their direction. They smiled benignly at her, curiosity fairly shining from their silver-blue eyes and sweet, wrinkled old faces. Zola couldn't very well ignore them since they were being shown to a table in the corner. Doomed to go right by the two biggest gossips in the whole county, she stopped short of their table and forced herself to smile. Forrest made a face and turned his back on them, leaving Zola to make introductions.

Mr?...God, I don't know his name. How can I introduce him, my new owner, when I don't know his name? Drat, drat, double drat.

"Good day, Miss Gladys, Miss Paulette," she managed to say.

"We watched the whole disgraceful display from here. How very mortifying for you, dear," said Miss Paulette, her lips drawn up in a tight pucker of disapproval.

"You must be so relieved Mr. Emory didn't get his way. He's a horrible man, just horrible," said Miss Gladys, her lace hankie pressed to her little nose.

"And you outbid him," she said to *Mr. whatever his name.* "My, my, you're a big fellow and such lovely, wavy, golden hair. Are you Swedish?"

Zola cringed and looked anywhere but at the man who stood next to her with his warm hand on her elbow. There were three more groups of diners scattered about the large dining room. Thank God, she didn't know any of them. She wanted to die, die right here on the spot.

"The name's Leif Kenyon," he said. "And yes, I am now the very proud owner of the Pretty homestead. My mother, she was Swedish and my father, Irish. They passed away when I was a boy."

Zola pressed her lips together, aware he was being deliberately condescending. She doubted the Abbot sisters would notice.

"Mr. Kenyon," Zola said, grateful to have his name fresh on her tongue, "these two ladies are longtime residents of Prettydale, Miss Gladys Abbot and her sister Paulette. They own the Abbot Emporium across the street."

"Pleased to meet you, ladies," Mr. Kenyon said. He tipped his hat to them in deference. "Please excuse us. Our table is ready," he said. His hat over his heart, his hand firmly on her arm, he moved Zola along.

Forrest had already sat down at their table. He waited, chin in hand, elbow on the window ledge. "Darned old busy-body tabbies," Forrest said. Zola poked him in the ribs with her elbow as she removed her shawl and draped it over the back of the chair Mr. Kenyon had pulled out for her.

Seated, the waiter filled their water glasses and left the menus.

"I'm sorry I couldn't introduce you. I didn't know

your name," she said once the waiter had left.

"There's a pair of those old tabbies in every town," Mr. Kenyon said, perusing the menu.

Forrest snorted in the midst of drinking from his glass of water. Again Zola poked her brother in the ribs with her elbow.

She tried to read the menu but found it hard to concentrate. Up close, the imposing, not exactly beautiful or handsome Mr. Kenyon's dark blue eyes pinned her down—intense and direct. His face, tan, had dimples, one on each side of his almost-too-big face, right where the cheekbone meets the jaw, and he had a cleft in his square chin. The way he walked and talked, he exuded authority and self-confidence. She envied him. These days, frightened all the time, day in and day out, she'd adopted a false cover of bravado that displayed itself in waspish retorts. The harder she tried to suppress her anger—angry at everything and everybody—the more it popped out like a prickly rash from eating too many strawberries.

The waiter returned to take their order. Zola hadn't decided, couldn't decide, and in the end, it didn't matter.

"I had the roast beef sandwich last night," Mr. Kenyon said to Forrest. "It came with mashed potatoes and gravy."

Forrest nodded, eyes big, "I'll have that," said her brother, nearly drooling like a hungry dog.

Not wasting time to give Zola a chance to speak, Mr. Kenyon spoke for her—and himself. "The lady and I will have the roasted chicken and asparagus with Hollandaise sauce. And coffee all round. Bring plenty of cream and sugar." And with that, he shut his menu, snatched her menu from her, gathered up Forrest's menu, and handed them to the waiter, who left them in a rush to reach the kitchen.

"I think it's time we properly introduce ourselves. My name is Leif Kenyon. I'm in partnership with my brother, Gunnar. We own a sawmill in Centerville on the other side of the mountains. I was a county sheriff for a few years. I'm done with that. I want to start up a sawmill on this side of the Cascades. As the crow flies, our Centerville Mill isn't all that far away on the other side of the crest. Eventually, we'll get a road through. All this will take a few years, but we've got time."

Forrest swallowed hard, eyes round, clearly impressed. He squared his narrow shoulders and said, "My name's Forrest Maxwell Pretty. I'm thirteen."

Zola sat mute, tongue-tied, and blinking while she absorbed Mr. Kenyon's ambitious plans for her home.

"Glad to meet you, Forrest," Mr. Kenyon said. He stretched his arm across the table and offered his hand for Forrest to shake.

Forrest eagerly shook hands. Mr. Kenyon grinned and folded his big arms on the table top. "So you'll need to go to school," he said to Forrest.

Forrest threw back his shoulders, chin up. He started to speak, but a squeak erupted. Blushing, he closed his mouth and cleared his throat. Dipping his chin, he lowered his voice an octave and said, "Nah, I'm done with that. I need to stay with my sister. Work the farm. Take care of things."

"Forrest, we talked about this," Zola said, using her waspish voice of authority. "You will go to school. And that is the end of the conversation.

"He will attend school," she said to Mr. Kenyon and held out her hand for a firm shake. "My name is Zola

Louise Pretty. I am past the age of having to attend school." He grinned at her. Her cheeks on fire, she found his grip surprisingly gentle, unnervingly warm— intimate.

Forrest opened his mouth, no doubt ready to argue with her or give Mr. Kenyon her age. It didn't matter. She had to stop him from doing either. Thank God Mr. Kenyon interjected to ask a question.

"Where were you two when I was looking around the place?"

To avoid looking him directly in the eye, Zola squirmed in her chair. "We were in the hayloft behind the doors. There are some knotholes, pretty big ones."

"Why? Why did you hide?" he asked her, golden brows furrowed, his blue-eyed gaze boring a hole in her head.

She hesitated to explain. Forrest started to say something. She elbowed him hard. He clamped his lips shut and glared at her.

"Mr. Emory comes around," she said, shoulders back, hoping to disguise her fear of the evil Mr. Emory by portraying a façade of indifference. "He's sent men around to check on us. The bank sent men around, too, to appraise the property. Afraid they'd send the sheriff, Forrest and I thought it best to keep out of sight, hide. When the bank foreclosed, they said we couldn't stay in the house. I begged Mr. Shaw to at least allow us to stay in the barn until we could find somewhere to go. When he said we could stay if we stayed on as hired help and put in an appearance at the auction, I took him up on his offer, at least for the time being. With winter just around the corner, at least we'll have a roof over our heads and maybe food. A few days ago, Forrest overheard some men talking at the stable. He found out the suggestion of our staying on as hired help had come from Mr. Emory. He intended to bid—become the new owner—take over the homestead and, we assumed, keep us under his dirty thumb."

Appearing to have lapsed into deep thought, chin in one hand, elbow resting on the table, Mr. Kenyon narrowed his gaze. The waiter served them their meal, and thankfully, Mr. Kenyon was distracted from the topic. Forrest set to with a will. Mr. Kenyon picked up his knife and fork and began to dissect his chicken.

Zola took a deep breath. Savoring the heady aroma of the well-prepared meal, she nearly swooned. Embarrassing her, Forrest applied a liberal amount of cream and sugar to his coffee. She really wanted to do the same. She was cold, chilled to the bone. The coffee smelled so good, and the lovely pitcher of rich cream had her mouth watering in anticipation—and the sugar, oh, the sugar.

Be damned pride—she drove her spoon into the sugar bowl three times, then poured a generous stream of thick cream into her cup until her black coffee turned a satisfying light beige. Sliding down her throat like fine satin over the skin, the first sip of the deliciously warm liquid settled her frayed nerves. Restraining the urge to dive into the food on her plate like a starving pig at the trough, she carefully, slowly, daintily began to enjoy the meal.

She didn't know if she should be relieved or insulted that all conversation had ceased, but in silence, she finished her meal and felt considerably better for it.

Mr. Kenyon sat back in his chair, pensive. The waiter came around and refilled their coffee cups.

Forrest shoved his plate back, put a hand to his mouth, unable to muffle the rumbling sound of his belch.

Mr. Kenyon tried unsuccessfully to hide his smile behind his coffee cup. He set down his cup on the table and said to Forrest, "I'm going to send you on a mission, so listen carefully. You're to go to the emporium." Fishing in his money belt, he pulled out two twenty-dollar bills. "Take this and buy yourself two pair of trousers, good trousers, long-lasting ones, two work shirts, two pair of woolen long johns, a winter coat, gloves, socks, and a hat if you need one. Oh, and a pair of good work shoes. If you have any cash back, you might want to buy your sister a pair of gloves."

Zola slapped down her napkin. "No," she said. "No." She laid her hand on Forrest's wrist to stop him from taking the money. "Mr. Kenyon, we have clothes. I'm refitting some of his father's trousers, and I'm going to take in a wool coat I think will fit him soon enough. And I don't need any gloves. We don't want anything from you. We'll work for our keep."

Forrest dropped his hand, his gaze passing from Mr. Kenyon's determined countenance to Zola's tight jaw.

"Miss Pretty, your brother is going to be under my employ, and I will not have him improperly attired. It's clear your brother has long since outgrown his garments. As you say, winter is coming. He's going to go to school. He can't go in rags."

Forrest opened his mouth. Zola, certain Forrest meant to restate his case as to why he no longer needed to attend school, pinched him, in no mood to hear it.

Mr. Kenyon stopped them both and addressed Forrest directly. "You will go to school. You will exceed all of your sister's and my expectations and master all of your subjects. You will also work for me. After you get home from school and when you're not attending school, you will earn a wage."

Mr. Kenyon trained his blue eyes on Zola. Unappreciative of his high-handed way of dealing with her brother, assuming he now had the authority to order them around, she glared at him.

"As for you, Miss Pretty...Zola, I want you to burn that dress you're wearing today. I presume you wore it on purpose to discourage Mr. Emory. I won't insult you by giving you cash as I know you'd spit on it and fling it in my face. However, I hope you have something more serviceable than that shawl to protect you from the elements. Otherwise, we'll have to go shopping for you, too."

Mr. Kenyon looked to Forrest, who sat there, mouth open, totally useless against the insults she'd sustained.

"Go," Mr. Kenyon said, waving him to be off. "Go now. We'll meet you in half an hour at the Emporium."

Forrest scooted his chair back, took the money, and sprinted from the room.

Zola opened her mouth, prepared to give Mr. Kenyon a piece of her mind. Holding up his hand, he stopped her. "Do you know Ephraim Gooding?"

The burning fires of her outrage summarily dashed to a hissing steam. She could do little but blink, blink, and sputter. At last, she gathered her scattered thoughts and answered his question, "Yes. Yes, of course I know Mr. Gooding. What has he got to do with my needing a winter coat, gloves, or—anything?"

"What's your opinion of his character?"

Flustered, she fussed and folded her linen napkin to give herself time to think. "I don't know. He's a hard worker, honest. He and his son helped us rebuild the barns. He does good work in a timely fashion."

"You trust him, then?"

She drew up her shoulders and huffed. "Of course I trust him. He's a decent man, and so is his son. Why? Why are you asking?"

"I'm going to hire him as my foreman for the farm if he'll accept the offer. I'll be busy getting the mill set up. I'm not a farmer or a rancher. You and Forrest will have to vacate your quarters in the barn for Mr. Gooding and his son."

Trembling, lips pressed tightly together to keep herself from throwing up, tears welling up in her eyes, clogging her throat, she said, or rather croaked, "I see. Well, thank you for the meal, I guess."

She couldn't bring herself to look him in the eye. It was all too dreadful. "You're willing to take on Forrest, and for that, I'm grateful. You'll see he goes to school, and that's good. It's me, then, me that needs to go, and I understand," she said. She brought up her gaze and caught him staring at her, a look of confusion on his face, lips pulled up to the side, golden brows drawn together.

He leaned across the table, his big face getting in her face, voice low and mesmerizing. "Miss Pretty, Zola, you and your brother need to move back into your home. You should never have left it. It is your home. Go home, Miss Pretty."

She shook her head, disbelieving her own ears. "The house? You want me and Forrest to move back into the house? Live? In the house, with you?" She sent a glance around the dining room, her voice barely above a whisper. The Abbot sisters had left the room, thank goodness, but there were still two tables occupied by diners. "No, Mr. Kenyon, we can't. I won't. We couldn't," she said, horrified by the very idea.

He put his hand on hers. "We can," he said. "As my wife, we can live under the same roof."

Indignant, Zola snatched her hand out from under his hand and gathered her shawl about her shoulders. "Thank you for the meal, Mr. Kenyon. Forrest and I will move out of the barn. You may have the house, the farm, the creek, the water in the creek, the timber, the flowers in the meadow, the rain, the snow, the blue sky, the eggs, the milk, and the fires in the grate on a cold winter's day, but you will never have me as your wife." Highly incensed and shaky, she moved to stand.

He latched his fingers firmly around her wrist. "Sit down, Miss Pretty. You and I have a problem."

Reluctantly, she sat down, not because he ordered it, but because her legs wouldn't hold her. It wouldn't do to make a scene. Somehow she would live through this nightmare—somehow.

His gaze fixed to her, he said, "I can't sit inside a big warm house knowing you and your brother are shivering with cold in a dark, rat-infested barn. I wouldn't be able to sleep. Either way, in the house or living in the barn, neither of us will be able to face our neighbors or ignore the whispers. Think of Forrest? How is he supposed to keep his head up in school? Bad enough he's lost his parents and the security of a loving home. You, I'm sure, don't want to shame him further. My solution is simple, we marry, and we all save face. You take care of the house, see to the gardens, the chickens, cook meals, and prepare food stores like you've always done. It will be a partnership arrangement. I'll provide for you in every way you will allow."

Zola wanted to scream. He held up his big hand again. She clenched her jaw so tight her ears hurt. She was beginning to hate that hand.

"Hear me out. You will be free to live in your home, warm and safe. I will not place any demands on you. This will be, as I said before, a partnership. There are benefits for both of us. Think about it, please, Zola. Talk it over with your brother."

Zola tipped her head to the side, lips in a tight line. She thought about it for a second and chose her words very carefully. "So far, you've been doing all the talking. When, exactly, is it my turn to voice my concerns? I thought this was going to be an exchange."

He had the decency to look chagrined, a flush coming to his strong cheeks. "I thought that's what I was doing. I was anticipating your concerns and addressing them straight on."

"What if I have a suitor? What if I'm betrothed, and I wish to marry? I can't very well do that if I'm stuck with you for the rest of my days. You assume I have no other recourse but to accept all of your *well-laid-out* solutions to my dilemma."

He did blush then and shifted in his chair. "Ah," was all he could say. "So you have a suitor? I didn't realize. I'm sorry. I didn't see him today. Did he not know of the auction? I would've thought he would want to help you."

Blushing furiously, she let him squirm a bit, then huffed. "I said, *what if.* I didn't say I had a suitor."

Chin up, she said, "I don't want one."

Using great restraint to keep herself from yelling at him, she said, "Men, you're all alike: dictatorial, heavy-handed managers, every one of you. You never think to listen or ask or consider. You just assume we're all too stupid, dimwitted, or weak to care or have a logical thought. Well, manage away, Mr. Kenyon. You're absolutely right. I have no choice in the matter. I'm in no position to argue or barter. But know this, I resent it. I resent having to hand over my future, my life, to you—my home to the bank. I know, I know I should be grateful and thank God and my lucky stars I don't have to put up with Mr. Emory. At least you look like you bathe."

To her everlasting chagrin, Mr. Kenyon leaned back in his chair and burst out laughing, a big laugh, big and loud, and everyone in the dining room gawked at them. Zola prayed the floor would open up and swallow her.

Chapter Four

Walking ahead of them, Forrest juggled all of his packages and entered the livery stable's dark interior. "Ephraim? Mr. Gooding? It's Forrest Pretty, Mr. Gooding. Are you in here?"

"Mr. Gooding and his son live in a shack behind the stables," Zola said. She scanned the busy street and nodded to the passersby. Blushing, lips pursed, she said to Leif without looking at him, "They both do odd jobs. Forrest is good friends with Oren, Mr. Gooding's son. They often go fishing and camping together."

They'd walked the full length of town together. Leif had taken her elbow when they stepped off the boardwalk and onto the dusty street. It felt right. Feeling protective, he kept her close to his side. They were stared at, of course, he, a stranger, and the newly auctioned off Miss Pretty at his side. She bravely nodded, acknowledging her neighbors, chin up and shoulders back. Leif suspected her predicament chafed her pride considerably. The woman had a lot of pride.

"Master Forrest," came a deep, resonating voice emanating from the deep shadows in the far corner of the stable. "I'm over here. Got to get this wheel back on Mr. Dorrant's wagon. Done busted right in two. I fixed it, though. A'course I done, like I always does."

A beam of sunlight from the open stable doors shone upon the straw-littered floor marking the center aisle. A dark figure, dressed in bib overalls over faded, red, long johns, broad-shouldered, thick arms and legs, stepped into the light and started towards them.

Ephraim Gooding was ebony dark, black eyes swimming in pools of pink, bloodshot sockets. Exposed in the smile he offered Forrest and Zola, his teeth shone white against the black of his complexion. He dipped his head slightly and did a little bow coming within a few feet of his guests. "Ma'am, Miss Pretty, how are you and Master Forrest? I worry for you."

Zola folded her hands at her waist and smiled. "We're fine, Ephraim. This is Mr. Kenyon. He bought our...*the*...homestead."

"Yes, Ma'am, I watched him do it," Ephraim said without giving Leif a glance. "Mr. Emory, he didn't get his way this time, no sir."

Leif stuck out his hand to the man. "Mr. Gooding, Mr. Prine recommended you to me, as did Miss Pretty."

Ephraim furrowed his meaty brows and shook Leif's hand in a crushing grip. "Yes, sir? I do odd jobs for folks. You got work for me?"

Leif, well aware colored folk were not allowed to buy or own land or property in Oregon, now understood why Mr. Prine had suggested Mr. Gooding as a good prospect for the job he had in mind.

"I'll be setting up a sawmill on the Pretty homestead. It'll take up a lot of my time for the next few years. I'm not a farmer or a rancher. I need a good man to act as foreman. I understand you've got a son?"

"Yes, sir. He's finishin' out to the Nolan place, puttin' in a new privy."

Leif smiled. Zola stepped back, allowing him to speak more one on one with the man. "I can't give you a house, but Miss Pretty and Forrest, from what she's told me, have set up a living space in the barn. I haven't seen it. You could do it up to suit your needs, Mr. Gooding. I would see you have the lumber and whatever it takes to make you comfortable should you decide to take me up on my offer and become Pretty homestead foreman."

A huge tear wended down Ephraim's brown cheek. He scrubbed it away with the back of his hand and wiped the moisture off on his coveralls. "I'd be proud to take your offer, sir. I surely would. And thank you."

Leif put out his hand again, prepared to take the bruising grip to seal the deal. Ephraim shook his hand and pumped it up and down. When he let go, Leif flexed his fingers to encourage circulation. "Good. I'm hoping you can start right away, tomorrow. I have to get back to Centerville and organize the move of my equipment. I'll be consulting with you on good men to work as logging and mill crew. We'll talk wages tomorrow for you and your son. I'll want to hire him as lead hand. Forrest is going to work when he's not in school. Your son, does he attend school?"

Ephraim shook his head. "Nah, my boy is a grown man of twenty years."

"I hope he'll want to stay on, live on the homestead and work for me."

"I can't say, but he'd be a fool if he didn't."

"Right. It's getting late," Leif said, noticing the sun had shifted the light to an angle in the doorway. "I'd like to rent a buggy for Miss Pretty and Forrest to use to see them home."

****

"I'm taking the reins," Zola said and gave Forrest a little push to move over. She hoped Mr. Kenyon hadn't heard her. She had held back the tsunami of bitter emotions, but she didn't know for how much longer she could control her calm façade. In less than a half a day, she'd lost her home, been put up on an auction block, sold to a stranger, nearly kidnapped, rescued, and proposed to—albeit in a benign business-like fashion—and now she desperately needed to take control of something, even if it was only a cob horse and buggy.

Forrest waved to Ephraim. Mr. Kenyon gave her a nod and tipped his hat. She set the horse in motion. Leaving the town and all its curious eyes behind, the peace and serenity of the woods, shadowy and cold, called to her, urging her to run, run away.

Forrest, hanging on for dear life to the back of the buggy, had to shout to be heard, "It's getting dark, can't see the road that good, you might want to slow down. Deer out this time of day. Come down to the creek for a drink. You mad or somethin'?"

"Yes," she said.

And yes, he was right. It was getting dark.

And no, she couldn't see the track very well.

And yes, the buggy was bouncing all over the road. It would be easy to lose control.

"No," she said, changing her answer. "No, I'm not mad, I'm…I'm oh, I don't know, resigned. I can't fight this or find a way out of it." She pulled back on the reins, slowing the winded horse down to a nice, safe gait.

Forrest let go of the back of the seat and settled himself. Looking forward, he hugged all of his parcels, arranging them on his lap. "Well, I don't think it's so bad. Mr. Kenyon seems all right to me. I got some good clothes to wear. Now you don't need to worry about me so much. I'll be goin' to school and workin', makin' a little money for us. And Ephraim and Oren will be better off livin' on the homestead with us, than in that old shack in back of the stable. Mr. Kenyon don't strike me as a mean man, not like Emory."

Zola groaned. Forrest had lapsed over the last few months into very poor grammar. She'd heard him swear too. Papa and Mama would not approve. "It's *doesn't*. Mr. Kenyon *does not* strike you as a mean man, Forrest. I know you know better. You've missed the first week of school. If you want to stay on the good side of Mr. Kenyon, you need to start Monday as you mean to go on."

"You don't like Mr. Kenyon, do you?" he said, more as a statement than a question.

"It isn't a question of liking him or not liking him. The problem I'm having is I…*we*…don't have a choice."

Forrest went quiet. They were nearing the gates to the Emory place. Zola hoped Mr. Emory wasn't lying in wait for them.

Reading her mind, Forrest said, "He's probably passed out drunk on his corn liquor by now."

They sailed past the Emory farm gate, and both of them breathed a little easier.

"Hey, I just thought of somethin'," Forrest said. Bouncing on the seat, he set the buggy to rocking. "Ephraim and Oren are gettin' the room in the barn. Is that what's got your dander up? Kenyon gave Ephraim our room in the barn. Is that why there's steam comin' out your ears?"

"There's no steam. What a silly thing to say." She looked off into the trees and to the creek running to the side of the road. The dead-end lane up to the homestead was near now. She hesitated to tell Forrest how Mr.

Kenyon planned to solve all of their problems, but now was as good a time as any. "Mr. Kenyon wants us to move back into the house. We'll do it in the morning before Ephraim and Oren arrive."

Forrest didn't immediately reply. She hoped she wouldn't have to give further explanation. She could feel the blood rushing to her cheeks.

"Butttt…Mr. Kenyon will want the house, won't he? That don't…*doesn't*…seem right. Us…you…living…and Mr. Kenyon living…and Ephraim and Oren all us men…living—there'd be talk. There will be talk, won't there? I mean, we heard about Rosemary Baker and that salesman she took in." Forrest gasped. "That's it, isn't it? He…Mr. Kenyon, he cornered you into makin' a deal with him. He did, didn't he? Damn him. And here I was thinkin' him a nice kind of fella, and us lucky he bought the homestead instead of Emory. He's no better than Emory. He's just prettier."

"Oh, Forrest, no, it wasn't like that at all. He simply thinks we should marry to put a proper face on the situation. And that's more than Emory was going to offer. Mr. Kenyon is right, of course, but it feels like duress, all the same."

"It sure as hell is. He can't force you. I won't let him, the skunk."

"We wouldn't be man and wife, Forrest, not like Mama and Papa. I'd sleep in my room, and he'd take their room—I guess. If I marry him, we'd have a home, a good home with security and standing in the community. He's going to create a new business. It will bring in a lot of money and prosperity for a lot of people in Prettydale. We need men like Mr. Kenyon. We, you and I, could be part of that. If Mr. Kenyon had come along while Mama and Papa were alive, and he courted me proper, and I…I liked…it…and he asked me to marry him, our parents would have told me I would be a fool to turn him away. He's what is known as a catch. I need to think about this. Think it through."

"But Zoe, marriage, that's for life, ain't…*isn't* it?" Forrest said, and put his hand on her shoulder.

Twilight held as they crossed the Pretty Creek bridge. The wooden slats clattered and echoed in the cool evening air. Ahead, less than a half mile, was home.

The gate's open," Forrest said.

"I see that." Zola drew back the reins and brought the buggy to a halt before turning into the lane.

"I smell smoke," Forrest said. He jumped out of the buggy before Zola could stop him. She whipped the horse into action and arrived at the barn in time to see him throw open the barn doors and disappear in a gray ghost of deadly smoke. Screaming his name over and over, she fell out of the buggy and landed on her knees.

In what seemed an eternity, coughing and gagging, Forrest reappeared and crawled down the ramp of the barn and into the yard. "No fire. Manure. Horse shit in the stove. Damper closed. Door open. He set it. Emory set it. Heard us coming. He did it," Forrest said and retched and gagged.

She recognized the smell of it now, sharp and a sickly sweet, a hot barnyard smell. The smoke started to clear, wafting out the door and the hayloft above, obscuring the first stars of the evening. She rushed to the well and returned with a ladle of water. Holding his head in her lap, Zola urged Forrest to drink. Stunned, they sat there in the yard, Forrest's head resting in her lap, smoothing damp hair off his brow.

Everything they owned, their clothes, their bedding, and a few meager mementos were in the tack room in the back of the barn. Thank goodness Forrest had new clothes he could wear. There were a few of her mother's things in an old trunk. Perhaps they could be salvaged, spared the stench of the smoke. She'd have to wash them. They could go to the house to sleep, but they had no bedding now, no blankets to keep them warm, no mattresses. She doubted the stench would ever go away. It would soak into the wood of the walls.

****

On the walk back to the boarding house, Leif passed by the big window display at the Emporium. A mannequin with red hair, wearing a hideous green bonnet covered in a vomit of silk roses on her inanimate head, stared unseeing out the window into the street. But, the olive green, empire-waisted coat with the red fox fur collar and gold buttons stopped him. The color would be perfect for his Miss Pretty.

His Miss Pretty?

The idea made him stop and shudder.

What the hell? I don't want a wife. I don't need a wife. But...she should have that coat."

Paulette Abbot tapped on the window and waggled her fingers at him to come inside.

An hour later, he exited the Emporium, the lady's coat with the fox fur collar, two pairs of kid gloves, a fox fur hat, two cashmere dresses suitable for a northwest winter, and two pairs of heavy cotton stockings bundled up in boxes. All, Miss Paulette and Miss Gladys assured him, were Miss Pretty's exact size.

On his way to his room at the boarding house, he held no illusions Miss Pretty would thank him for presuming to shop for her, let alone shop for such personal items. He chastised himself for his impetuous purchases and for his big-mouth proposal. But what else could he do?

He faced a sleepless night. Therefore, in his room, he sat down to make lists of the must do's and don'ts. The hall clock struck half past the hour of two a. m., and he laid down on the lovely, downy bed, arms behind his head, eyes wide open to stare at the dark ceiling.

He'd spent more than he should. Now, being Sunday, the bank would be closed, so he might as well go out to his new home with Ephraim and his son. Deciding he could postpone his departure until Monday, he closed his eyes.

That was the excuse he gave himself, but in truth, he wanted to be sure Miss Pretty and her brother had made it home without incident. He didn't trust Amos Emory. He felt pretty certain Ephraim had Emory's number, but to be sure, he'd make it plain Ephraim had his permission to do whatever he had to do to protect not only the homestead property but Zola and Forrest as well.

Funny, he couldn't stop thinking about Zola Pretty, how she'd stood up to him, faced the auction. She was a strong woman. He liked strong women. He'd run across a few. If he had to marry, then Zola wasn't a bad prospect. They'd find their way as partners. She'd keep him on his toes. He chuckled at the thought. Yeah, she'd be a pain in the neck most of the time, but he didn't doubt for a minute once she said her vows she'd be true to her word.

Chapter Five

Fully clothed, boots on, lying on the boarding house bed, Leif awoke at dawn. He blinked several times to orient himself and clear his head. He'd gotten the timber and the land he'd set out to acquire at a good price, but the conditions of the bargain stuck him with a female and her sassy kid brother, neither of which he wanted or needed. He swung his legs over the side of the bed and scrubbed his head with his knuckles.

Face washed, hair brushed, dressed, he gathered up the boxes and packages filled with the things he'd bought for Miss Pretty. He bundled them together with the lengths of twine salvaged from the smaller packages to make it easier for him to carry. Downstairs, he checked in with the landlady to let her know he meant to stay another night.

Outside, the streets were quiet, and he noticed Prettydale didn't have a saloon. Come to think of it, Saturday night had been very quiet. Centerville had two saloons. Saturday nights were wild, with fistfights, drunks, squealing women, out-of-tune pianos, the air smelling of cigars, sweaty bodies, puke, and beer.

At the end of the street Ephraim, out front of the stable, was loading a large Saratoga traveling trunk, two cots, and two mattresses into a wagon. "Quiet around here," Leif said upon approach. "Got a few things here for Miss Pretty. All right if I put them under the seat?"

"Good mornin', Mr. Kenyon. Sure, go 'head." Offering Leif a brief nod of approval, Ephraim went on to say, "There's no liquor for sale in this town. Mr. Pretty, he was a Quaker gentleman. He married outside his church, but he set up the bylaws and platted the town, staying true to his faith. Mr. Emory, now he's got a still. A lot of folks buy his corn. You a drinker?" Ephraim asked, stopping his work.

"No, I was a sheriff, and I've dealt with too many drunks, cleaned up their jail cells after a night of drying them out. Can't stand the smell of the stuff. Part of the reason I decided I'd had enough."

Coming out of the barn, balancing a large wooden tool chest on his huge shoulders, there appeared a young man Leif assumed to be Oren Gooding, Ephraim's son. He was just as dark as his father, but he had to be twice as wide as Ephraim. The man shoved the big chest into the bed of the wagon with no effort at all.

"This is Mr. Kenyon, Son," said Ephraim.

Oren, black eyes narrowed, broadcasting his disdain, offered Leif a curt nod.

"Oren," Leif said and stepped forward, hand extended, "you look like you could break my hand. I hope you don't. I like my hand."

Oren lowered his strong chin a fraction and shook Leif's hand, giving it a good pumping. "Pa said you offered him a foreman's job at the homestead?"

"I did," Leif answered. "I'm offering you lead hand. I'll pay Ephraim twelve dollars a month and found. And you ten dollars a month and found. Living quarters? You build to suit in the barn or out, makes no difference to me. I understand you two built the barn, so you know its layout better than I do. You two know a lot more about the whole property than I do. I'll supply the lumber, pay for whatever you need to make it livable. You can read and write?"

Oren snorted. "Course I can read and write and do ciphers in my head. I got to or get cheated."

Leif nodded. "Good. Before I leave town, I'll set up an account at the mercantile. I'll leave instructions only you two men, Miss Pretty, or Forrest can sign. I'll be keeping accounts. Miss Pretty will keep track of household inventories, and you will have to maintain the inventories to keep the homestead running. We'll all work to keep ourselves fed, warm, and dry."

Oren snorted again. "While you get rich," he said under his breath.

Leif offered the young man a sheepish grin. "Eventually, yeah, I hope it works out that way. But for the first two or three years, I don't expect to see much profit. As a matter of fact, I'll be lucky to break even. Right now, I have a time problem. I have to leave, go back over the mountain, get equipment, and God knows what all, packed up and ready to ship over here. I'm counting heavily on you two to keep a watch over the homestead, especially Miss Pretty and Forrest."

"You don't know us," Oren said, wide nose in the air, chest out.

Leif narrowed his gaze. "Oh, I think I do. Mr. Pretty hired you to rebuild his barns. You take Forrest fishing, don't you, Oren? Miss Pretty says she trusts you.

"Ephraim. You come highly recommended by Mr. Prine at the bank.

"I need you two. I need you because you know the people here. You know who you can trust and who you can't. I already know about Mr. Emory. I liked Mr. Prine, but I'm not too sure about Mr. Shaw, the owner of the bank. I'm going to need a crew, a hard-working crew, to work the mill. I'm gonna depend on you two to help me when it comes to the hiring. I can't think of a better choice for foreman and lead man than two men who've worked for most of the folks around here."

Oren, his big head tipped to the side, chewed on the inside of his well-rounded brown cheek. His sloe-eyed gaze never left Leif's face, and he nodded. Finally, he said, "Got some tools I gotta load up, then I'm ready to go," and he stepped around Leif and the wagon with a purpose.

"Good, Son," Ephraim said and shrugged his shoulders.

"That's as close as you're gonna get to an agreement with the boy, Mr. Kenyon." Ephraim unearthed a skein of rope from his hip pocket and tied a knot on the front loading hook, preparing to tie down his possessions. "You mean it about protectin' Miss Pretty?"

Leif went to the other side of the wagon, waiting for Ephraim to send the rope end across. "I do."

"Then I have to ask you this if I'm gonna be livin' and workin' the homestead 'cause Miss Pretty and her brother is left on their own, so to speak." He leaned his big arms on the side rail of the wagon, pinning Leif down with his gaze and asked, "You movin' us to the barn? Where's that leave the Miss and her brother?"

"The house, of course. They never should've moved out. It's their home." Leif caught the end of the rope Ephraim sent his way and tied it to the hook on his side of the wagon, then sent it back to Ephraim.

"I'm gonna ask you straight out. You plan on beddin' her?" Ephraim asked, his voice a low, threatening growl.

Leif took a deep breath and let it out, and looked the man straight in the eye. "I've asked Miss Pretty to be my wife. I promised her a partnership with no demands on her person. Should, in time, we form a compatible fondness for one another, well, I would, yes, bed her if she would allow me the pleasure."

Ephraim clicked his tongue and tipped his head in a show of approval. Oren brought out more tools, then another big trunk and they started for the Pretty homestead, Leif on a borrowed horse from the stable.

The creek this morning took his attention. It was moving, but at a low level. This was fall, and they hadn't had a lot of rain on either side of the mountains since spring. A pond, the homestead needed a pond. Mr. Prine had mentioned the county had given approval for a pond.

Today Leif looked closer at the Emory farm, the gate, and the fence line. The house was imposing, with a big porch and lots of windows. A lot of house for one person, Leif thought. They crossed the rickety, loose board bridge that crossed Pretty Creek, and he made a mental note to get it reinforced. Traffic, heavier traffic, would soon destroy the bridge, and it needed to be wider.

Ephraim took the wagon through the gates to the homestead. Leif reigned in his mount and dismounted to take his bearings. He planned a road to go around the farm and up the mountain. A lot of good timber would have to be removed. It would be a good start and a good test for his mill.

He led his horse through the gates to find the wagon abandoned in the yard. Hearing voices coming from the stock barn, he entered and instantly smelled the smoke-saturated wood. The smell had a tang to it, unfamiliar and yet familiar. The door to a small room at the back stood open, and that's where he found Ephraim and Oren standing at the back of the room looking down at Forrest, who was on his knees shoveling ash from the little pot-bellied stove into a coal scuttle.

"Emory set the fire. I know he did," Forrest said to Ephraim. Leif hung back to the side of the door. "He put a shovel full of horse flop on top of hot coals, then closed the flu and opened the door. He must'a heard us cross the bridge when we come…came… home last night. He was here waitin' for us. You should see the garden, Mr. Gooding. It's all tore up. Zoe cried and cried. I'm gonna kill the son-of-a-bitch. I swear I will."

Ephraim put a big hand on the boy's shoulder. "We're here now, Forrest. Oren and me, we'll get this place slicked up smart in no time."

"I gotta finish cleaning out the stove and wiping down the walls with vinegar water. I told Zoe I'd do it, and I'm gonna." He wiped his nose on his shirt sleeve. "Zoe's around back. We dragged our cots and all our clothes out back last night. We slept on the porch wrapped up in Pa's coat and a tarp."

Leif didn't wait to hear more. He started across the yard, heading for the back of the house.

Hunched over a huge caldron of water set over an open fire pit, still wearing that horrible brown dress, Zola stirred a pot full of gray, soapy wet clothes and bedding. Tears in her eyes, steam curling her damp hair, she sniffed back a sob.

Leif stopped and looked beyond her clothesline to her garden. The signs of a horse's hooves and horse shit were everywhere, the lawn torn up, turf turned over. String, poles, vines uprooted, cabbage and collards torn to shreds, beets mashed, and beans were everywhere. The rider had ridden up and down the rows of corn, slashing and stripping them, mowing them down. It was hard to comprehend what kind of madman would do such a thing.

"He broke through the fence," Zola said without looking up from her wash. "That's our fence across the field. Luckily, Forrest and I had put the plow horse and the team in the corral, and the milk cows in the shed, before we left for town yesterday morning. The rider came from Mr. Emory's farm and returned in that direction." She swiped her arm across her forehead and pushed her hair out of her face. "Help me wring this out?" she asked, winding the quilt around her paddle.

Leif fished one end of the quilt out of the water, and Zola found the other end. Together, they wrung the hot water out of it and hung in on her line. They did another quilt and two wool blankets, then Leif excused himself.

"Where are you going?" Zola asked him.

Leif shoved his hands in his pockets, jaw tight, unable to look her in the eye. "I think I need to pay a visit to Mr. Emory."

"No, no, Mr. Kenyon," she said, grabbing him by the arm.

Rage got the better of him, and he pulled her close to his chest, his chin resting on her soft, sweet, damp, carrot-red curls. "He trespassed and did damage to my...our...property, Zola. I can't let it pass." She stayed in his arms, even wrapped her arms around him. Then, as if coming to her senses, she shoved away from him, and he let her go.

"No violence, I won't countenance violence," she said, her little chin up, cheeks flushed pink, perspiration highlighting all the freckles across the bridge of her nose.

"Violence?" he said and burst out laughing. "I won't leave a mark on him, I promise."

"Men," Zola said and returned to her chore.

Chapter Six

Leif caught Forrest emptying his bucket of stinking ash over the paddock fence near the wood pile. "Come with me. We're going to harness our wagon to Ephraim's team. Then we're going to pay Mr. Emory a visit."

"You and me?" Forrest asked, skipping to keep up with him.

"You, me, Oren, and Ephraim."

Forrest gave out a whoop and spun around. "I'll let Zoe know we're gonna see Emory gets what's comin' to him."

Leif caught him by the collar. "She knows."

Oren and Ephraim helped harness the livery team to the homestead wagon in short order. "Miss Pretty has asked for no violence," he told them. "I'm going to call it persuasion with a strong emphasis on reasoning non-violently."

Oren grinned and nodded, but Ephraim remained sober and silent and set the wagon and team in motion. Ephraim and Leif sat up front, and Oren and Forrest stood up, leaning over the seat.

"Forrest, how many men does Mr. Emory keep on hand at his farm?"

"None that I know of. He hires men to do the haying and harvesting and most any other chore that needs done. But none of them live at his place."

"Would any of these men be around the place

today?"

"Nah, it's Sunday. Not many men will work a Sunday.

They pulled the wagon up to Emory's front door. "Forrest, you go to the barn and find some rope, some short pieces and some long. Don't show your face back out here. You stay out of this."

"But…"

"No but's. You take orders from me now. Understand?

"Yes, sir."

The boy jumped down off the wagon and made a dash for the barn.

In his long-johns, bleary-eyed, Emory staggered out of his house. The way he stood, swaying, shading his eyes from the bright morning sun, Leif would bet a blistering hangover cursed the man.

"Good morning, neighbor Emory," Leif said, being purposefully cheerful, hoping Emory would find it irritating.

Hearing Mr. Emory's snarl, it pleased him no end he'd managed to do exactly that. "The name's Leif Kenyon. I'm your new neighbor. We weren't properly introduced when we spoke yesterday. I'm here to remedy that. You have a mighty fine place here—big house for one man," he said, sizing up the house, taking his time to study its gabled, two-story construction and Dutch style. "I'd like to see your barn, your stock. I'm not familiar with what animals do well here. Perhaps you could guide me. I'm more of a lumberjack, not a farmer. I'm sure you have only the best."

Emory ran a big, dirty hand down over his face, swallowed and hooked his thumbs in his armpits, and stuck out his chest. Eyes scrunched, squinting against the morning sun, he answered, "I do. Nothin' but the best. Recently acquired a pretty little mare. Gonna' breed her with my stallion. He's a purebred Tennessee Walker."

"Well, I sure would love to see her and your stallion too. And I'm sure Mr. Gooding would be interested."

While Emory sat down on his bench to pull on his boots, Oren and Ephraim got down off the wagon. Stepping off the porch, Mr. Emory beside him, Leif started across the yard. Emory cast a nervous glance over his shoulder to Ephraim and Oren, who followed close behind like two giant shadows.

"Ephraim's going to be acting foreman on the homestead, and Oren will be my lead hand," Leif said.

They all stopped inside the doorway to the barn, allowing their eyes to adjust to the sudden dimness. Ephraim went around them, going down the line, stopping before a stall that housed a big sorrel stallion.

"That's a good-lookin' animal," Leif said, moving closer. Emory followed. Oren, right on his heels, trailed him.

Ephraim touched the beast's nose. The horse tossed his head. Ephraim said something indistinguishable, more of a purr, and stroked the animal's jaw, then his ears, smoothing his hand down the animal's strong neck.

"You look out. Snake don't take to darkies," Emory said, a sneer on his lips.

Leif balled his fists, itching to punch the man's teeth down his throat.

Ephraim grinned. White teeth bared, he defiantly opened the stall gate. The horse whickered, backing up.

Leif, Oren, and Emory moved closer to look over the stall gate. Ephraim ran one big hand down Snake's powerful neck and the other down his front leg. Lifting his hoof a couple inches off the floor, he extracted a piece of twine, a few leaves from a root of some kind. Using his finger, he dug out a clump of really dark, rich soil and grass. The powerful horse stood quietly, head down, eyes shuttered, in repose.

Ephraim nodded to Leif, backed out of the stall, and shot the bolt. In a sudden and surprising move, Oren locked Emory's arms behind his back, shoving him to the ground, causing him to land on his big belly.

"Ooofff." A wad of bile jumped out of the man's mouth.

Forrest jumped out from behind an open stall door and handed Oren a piece of rope. Oren tied the man's wrists behind his back. Emory cried out a couple of curses, struggling to roll over. Ephraim helped him, toeing him in the side like you would a log. Once on his back, Ephraim put his big, booted foot across Emory's Adam's apple to convince him he should stop thrashing around. Grinning, Oren shoved his booted foot between Emory's legs, putting pressure on the man's crotch.

"Tsk, tsk, tsk, Mr. Emory. You left my garden in a state of disgrace," Leif said, motioning Forrest to hand him a long length of rope, which he handed off to Oren with a silent nod, pointing to the strong beam overhead. "That wasn't at all neighborly," Leif said, bending down, dangling the string and the bits of vegetation in front of Emory's nose.

Oren made quick work of tying the rope around Emory's ankles. Ephraim tied a knot in the loose end and threw it up and over the beam. He and Oren hoisted Emory off the barn floor, bringing the man up to hang upside down like a big ole' side of beef in the middle of his barn.

Wriggling, howling, Emory cursed his tormentors but to no avail. "You son's-a-bitches. Let me down."

"Not until we come to an understanding," Leif said, voice calm and smooth. "A good neighbor does not destroy fences or gardens. And they do not throw horse shit on burning coals to make a nasty smudge pot in their neighbor's stove. Those types of transgressions create animosity, hostility, and inspire revenge in me. As do insults and slurs made to those in my employ and under my protection. It is my natural inclination, as a former man of the law, to haul you up before a court and let them toss your sorry butt in jail. I have evidence right here in my hand and I have witnesses.

"But…and this is a very tenuous, fragile *but*—and by that I mean you stick to the terms of the deal, or I see you behind bars before you can spit—*but*—we can come to some kind of agreement—neighbor to neighbor, this morning, right here, right now.

"So listen up, you piece of scum, I've already expressed myself concerning Miss Pretty and her brother. Perhaps you dismissed my warning as an empty threat with no bite. So I repeat," he said and grabbed Emory by the ears, cranked his neck around and gave him a spin that sent him swinging across the center aisle and slammed him into a stall post. Above Emory's howls of pain and distress, Leif shouted his terms. "Leave them alone. Leave Miss Pretty alone. She will soon be my wife. You touch her, you harm one hair on her beautiful head, look crosswise at her, and I will throw your bloody carcass to the pigs. The same goes for her brother. Leave him alone. Stay the hell off my property. Stay the hell away from the Pretty homestead." Emory's body swung back in his direction, and Leif gave him another twist and grabbed hold of his hair, giving him a push. "Now, do we have an understanding?"

Ephraim caught Emory and shoved him out, changing the direction of his trajectory. Oren caught him, and the two played catch the hog.

"Yes," Emory cried, twisting like a snake.

"Yes, what?" Leif asked.

"Yes, God damn your dark soul to hell. Yes, I understand."

"Understand what," Leif asked.

"Leave Miss Pretty alone and…and the boy."

"And…"

"And…and stay the hell off your cursed property."

"Ah, well, that wasn't so hard, was it?" Leif said and stepped in to put a halt to the game of catch the hog.

"Untie me now. Let me down," Emory cried, slobbering, sounding pitiful.

"No, no, now, not so fast. We've come to the part of the deal where you make restitution."

"What?" Emory squealed, "Jesus Christ-a-mighty. I can't think. You gotta let me down. I'm gonna puke."

"You created a great deal of damage to the garden. Beds, walls, and clothing were ruined by nasty-smelling smoke, smoke that probably will never be completely removed. As I said, we can settle this quickly, right now, between us, or I can take you to court and exact—no—demand, an exorbitant amount of money to replace all that was lost and to heal the anguish you've caused Miss Pretty and her brother."

"What? What? You want money. I got money. I'll get you all the money you want tomorrow when the bank opens."

Leif rubbed his chin, lips twisted to the side in thought. "No, I don't think cash will cover what was lost."

"Beds, you said beds. I got beds. Take'em."

"Now that's more like it. Mattresses, too, and pillows, quilts, and comforters."

"Hell and damn. Go. Loot the damn house. Just let me down."

"First, let me hear you apologize for the damages, and then apologize to Mr. Gooding and his son, beg their pardon for your insulting language."

Mr. Emory started to protest. Leif raised his foot and set it against Emory's backside, prepared to give him another shove to the far side of the barn. Oren got in a position to catch him.

Mr. Emory cried, actually whimpered, and apologized for the damage to the barn, the cabbage, corn, beans, and profusely begged Mr. Gooding and his son's pardon.

Leif, satisfied, waved to Ephraim and Oren. "Lower our good neighbor, Mr. Emory, down. But, as a precaution, leave his hands bound behind his back. We don't want to have to resort to physical blows. Let's go to the house and choose some items to replace what was lost. What a good neighbor you are, Mr. Emory," Leif said and helped the man to stand, his arm around Emory's shoulder while Oren untied his ankles.

Chapter Seven

Zola turned her back on Mr. Kenyon, dismissing his intent to pay Mr. Emory a visit. Men will do what men will do, so her mother had said many, many times over. Hanging up the last sheet, it occurred to Zola, Forrest must not go with them. Running around the side of the house in time to see the wagon pass between the home-gate, frustrated, she stamped her foot.

Harassing Mr. Emory would only accomplish one thing—more vicious and subversive attacks. How dare Mr. Kenyon allow Forrest to become involved in a senseless and potentially dangerous, most certainly violent, mission to extract justice from a man who had no moral compass what-so-ever.

Combing her fingers through her tangled curls, she considered it could very well be time to admit she'd lost control of her little brother. Sadly, now thanks to Mr. Kenyon's influence, he'd set off to rough up their neighbor. Last week he'd skipped school. She'd heard him curse the rooster and blaspheme, and now this.

And speaking of losing control, what about that embrace she'd shared with Mr. Kenyon? Shamefully, she'd absolutely reveled in the heavenly feel of his strong arms around her—the solidity of his chest beneath her cheek. Blushing, she called herself a hussy and a fool. She'd brazenly put her arms around his waist. Out of control, she and Forrest were out of control, swimming in some very swift-moving waters.

A distraction, something to do, she would do something she knew how to do—anchor herself in useful occupation. The sun cast the barn in a giant shadow across the yard, reminding her the men, when they returned, if they returned alive and in one piece, would be hungry. The one thing they had here on the homestead was plenty of vegetables, fruit, meat, and flour. However, this morning, nerves on edge and both of them upset, neither she nor Forrest had much of an appetite. They'd dined on butter, honey, and three-day-old biscuits.

For the next hour and a half, Zola baked. And while she baked, she conjured up all manner of horrific scenarios in her head—Forrest broken and bloody, Mr. Emory broken and bloody, Mr. Kenyon and Ephraim and Oren dragged off to prison for murder?

Leaving the carnage in her head, she traveled out of the dark into a state of panic—*where the heck will we eat and on what and with what*?

No table, no chairs. They could eat on the porch. She'd enough forks for the men, she could manage with a spoon. Plates? No plates. She had tins and two bowls. She prayed her ham and potato pie with ham gravy would be good enough. Mr. Kenyon wouldn't notice, probably wouldn't even care what he ate.

Well, no, she didn't care if he cared or didn't care. She didn't need or want to impress him. But then she caught herself fussing over the crust to make it look decorative. Ephraim and Oren had eaten at their table many times. She knew they would appreciate whatever she served. And Forrest barely chewed his food. He simply shoveled and swallowed.

Well, her pie was nice and brown and bubbling, and the same with the crisp. She removed them from the oven and set them on the warming rack. The stove was the one thing she'd not sold over the last few months. Everything else, furniture, all the bedding, except what they were using, even the tableware and most of the kettles and pans were gone.

Every dream she had revolved around this house. Even the nightmares usually began and ended in this house. This last month, she could barely stand to look in the direction of the house. The bare windows made the house appear in shock, staring at her with wide, accusing eyes.

This morning she stayed in the kitchen, avoiding the empty rooms and the echoes of a house haunted by memories. But the memories and the ghosts invaded every corner. While she baked, in her head, she heard her mother humming her favorite hymn, and she hummed along with her. And when she'd picked up a fork she'd dropped on the floor, she smelled her father's pipe tobacco. He used to sit at the kitchen table in the mornings after doing his chores, drinking his morning coffee. The table was gone now, sold.

The walls, stripped bare of family portraits and childish art, showed outlines, voids, as reminders of what used to be. Standing in the doorway, she gazed into the formal parlor beyond the entryway. She sighed, tears coming to her eyes. She especially missed seeing Grandmother Pretty's beautiful painting of Holland's wetlands, windmills, and storms. You could see that painting from the kitchen doorway and the stairwell. Proudly displayed in the parlor over the fireplace, the vacancy now accentuated the smutty, sooty wall that had surrounded it. All the while growing up, several times a day she'd stop to admire the painting and read the homily her Grandmother had incorporated into the painting. *"A good name is to be chosen above great riches and loving favor above silver and gold."* But now the handmade rugs were gone, the lovingly sown curtains were gone, and the rooms echoed in the emptiness.

Forrest crashed through the back porch. The screen door slapped shut behind him. "Zoe, c'mon, c'mon, you gotta see what we got."

"Someone's hurt. I knew it. I knew something bad would come of it—God, Ephraim, dear sweet Ephraim, or is it Oren?" She stopped herself from saying it out loud, but—*God forbid, Mr. Kenyon*? Picking up her skirts, she followed Forrest to the front porch.

"Ah, Miss Pretty," Mr. Kenyon said, a broad, annoying grin on his lips, dimples deeply entrenched in his cheeks, "Mr. Emory has proven himself to be an excellent neighbor. After a bit of persuasion, and after I described the damage his horse had done to your garden and the damage he'd caused by creating a stinking smudge-pot in your sleeping quarters, he begged to make restitution. Rather than vulgar cash, look what he's done. He's donated all of this to express his deep shame for his actions."

No words, Zola could find no words that would come close to expressing the jumble and mishmash of emotions seeing her family's things loaded in the back of the wagon. Chest aching, throat constricting, she covered her mouth with both hands to muffle her sobs.

"You should'a been there, Zoe," Forrest said before Oren put his big hand over the boy's mouth.

"Yes, Ma'am, Mr. Emory proved mighty generous,

he did," said Ephraim. "We'll take these beds upstairs and set the table up in the kitchen where it belongs."

"What is that heavenly smell?" Mr. Kenyon asked, sniffing the air, untying the last knot holding the load in place.

Zola answered without thinking, "Ham and potato pie and apple crisp."

"Mmm, mmm, I'm ready. Forrest, you take a couple of chairs, and I'll take a couple. Let's get this in the house. Didn't expect you to prepare a meal for us, Miss Pretty," Mr. Kenyon said, helping Oren get the table out of the wagon, "but I'm sure glad you did."

In a daze, Zola stepped out of the way and stumbled down the last step to the yard. Slipping to the side of the house to the bench under the willow tree, she plunked down to indulge in a good cry.

The brass bed, her mother's and father's, Forrest's bed, her bed, their mattresses, the quilts she and her mother had made, the table and chairs, Mr. Kenyon had brought them home.

Mr. Emory had bought a lot of furniture, even Grandmother Pretty's painting. He'd bought a wagon load for a song, paying one hundred and seventy-five dollars, not enough to make any difference to the bank or put a dent in the loans. But, the painting? She hadn't seen it among the things Mr. Kenyon had retrieved.

Closing her eyes, she shuddered, recalling the feel of Mr. Emory's sweaty, hot hands on her backside, kneading her bottom through the fabric of her skirt. He'd cornered her beneath the stairwell, his ugly lips pressing against her mouth, the stubble on his upper lip scratched. The memory of him, she could still smell his breath— bile bubbled up into her throat.

She couldn't shake the ugly look in his dark eyes. They would haunt her for the rest of her days. She would never forget what he'd said, never, "You want to sleep in your own bed, you sweet little ginger cookie, you come over to my place, I'll keep you nice and warm. We'll have a little fun. I got a big house. I'll see you dressed fine in furs and satin. You won't have to lift a finger 'cept keep me happy, and that won't be a chore. I think you and me would get along just fine. I'll see your brother taken care of. Get him in a good school back east. C'mon," he'd urged her, slobbering on her neck.

She would be eternally grateful to the people who'd arrived at that moment to pick up the wardrobes and sideboard, because he would've raped her for certain then and there.

"Zoe, did you see? They're our beds. Mr. Kenyon got him to give'em back," Forrest said, excited, rushing around the side of the house.

Zola turned away and swiped the moisture from her cheeks. "Yes, I saw. It's wonderful."

"I'm hungry. Can we eat now?"

"Yes, yes, coming."

****

So quiet, she went about her work. Leif had hoped to at least get a smile from her. Instead, he could swear she'd been crying. Tight-lipped and stoic, she laid the table without making eye contact or saying a word. Forrest had shown them where they could wash up. And now Leif had a good look around at the bare walls, floors, and windows. He had a better understanding as to why Zola balked at moving back into the house. There was nothing here. He'd like to look in the larder. He'd bet there wasn't a lot there, either.

Ephraim said grace, and they tucked in. Leif had never tasted anything so savory as Zola's ham and potato pie. The crust had some kind of green herb in it, and the filling was more than just ham and potatoes. All the vegetables of the garden were in there, he'd swear it. "You butcher and render the lard from your hogs?"

"Yes," Zola replied, no further embellishment offered.

"When do you do that?"

She put down her spoon, clasped her hands in her lap, and challenged him with her gaze. "Mr. Emory? Is…he…? Did you…hurt him much?"

Leif put his fork down and met her gaze. He answered truthfully, "He has a few bruises. His head hit a barn post. But not due to a blow by my fist or Ephraim's or Oren's fist. We never landed a blow on the man."

Forrest ducked his head. Stifling a snicker, he pressed his lips together. Oren elbowed him in the ribs, and the boy sobered.

She narrowed her eyes, giving them all a hard look, and squared her shoulders. "I see," she finally said.

Taking a breath and letting it out, she finally answered his original question, "We butcher our hogs in late October, sometimes November. Anyway, as soon as we get the cooler days and freezing nights. Right now, we only have the sow and the boar, and two wiener pigs. We'll have to wait until next year to butcher. We have plenty of lard in the ice house, five hams, six sides of bacon in the smokehouse, and six racks of pork ribs. We have three wheels of cheese, preserved pickled pigs feet in jars, dried beans in jars in the root cellar, and a few of last year's potatoes and winter squash. I can give you a full inventory if you like," she said, nose in the air.

"Not necessary," he said. He pressed his lips together to hold back the smile.

God, the woman was a prickly little cactus.

"When I was here before, I looked around. I could see you've sold off a lot, but I had no idea as to the extent. I told Ephraim and Oren I'll set up an account at the mercantile in town for you to use to replenish whatever you need here, and that includes fabric for curtains, rugs, tableware, kitchen utensils, and cooking pots."

Beautiful dark brown eyes blinking, mouth open, she nodded, then licked her lips and swallowed. "In the past, we've done a lot of trading there, eggs, apples, potatoes. This afternoon Forrest and I will see what we can harvest from the wreckage."

"Keep accounts," Leif said and went back to his meal.

"Of course, I will keep accounts. I *do* keep accounts. We always have, Mr. Kenyon."

He looked up from his plate, which was a flat lid from some kind of pan, and said, "Good."

The meal continued in silence. Forrest asked to be excused, and Zola began to clear away his pie tin. Oren raised an eyebrow, signaling Leif he needed to talk to him. They rose at the same time and went out on the front porch.

"Maybe this is none of my business, but when we was in Mr. Emory's house, Forrest says to me them beds is theirs. That man bought them when Miss Pretty sold off to raise money for the mortgage. I reckon there's lots more things in that house he bought for a song. Forrest says he heard Mr. Emory say to Miss Pretty many times how she could come sleep in her own bed whenever she wanted. He'd be there waitin' for her."

Leif stood silent in thought, wishing he'd smashed the man's face in when he had the chance. "Thank you, Oren," he said and put a hand on Oren's shoulder. "I left a bundle of packages under the wagon seat when we left town. Would you bring them into the kitchen and set them on the table?"

Ephraim came out of the house. "Oren and me, we'll make a settee for Miss Pretty so she can set by the fire of an evening. Nights are gettin' colder. Soon as we get the tack room cleaned out, we'll settle in fine. Don't you worry none. You did good this mornin'. I got a good feelin' about all this. Gonna change things around here. Yes, sir," Ephraim said. Waving his hand over his head, he headed for the barn.

Leif followed Oren into the house but hung back in the kitchen doorway. Zola stood over a pan of water, washing the last of the odd assortment of lids and pans they'd used to eat their meal.

"What's all that?" she asked, giving the bundle Oren had deposited on the table a brief glance.

"I think you're going to call it a mistake," Leif said but held his position in the doorway.

She stopped, folded a tea towel, and set it aside on the warming rack above the stove. "Then why leave it on my table?"

He shrugged his shoulders. "Had to do something, couldn't let you suffer because of your pride."

"I am not proud, I'm…I'm humble and self-reliant, I have a strong sense of self-preservation."

"Humble? Hardly. You'd rather go naked in the middle of winter and starve before asking for help. Zola.

You snarl and snipe at anyone who tries to do anything for you."

"You're a bully, Mr. Kenyon, always ordering people around, telling them what to do and when to do it. For your information, self-preservation is not a sin, and it is not to be compared to pridefulness. If I snarl and snipe, it is a self-defense mechanism. I have learned, over the last few months, no one gives without expecting something in return. And, as I'm without resources to pay, that means favors. Personal favors, which I'm not prepared to give. You didn't think I understood that, did you? Well, I do."

Her fine, pale, honey-colored eyebrows rose over her sparkling brown eyes, and her pretty lips formed a tight little pucker. He wanted to kiss those lips, loosen them up and dive into that mouth like a thirsty bumble bee. Inwardly he chastised himself for being no better than Emory.

Removing his pocket knife from his right front trouser pocket, he cut the string that held the bundled packages together. "The only favor I want from you is for you to forgive yourself. There was nothing you could do to stop your home from going to auction. There is nothing you could have done to change anything. Do yourself a favor and stop being so bullheaded.

"All of these are for you," he said and spread the packages around the table. "Burn'em, do what you will. But if you burn'em, you did this to you. No one made you do it. No one, especially me, expects repayment of any kind.

"I'll be gone shortly. I'm going to have another look around now before I leave to return to town. You won't see me until I return from Centerville. We'll see the judge and get married as soon as I step off the train. And, by the way, I've never tasted anything like your ham and potato pie. You are a wonder of a cook, Miss Pretty. I think I'm going to enjoy getting very fat."

She stood there, her little heart-shaped face all stormy, freckles bright against her pink cheeks, and he longed to hear her laugh, see her smile just once before he had to go.

"Mr. Emory promised not to bother you anymore. Ephraim and Oren will mend the fence rail today so you can let the animals out."

Slowly, he made his way toward her. Speaking softly, he said. "You'll be safe now. You're not alone. You don't have to do it all, Zola. You're home. You'll sleep in your own bed tonight, and no one will hurt you or come take anything from you." He touched her cheek with his finger. She closed her beautiful brown eyes and turned her face away.

"I won't hurt you, Zola. I won't try to buy you with promises or things or threaten to take anything from you that you aren't willing to give," he said and kissed her cheek, then left the kitchen.

****

The kiss to her cheek paralyzed her. In an odd way, the big and physically imposing Mr. Kenyon reminded her of her father. He was firm, pragmatic, diplomatic in an autocratic way, and very charismatic. In short, she found it hard to *not* like him. She did like him, a little too much. She really didn't know him. It would be wiser to withhold judgment.

The packages drew her to the table. The first one, the biggest one, opened easily, and she recognized the lovely fox fur and the green wool of the coat. The sight of it took her breath away. Holding the coat up, tears blurred what her eyes were seeing. She couldn't believe it. How could he have known this coat was one of her most sinful, secret desires? She'd seen it a week ago when the Abbot sisters first dressed their window for fall. She pressed the fur collar to her cheek and hugged the coat to her breast. Oh, it was so wrong to desire, long for, material things, but she'd longed to press her cheek to this fur collar.

****

Leif smiled to himself. Peeking through the back door of the kitchen, he watched her hug the coat to her breast. She tried it on, a smile on her face. Turning the collar up, she pressed it against her cheek. Eyes closed, obviously in absolute heaven, she twirled around—she even giggled. Oh, he could leave now. Yes, he could leave now. He'd made Miss Zola Pretty smile.

Chapter Eight

Two forty-three, according to the station clock left him less than twenty minutes to get to the judge's office, and still no sign of Ephraim. Pacing the length of the Prettydale railway station didn't help make the waiting any easier. But he had the cargo car to unload, and he could do that to make the time go a little faster.

He'd wired Ephraim at the end of last week, notifying him of his arrival on Tuesday the twenty-seventh of September, and sent a separate wire for him to deliver to Miss Zola, but who could say if she'd meet him. He didn't like it that Ephraim hadn't made a showing. He should've arrived by now. Something could've happened—Emory could've happened. The thought had him grinding his back teeth.

He'd very carefully worded his telegram to Zola. Couching his request to make it sound less demanding proved beyond him. No matter how he put it, it sounded like an order—which it was. At the risk of proving her assessment of his character as a bully to be true, he requested she meet him in Judge Lancaster's chambers in Prettydale at three p.m., where the judge would perform the ceremony. Unsure, afraid of sounding cold or too warm or too familiar, he'd signed the telegram, *Regards, Leif.* At the moment, he wasn't even certain she'd gotten his message. He hadn't received a reply, other than Ephraim's terse, *got it.*

Leif, and three other men set one of the steam saw's drive belts down on the loading dock. The station clock said two-forty-five. He had fifteen minutes to make it to the judge's office, where he hoped he'd find his bride waiting for him. But where the hell was Ephraim?

The rattle of harness and wagon wheels turned his attention toward town. Ephraim whipped his team up to the cargo car. "Sorry, Mr. Kenyon. Oren's comin' with another wagon, and Forrest's got the homestead team and wagon. Two boards on the bridge gave way. We had to replace and reinforce. I think it'll hold now. Then a'course we had to drop Miss Pretty off at the judge's."

Leif set his hat more firmly on his head. "That bridge needs to be taken care of right away. We'll widen it. I've got to get to the judge's office. There are four horses up there in the cattle car. Tie them off behind the wagons. Be sure to get my saddle, trunk, and my boots in a wagon somewhere. There's still some equipment in this car. These men will help you. I gotta get."

"Sir?"

"Yes."

"Me and Oren, we wish you and Miss Pretty all the best."

"Thank you, Ephraim."

****

Judge Lancaster's secretary, Mr. Patterson, eyed Zola over the rims of his spectacles. "Sign the register, please. We'll need the groom's signature." He looked around her for the groom. "Where is your groom?"

The clock struck the hour of three o'clock. Zola removed her tan kid gloves. Hands shaking, she dipped the pen in the inkwell to sign her name. "He's at the railway station. He'll be along shortly, I'm sure," she said, not at all sure of anything.

Married? I'm getting married, married to a man who doesn't want to marry. A man who looks upon this union as a necessary partnership to save face, not only my face, but his.

In her head, her father's voice mocked her, parroting his favorite homily *"A good name is to be chosen above great riches and loving favor above silver and gold."* Well, the choices given to her these days were limited and came with hidden strings attached.

Her groom was late, and she was starting to regret her decision to wear the coat he'd given her and the little fox fur, pill-box hat that matched. She'd thought to please him, hoping to assure him he wasn't getting too bad a bargain. Two weeks of good rest and regular meals, and a more normal existence, had done a lot to soften Zola's disposition. But, at the moment, she could feel the cords in the back of her neck tightening up. She'd give him five more minutes.

The clock ticked away. Mr. Patterson cleared his throat. "The judge has another appointment at three-thirty."

The door to the office opened and, in a flutter of frilly lace and a cloud of sweet-smelling perfume, the Abbot sisters, twittering like a couple of silly barn swallows, entered the room. "We saw Mr. Gooding and the wagons going by," Miss Gladys said.

"We knew they were headed for the railway station. We put the closed sign in the door, and down the alley we went just as fast as we could," Miss Paulette said.

"He's coming, my dear. We saw him. Such long legs and big strides he does take. Very striking man, very striking," Gladys said, waving her hanky in Zola's face, her cheeks bright pink and silver-blue eyes full of sparks of delight.

Miss Paulette put her lace-encased fingers on Zola's wrist and said very sincerely, "Now, I know you're surprised to see us. But dear cousin Clarence, the judge, you know, let it slip, you and dear Mr. Kenyon were seeing him today, and we put two and two together."

Miss Gladys dabbed at her little nose. "We just think this is the most romantic thing ever to happen here in Prettydale."

"We're here to lend you support, Dear, as you have no family other than your little brother," Miss Paulette said.

Zola, blushing, flustered, opened her mouth to thank them and send them on their way, but no sound came out. She'd assured Forrest he need not attend. The last thing she wanted was the gossiping, gabby Abbot sisters witnessing this farce.

Mr. Kenyon, looking large, handsome, and powerful in a long black dustercoat, black hat, blindingly white, ruffled shirt, with a black string tie at his neck, entered the office, filling the room, making it seem ridiculously small and cramped. He immediately removed his hat and greeted the old dears.

"The judge is waiting," said Mr. Patterson. "I presume you are the groom? Please sign the register."

Leif sidled his way around the ladies and took Zola by the hand, his gaze traveling from her fur hat to her shiny, black, new shoes, and said, "I knew that shade of green would suit you. And the little hat, it is a perfect foil to set off your spectacular curls. I'm late. I apologize for keeping you waiting."

"The judge is waiting," Mr. Patterson said. "Sir, if

you would, please sign the register. Miss Gladys, Miss Paulette sign as witnesses." And to Leif, he said, "Two dollars, please."

The judge waved them into his chambers and took his place before his brick hearth. He peered over his spectacles at them, first nodding to Leif, then to Zola. The clerk handed the judge the register book and a pen. The judge signed and handed it back and cleared his throat. "This is a solemn oath you are about to take. Marriage is for life and not to be entered into without considerable thought. It is a bond not easily broken. It is a legal contract. With that said, Zola Louise Pretty, do you promise, before this company, to take this man, Leif Allen Kenyon, as your lawfully wedded husband in sickness and in health, to love honor and obey unto death do you part?"

Zola opened her mouth, then pressed her lips together. "No," she heard herself say aloud.

The Abbot sisters gasped in unison, and their lace hankies went to their bosoms. After that, the room went silent.

Zola stammered, realizing she needed to explain her objection to the judge. "*Obey*? I can't promise that." The Abbot sisters nodded and huffed in agreement, or at least Zola assumed they agreed with her. "I don't think blind obedience is in me. If I'm to be truthful. I have to be truthful, don't I? I certainly wouldn't ask Mr. Kenyon to obey me."

"We don't ask the groom to obey, just the bride," said the judge, his salt and pepper brows forming a hairy hedge over his dark eyes.

Muttering the injustice of it, she shook her head. "I really do have a problem with that," she said, shoulders pulled back, chin up and out.

"Perhaps some editing is called for," the groom said, lips twitching, obviously struggling to maintain a sober countenance. "Give me a minute to think."

The Judge frowned. "Well, hurry it up."

"I know, I know you have an appointment," Leif said.

Leif turned to her, took a deep breath before saying, "Zola, can you promise compassion during sickness, respect and consideration through the hard times, and loyalty and fidelity unto death us do part?"

Gazing deep into his eyes of blue, Zola thought about it carefully, weighing the ramifications of such a promise. "I can, if you can."

He smiled down on her and nodded. "I do, and I will. Done."

The judge took a deep breath and said in a rush, "By the power vested in me, I pronounce you man and wife. You may kiss your bride," the judge said to Leif.

Zola held out her hand for her new husband to shake.

Leif shook his head. "This is a very important pact. I don't think a handshake will seal the deal. The Judge has ordered a kiss. A kiss of trust, Zola."

"Agreed," she said and closed her eyes, preparing for his touch.

Arms to her side, his lips touched hers, his breath smelling of cloves and spice. Lightheaded, she swayed. To steady herself, she placed her hands on his solid chest. He cupped her chin with his fingers, encouraging her, applying more pressure. She came up on her toes, seeking to deepen the pleasant sensation.

The giggling Abbot sisters broke the spell, and the kiss ended. Taking advantage of her lost-in-another-world state, the sisters kissed Zola's cheek, then the jaw of the grinning groom.

"You'll come to the hotel, and we'll toast the happy couple," Gladys said.

"I'm sorry, ladies, but it's getting late in the day, and I have equipment to deliver to the homestead. Perhaps when next we're in town."

"Yes, yes, of course," Miss Paulette said. "Your mill, how exciting."

****

It wasn't easy to break away from the Abbot sisters. They followed Leif and Zola, all of them trooping outside and finding Ephraim, Oren, and Forrest sitting on the edge of the boardwalk. The sisters finally, twittering away, gave them their blessings and rushed back to their store. Three loaded wagons, three teams of strong horses stood heads down at rest, and Leif's four riding horses waited patiently tied off to the end wagon. All in all, they made quite a spectacle. A small crowd had gathered around. Ignoring the gawkers, Leif folded the marriage certificate and tucked it away in his inside coat pocket. He picked Zola up and helped her to take her place on the wagon bench.

"You're married now?" Forrest asked him, coming to his feet, a challenge in his eyes.

"We are," Leif said and placed his hand on the boy's boney shoulder. "Which makes you and me brother's-in-law. Let Ephraim take the reins, and you get up on that chestnut gelding back there. Let's go home. I want to get a look at the bridge before we lose daylight."

"Ephraim told you about the loose boards?" Zola asked. Leif boarded the wagon and slapped the reins over the rumps of the team of dray horses, setting the wagon in motion. The crowd stood back. "He did. It isn't wide enough. It'll have to be fixed."

"Ephraim almost threw the boards away. I put them aside. I think they were sawed in two."

"Have you had any trouble with our neighbor since I've been gone?"

"No, he's been very quiet." She nodded at some ladies who stood staring at them in the doorway of the mercantile.

"He has a big house and expensive animals. Do you know where he gets his money? It's not from his farm." Leif tipped his hat at the gawkers.

"No. He and Mr. Shaw, the owner of the bank, have investments in the North Pacific Railway. So does the judge."

"How long has Emory lived next to you?"

"About six years, maybe seven." They left the town and headed up a slight rise, and entered the tree-lined road. "He murdered my father," she said, her voice flat and emotionless.

"What makes you think so?"

"Papa was hale and hearty," she said. Shrugging her shoulders, she straightened her coat, lining up the gold buttons on the front. "There was nothing wrong with his heart. The day he died, Forrest found him near the fence line at mid-morning between Emory's property and ours, face down in the mud. He had mud and blood in his nose and mouth, blood on his cheeks. The back of his head was caked with mud and blood. He had mud under his fingernails. The sheriff called it a heart attack."

"What was he doing out there, at that spot?"

"We'd had a lot of rain, a freeze, and more rain. All the animals were in the barns. There really was no reason for him to be near the fence. The ground at that spot was all torn up and muddy."

"Torn up? What do you mean?"

"Well, like the garden, you know, but wet, really wet and…and stirred up into a slurry."

"Have you ever heard of anyone taking gold out of Pretty Creek?"

Zola laughed, and the sound of her girlish giggle did funny things to his innards. "Forrest, he came home one day a year or so ago all excited, wet. He'd fallen in the creek. He had grit in his boots and the cuff of his trousers. It sparkled. He thought it was gold. Papa assured him they were mica flecks. We'd heard they'd discovered gold south of here about three or four years ago. Several men caught the gold fever but returned to their farms no richer but no poorer because they'd left their hard-working wives and children home to keep their farms going."

Traveling beside the creek, sunlight playing hide and seek between the fall leaves and the boughs of the tall pine, Leif noticed the water in the creek, running a little higher than when he'd been here before, appeared murky. He mentioned the color of the water to Zola. "Is that unusual?"

She twisted to the side, leaning over, looking down into the stream bed. "It was clear when we left home. Sometimes, if there's erosion, it gets murky like that. You should watch the road. With all these shadows, it's hard to see. The road might have fallen into the creek."

"We'll stop at the bridge. I'll take a look at it before we try to take the wagons across." They passed by Emory's gate, and the water in the creek flowed brown as coffee with heavy cream, spilling over and around the boulders and fallen logs in the stream.

Leif pulled up his wagon and held up his hand for Ephraim and Oren to halt.

"I laid the broken boards over there at the base of that big oak," Zola said.

"Hold the team. I'm going to walk across, test the wood."

He picked up the boards and agreed with Zola. The boards had been sawed in two. He stopped short of the puncheon logs and planed boards of the bridge to look over the left side and into the muddy stream, then to the right. The water was clear upstream on the right. The source of the mud lay beneath the bridge. He started across, stomping from one board to the next. On the other side of the bridge, again the water was disturbed on one side but not the other.

"We got trouble, ain't we?" said Ephraim, crossing the bridge and coming up beside him.

"I'd say," Leif said. "I don't think we can take the wagons across. It's getting too dark to see what's happened under there. We'll put the teams on a line and lead the other horses across one at a time. Take them to the barn."

"Oren and me, we'll set up camp here. Keep watch over the wagons tonight."

"Yes, I think that would be best. It's a clear night. Do you have a gun?"

"I do. She's a sweet little over and under I use for shootin' vermin. I recon Emory is vermin if he done this."

"I'll see Zola and Forrest across, then come back and keep watch until you and Oren gather up what you need to be comfortable out here. I don't want to leave this bridge or the wagons unattended."

"What's going on?" Zola asked, sneaking up on him.

Drawing in his breath, Leif straightened his shoulders and exhaled slowly to give himself time to think of a way to minimize the situation. "Could be the flow has washed away some dirt and rock supports from beneath the pylons and weakened the bridge. Anyway, I don't want to take a chance and bring the wagons across. And we can't work on fixing whatever is wrong, not with daylight fading. It's safe for foot traffic. So I'll take you and Forrest up to the house. Ephraim and Oren are going to camp here tonight to watch the wagons."

Surprising him with her compliance, she said, "I'll bring down some supper and coffee."

He retrieved his valise and his work boots from the end wagon and took Zola by the arm to escort her to the house. She called for Forrest to follow, but Forrest balked, and that brought them to a standstill. "I don't want you down here, Forrest."

"He'll be fine," Oren said.

"But, if...if...there's trouble..."

"He'll be fine, Zola," Leif said. "He'll have Ephraim and Oren and me to keep him safe. I don't think I'll sleep at the house. I'd be worrying about what's going on out here." He tugged on her arm, and reluctantly, she allowed herself to be led away.

"You know there's trouble, don't you, Mr. Kenyon?" she said and jerked her arm away to loosen his grasp.

"You know who's behind this?" she said once they were safely across the bridge.

"Could be the recent rains, or some animal's been

digging under there," he said and kept her moving.

They passed through the homestead gate, and she swiped his hand away from her elbow. "I don't believe for one minute the recent rains washed out the pylons. They've been tampered with. And I don't believe for one minute you believe that either."

He heaved a weighty sigh, arms at his side. "I warned our neighbor to stay off the homestead. Perhaps I need to be more specific."

She snorted, dismissing his comment, and marched toward the house without him. He followed her into the house.

The change in the interior of the house brought him to a standstill. The walls in the front parlor had a fresh coat of whitewash. A settee and two bench seats sat close to the fire. A hooked rag rug on the floor before the hearth gave the room warmth.

Zola stood quiet while he looked around. The walls remained bare, but at least it now looked inviting, hospitable.

All of it brought a smile to his lips and gave him hope. "You've been busy. It looks like home now."

Cheeks bright pink, she avoided his gaze. "The big bedroom, your room, is the first door at the head of the stairs. The windows look over the yard with a view of the barns. My room is the middle bedroom. I'm sure you'll be wanting to change your clothes."

He fully grasped the underlying warning behind her pointed reference to *his* room and its location in relation to *her* room. Her barely veiled dismissal did not go over his head. He understood perfectly—he was to stay in his place, keep his distance. Finding it difficult to hide his amusement, he ducked his head and proceeded up the stairs.

It did not portend to be a wedding night a man could brag about, but he hadn't expected more, not really. He'd thought a lot about Zola over the last couple of weeks. He'd told his brother about her, how he had no choice but to marry her. Gunnar laughed, finding his predicament highly amusing and somehow proper punishment for all the broken hearts Leif had left behind over the last ten years.

He'd tried to describe Zola to his brother but stopped, realizing she had a rare, one-of-a-kind beauty that was more than attractive features put together in one body. It was more of an inner beauty words could not describe.

When he kissed her today in the judge's office, he no longer had any doubts. He was doing the right thing, the best, and for all time—the right thing.

Chapter Nine

The footsteps overhead echoed inside Zola's head like thunder rolls. Mr. Kenyon—her *husband*, Leif Kenyon, now occupied her parent's bedroom. Her *husband?* No, just a man. But not just any man, this man now owned her and her home. If he demanded his husbandly rights to her body, what would she do? According to the law, she had no legal right to deny him those rights.

The pragmatic side of her mocked her puritanical side, asking why she should object to consummating their union? What, or who was she saving herself for? Here was a man, a beautiful man, whom she instinctively felt was a gentleman at heart. He would be a kind lover. If only she knew what a lover actually did. Oh, she knew the basics, being a farm girl, but surely there was more to it. Well, whatever the process entailed, it wouldn't happen tonight. The devil Mr. Emory had seen to that.

Footsteps on the stairs set her to buttering more slices of bread than needed to make bacon and tomato sandwiches for Ephraim, Oren, and Forrest.

Dressed in canvas trousers, knee-high work boots, and a flannel shirt, Mr. Kenyon headed for the front door without casting a glance in the direction of the kitchen.

"You'll need a coat," she said, wiping her hands on her apron and coming into the foyer. "Papa's mackinaw? I'll get it for you. I saved it back for Forrest. But he doesn't need it now, thanks to you."

"I have a coat in my trunk," he said, his hand on the door latch. "I'll be fine."

"The coffee and sandwiches, I almost have them ready. Wait, and I'll go with you."

Leif followed her into the kitchen. "I've been thinking about you here in the house alone tonight. I'll send Forrest up before it gets too late. Do you have a gun, Zola?"

"We have Papa's rifle. Why?"

"I think you should keep it handy. You could fire it off if you thought there was trouble. Have you ever shot a gun, Zola?"

Her chin went up, "No." The lie came quickly, suddenly, unexpectedly to her lips. He didn't need to know she knew how to shoot a gun, that she was a crack shot, that her mother had taught her, not her father. Her father, who abhorred guns, abhorred violence of any kind, would not have approved of her skill. She'd never told her little brother she knew anything about guns. Forrest hunted, of course, and bragged about his skill, but she'd never let on she knew anything about guns.

"You need to know how to handle a gun. I'll show you. After we get the bridge repaired, I want to explore the meadow, have a look around. Come with me. We'll take the rifle. I'll look it over, make sure it's safe."

The meadow was one of her very favorite places. She went there all the time to think and dream. But did she want to share it with Mr. Kenyon? He was invading all of her spaces—now the meadow. He owned it. Nothing to do but accept. "Yes, yes, of course I'll come with you, if you like."

"Good," he said, and relieved her of the big coffee

pot and hamper full of food.

****

Ephraim and Oren had set up their camp near the bridge beneath an old Douglas fir where there was little brush and stones to build a fire pit. The sun had gone down, but twilight lingered.

Oren sat near the little fire, feet bare, pant legs rolled up to his knees. "I waded in to get a look under there," he said, waving his arm to the stream. Leif set the coffee pot down on the stones that ringed the fire. Zola took the hamper from him.

"Could you see where all the mud is coming from?" Leif asked.

Oren pulled on his well-mended socks and rolled down his pant legs. "The creek is narrow at the bridge with a deep channel on this side before it swings around to follow along the road. I could see someone's dug out the boulders, rock, and dirt from under the sill logs on this end and on the other end across. It took some doin'. Wouldn't be easy to dislodge them boulders."

"We'll do repairs as best we can in the morning— good enough so we can get these wagons across. Is the stream eroding more of the soil right now?"

"Well," Oren said, "that's the funny part." Coming to his feet, he tucked his shirt into his trousers. "Right now, the water level is a good four, five feet down from the sill log and where those boulders was. The water never reached that high, not yet anyways. I'd say the damage was done a'purpose."

Ignored, Zola set the hamper of food on the ground next to Ephraim and turned back for the house, mind racing. *Mr. Emory truly is the devil. He covets the homestead. That's plain. Mr. Kenyon mentioned gold.*

Surely Mr. Emory couldn't believe there's gold here. The gold lay in the land, the water, the trees, and rich earth like Papa always said.

Passing through the gate, a hand landed on her shoulder. It had gone almost full dark. Her thoughts dark and full of Mr. Emory and his evil ways, she startled, jumped, and slapped at the hand.

"Shhh, easy, Zola, it's me," said Mr. Kenyon, soothing her arms, stroking her with gently gliding hands. "I wanted to wish you good night. I'd rather spend our wedding night sitting with you by a warm fire, talking, getting to know you. I have so many plans for this place. I'd like to share them with you."

Grateful for the darkness hiding her crimson cheeks, she exhaled and willed her heart to slow to a more natural, easy pace. "I'm sorry. You startled me. I was thinking of Mr. Emory," she said. Shaking her head, she tried to free herself of her fears.

"Don't worry, we'll keep watch. He's a coward. He won't show his face while everyone is about. I need to...to kiss my wife good night," he said, and even in the dark, she could see the mischievous sparks in his blue eyes—he had the bluest eyes.

His naughty chuckle sent tingly ripples throughout her body. "Oh, I don't think a kiss is necessary. Surely a handshake will do," she said. Pressing her lips together to stifle a giggle, she held out her hand.

Taking her hand, she resisted a little, just a little, when he pulled her into an embrace. On a sigh of surrender, she fell in love as their lips met in a soft, gentle kiss. So in love. Instantly in love, longing to stay right here, in his arms, she knew herself for a traitor. A traitor to her parents, to the history of the homestead, to herself, and her resolve to remain defiant and impervious to this trespasser, this invader.

****

Absolutely shameless, unrepentant in his triumph, Leif marched across the yard confident he could easily win Zola Pretty's trust and her admiration. He had absolutely made headway, breaking through her prickly wall of pride. He couldn't decide if it was the challenge she presented or if he was truly infatuated. But breaking through her barriers had become a priority. The sound of her sigh of surrender pleased him out of all proportion.

Getting Emory to surrender, that would require a bit more patience. He'd dealt with men like Emory before. They rarely came at you in a straightforward manner, preferring sabotage. The only way to defeat them was to proceed and succeed. But, leaving Zola alone at the house when Emory probably knew they were all camped at the creek made him uneasy.

Probably what the man wants. He wants us always on edge, scattered, living in fear of what he'll do next. I've got the place I want, but the devil comes with it. The devil and Miss Pretty. Miss Pretty? Why is the devil so intent on destroying her and her family? And where in the hell do I fit in?

He stopped at the bridge. Oren, Ephraim, and Forrest hunkered around the fire pit, the flames lighting up their faces in the dark, and it hit him—they were his responsibility now, his family. And Zola, Zola was his wife. He wanted her in every way a man wanted a wife—in every way. The question chipped away at his confidence; when, if ever, would Zola accept him in every way as her husband? And could he keep them all safe?

****

Zola banked the fire in the parlor grate and wandered over to the double window facing the yard. A flicker of lantern light danced between the blackberry vines and the gate, and she guessed someone was coming to the house. Footsteps sounded on the porch, and Forrest entered. "I was thinking of making some cookies. Would you like to help?" she asked him.

"I'm not a little kid," he said. He doused the flame in the lantern and set it down by the door. "I should be with the men, not in here baking cookies, for Christ's sake."

"You will not take the Lord's name in vain, Forrest Maxwell Pretty. If you don't want to be treated like a child, then you will stop acting like one. I need you here. I can't sleep. I'm scared, and you're here to protect me. Emory isn't going to leave us alone. I have to do something. Baking cookies seems like a good way to pass the time."

Forrest huffed. Begrudgingly he apologized for his transgression and shrugged his shoulders. "Ah, Emory ain't...isn't...no match for Leif."

"We can hope. Well, anyway I'm glad you decided to come to the house. You need to get some sleep tonight. School tomorrow. You skipped today, and I understand. You were needed to help, but you can't skip any more days this week."

He grunted and followed her out to the kitchen. "What kind of cookies?"

"I was thinking molasses and walnut pin-wheels."

"I'll get the eggs," he said on his way to the pantry on the back porch.

****

Pacing back and forth before their puny fire, Leif said aloud to himself, "This doesn't feel right. What's he after? Why would Emory mess with the bridge, Ephraim?

Ephraim tossed another chunk of cord wood on the fire, and sparks shot up into the darkness.

They'd been out here several hours now and not a sound. Oh, a couple of owls were sending coded messages back and forth across the creek to the barn, but other than that, even the leaves on the trees had gone dead quiet. It was cold, and frost was starting to form on the dry grass and brambles.

"I been thinkin' about it," Ephraim said.

In the shadows, to the side of the fire, Oren snuffled and snorted, eyes closed, big feet stretched out toward the fire, arms akimbo across his big chest.

"You got married today. This is your weddin' night. Mr. Emory knows it. The whole town knows it. He don't like that. He don't like lookin' like a fool. I think this here is a stunt to keep you from your bride and to let you know he don't give you his blessing. And he ain't gonna give you no peace."

Leif laughed off Ephraim's theory, even though it pretty much matched his own. "Well, the bride is keeping me at arms-length, so Emory hasn't got anything to worry about. But there's more to this than his coveting Zola, surely? There has to be. No, he's up to something. He knows we're down here away from the house, away from Zola. Forrest is a good kid, I like him, but he's no match for Emory."

Ephraim poured himself more coffee. "The man drinks his own corn. It twists up his brain into a ball of vipers. He's mean, and when he gets a snoot-full, there ain't nothin' gonna stop him from his meanness."

Leif poured the coffee out of his cup to the side of the fire and picked up the rifle he'd left leaning against the back of the tree. "I'm going to the house."

Ephraim didn't say a word.

The house looked quiet, no lights. Pulling the ax out of the chopping block, Leif sat down to focus on the field between the Emory property and the homestead fence. The big moon helped illuminate the landscape. Up on the hill behind the house, a pack of coyotes was on the hunt, yipping and laughing. The kitchen window, to his right, stood open a crack. The smell of fresh baked cookies sweetened the air. His stomach growled in response.

After an hour, chilled, the backs of his thighs began to scream with cramps. Shivering, he came to his feet to stretch and shake some blood down to his toes. The sky had started to lighten, the moon low to the west. About to give up his vigil, Leif caught sight of a dark figure way off on the other side of the homestead fence. It wasn't a cow or a horse or a dog. He tucked himself back between the wood pile and the ash bucket to wait and watch.

A man? Definitely a man reached the homestead fence near the paddock gate and the house. He tossed a long stick through the fence rails and climbed over. A few yards from the fence, he pulled a rag out of his back pocket, and wrapped it around the end of the stick. Stooping down, he gathered several handfuls of long, dried grass and twisted them around the cloth and the end of the stick.

Leif didn't wait for the next step. He'd seen this before. Stepping out, away from the woodpile, he raised his rifle before the man could light his deadly torch and fired a volley that landed a good yard from the would-be arsonist's feet.

The loosely formed, unlit torch dropped to the ground. The man scrambled back over the fence, stumbled and fell to his knees, got up, and ran toward the Emory farm. Leif couldn't swear, but he was almost ninety-nine percent certain the foiled arsonist to be none other than their neighbor, Mr. Emory.

Behind him, his hand on the paddock gate, the bang, and slap of the screen door on the back porch echoed in the crisp dawn. Barefoot, Zola raced across the lawn, her white nightgown hugging her full bosom, legs, and hips, wild red hair flying. She slammed into him, hands to his shoulders clutching, hysterical, crying, and none of her questions made it to the end of their sentences. Leif stood calm to quiet her panic. The feel of her warm body beneath his hands heated his blood. Her body so soft, so feminine. Everything about her, the smell of spice—cookies—in her hair, brought a lump to his throat.

"I heard a gunshot. Are you hurt? Who shot a gun? Why? What did you shoot at?"

"Shhhh. Yes, I fired a shot, nothing but a prowling wolf out there next to the fence. I'm sorry it woke you," he said, holding her close, forbidding himself to move his hands down to her hips, to her full bottom. He had to keep very, very still, and take nice, quiet, steady breaths.

"No. Wolf? No. We've never had wolves around here. Mountain lions, yes," she said, turning slightly within his embrace, her bosoms sliding across his chest. She attempted to pull away from him, but he couldn't allow that, not yet.

"Maybe it was a mountain lion. It was dark. Couldn't see him that well."

"Heard a shot," Forrest said, padding across the yard

barefoot in his long underwear, brown hair spiking out in all directions.

"Leif shot at something, maybe a wolf or a mountain lion," Zola said.

Leif let her go. Forrest might see the lust in his eyes.

"You shouldn't be out here in your bare feet," Zola said to the boy.

"Well, neither should you," Forrest said, giving her the once over.

Zola shoved out of his embrace, folded her arms across her chest, and turned away from him. "Oh, for heaven's sake. It's freezing out here."

To Forrest, she said, "It's time for you to be up and getting ready for school. I have to get breakfast ready." Fussing at her brother, she turned him around and shoved him back toward the house.

Leif, fascinated, thinking lustful thoughts, studying the way her nightgown clung to her hips and little round bottom, regained his composure at the sound of Ephraim's shout from the corner of the house. Father and son acknowledged Zola and Forrest with a nod. Mentally giving himself a shake to dislodge his fantasies, Leif waved to them. They followed him through the paddock gate. He picked up the torch stick and the box of *Lucifer's Sulphur Stix* where Emory had dropped them. "I believe our neighbor intended to burn us out," he said to Ephraim.

"Miss Zola? Does she know about this?" Ephraim asked.

Leif snapped the stick into several smaller pieces. "I told her I took a shot at a wolf. She preferred to think the critter a mountain lion. Either way, we have a deadly predator stalking this farm."

"Maybe we should make another call on good neighbor Emory," said Oren.

"I think my shot spoke loud and clear our position. We've got enough on our plate. He must know by now we're watching him, and we don't trust him."

They reached the paddock gate, and Zola called to them from the back door, her nightgown fluttering in the breeze, "I'll have breakfast on shortly."

****

Nightgown exchanged for a serviceable blue, chambray shirtwaist dress, Zola held her tongue and refrained from saying anything about the so-called sighting of the prowler. The men were suspiciously silent as well, even Forrest. Normally, the presence of a big cat or a wolf would require considerable excited discourse at the table. Forrest set off to school in good time, for a change. She cleared the breakfast dishes, dried her hands on her apron, and hung it over the oven door. Decision made, she went out the paddock gate to inspect the stick she'd seen Mr. Kenyon break into pieces, her gaze going to the clump of dried grass and the cloth caught among the stems. The grass lay flattened near the fence on both sides. An animal wouldn't have caused that. In deep thought, she went back to the house for her shawl. Juggling a fresh pot of coffee and a plate of her cookies, she started for the bridge.

They'd erected a high fence wall of woven sticks and branches across the road and the creek on the other side, where it met up with the homestead fence. Dropping the reins of the big workhorse, Mr. Kenyon wiped his arm across his brow, waved to her, and came across the bridge to greet her. "Wouldn't want anyone trying to cross the bridge until it's safe. I'm thinking of

91

leaving it up. We'll have to make it so it swings open, of course."

Glancing around, noticing they'd thinned the underbrush to make the fence, she saw they'd cut down a tree. She stamped her foot. "You...you've cut down the spruce," she said, pointing to the stump on the other side of the road, away from the creek.

Unapologetic, he nodded. "Yeah, we had to. Oren and Ephraim are under the bridge setting the sill logs in place before we brace them and reinforce with boulders. I think we'll have it safe enough to bring the wagons across by noon, or at the latest before Forrest gets home from school."

Setting aside the disappointment at finding one of her favorite trees sacrificed for the sake of the blasted bridge, she made an observation. "The water looks better this morning," she said.

"We're trying not to disturb it too much. Oren caught several trout this morning. We were hoping you'd fry them up for our lunch."

"Any sign of the cat or wolf or whatever it was you shot at this morning?" she asked, hoping to sound off-hand.

"No, I scared it off. I'm sure of it."

"I hope so. I let the cow and the horses out into the paddock and the chickens out of their coop."

Ephraim crawled up and out from under the bridge and greeted her, "Miss Zola. We've got this side all set right with the boulders and the sill set and braced."

Oren came out from under on the other side, face, hands, knees, and chest caked in mud.

"I brought down a fresh pot of coffee and some cookies," Zola said.

"I thought I smelled cookies this morning," Leif said, taking the coffee pot from her.

Zola allowed them to finish their first cup of coffee and several cookies before bringing up the events of the morning. "What was Mr. Emory's goal this morning– breaking windows or setting fire to the woodpile?"

Mr. Kenyon poured himself another cup of coffee, avoiding her gaze. Oren plucked the last four cookies off the plate, and Ephraim kept his head down.

"I know it wasn't a wolf. Wolves don't carry sticks. And by the flattened grass on both sides of the fence, I'd say it wasn't a cat. I saw where your shot landed, Mr. Kenyon. Did you hit him?"

"I told you, I scared the animal off. I missed him by a mile on purpose," Mr. Kenyon said. "I caught him before he could light the torch."

"This is ridiculous. Why did you lie to me?" she asked him, hands on hips. "How can I trust you if you lie to me?"

"You were scared. Or I should say, you continue to be scared. I want to give you some peace. Can you understand that? Let me worry about what Emory is up to."

"And you think that…that bramble fence of yours is going to keep him at bay?"

He shook his head at her and snorted. "No, I do not think any kind of fence will deter the man. But the fence draws the line I set. He's to stay off this land. This morning I punctuated my threat with a warning shot. If he continues his attacks, if he gets bolder, he'll leave me no choice. I will kill him like I would a marauding wolf or mountain lion."

"Kill? You will not *kill* Mr. Emory."

"I will if I have to. If I catch him trying to torch the house, poison the animals, weaken the bridge, or touch you or intimidate Forrest, I'll pound him to a pulp and then kill him."

She'd been taught to never raise her voice in anger. Her parents never raised their voices or argued, at least not in front of her or Forrest. How dare Mr. Kenyon defy her? Forgetting everything she'd been taught not to do, she stamped her foot and shook her finger up in his flushed face. In a voice bordering on a scream, she informed him, "I do not hold with violence under any circumstances, Mr. Keyon."

"It isn't violence if it's self-defense," he said, a stubborn gleam in his blue, blue eyes. "I'm going to defend you, Forrest, Ephraim, and Oren. And yes, damn it to hell, I may very well resort to violence to the point of death."

Shocked and stunned by his blasphemous language, holding her breath, she put a halt to this senseless argument. Clearly, trying to reason with the man would not work, and nothing she could say would change his mind. "Mr. Kenyon, I'm going to chalk up your, your outburst, to exhaustion. You haven't had any sleep. You've been working hard since you arrived yesterday. It is clear to me you and I will never see eye to eye on this subject.

"Oren, the trout? Give me the trout." She took the string of fish and held them out and away from her as far as she was able. To the men, she said, "You are all muddy, every one of you. I'll bring your meal down to you at mid-day. You're not stepping foot in my kitchen in all your dirt." She turned her back on them.

"You resorted to violence," Mr. Kenyon said behind

her back, very quietly. He'd said it so quietly, she wasn't sure he'd said it at all.

"I never," she said in her defense, pivoting to face him.

He grinned at her. "You did. You were kicking and pounding Emory when I came out of the bank. You bit him. You bit him more than once."

Shoot, she'd forgotten about that. "Well…well…well, yes, but that was hardly violence."

"You drew blood. You nearly bit his thumb off," he said, a smirk on his lips, eyes glittering, challenging her. "I would bet you would've done serious damage if you'd been able to connect with those feet of yours."

"But that was…."

"Self-defense," he said, finishing her sentence for her. "Self-defense, Zola. In self-defense, I will use violence, but first, I will use my head. This morning I couldn't shoot him dead, although I don't think anyone would've blamed me if I had. He was on our side of the fence, and his intent was clear. He was going to burn this farm down. I aimed my shot to hit the ground in front of him, not to kill him."

Suddenly, she found herself wrapped in his strong arms. Her cheek against his solid chest. Closing her eyes, she savored the moment. Fish dangling on a string in one hand, she patted his chest with her free hand and sniffed back the tears that dampened her cheek. "You have work to do. I have work to do," she said.

To free herself, she waggled the fish in front of him. "I'll be in the orchard picking apples and pears this morning."

"The orchard? That's up on the hill? No, Zola, not this morning."

"Yes, Mr. Kenyon. It's past time to pick the apples and the pears. I've promised them to Mr. Dockendorf at the mercantile."

"Fine, but take the rifle."

"Why?"

"Because, we live next door to a madman."

Voice raising an octave, she said, "What good would a gun do me? I told you I've never handled a gun before."

Yelling at her, he waved his arms in the air, "Use it like a club then, I don't care, just take the damn gun with you."

"I'll take it, but I refuse to load it," Zola said.

In a huff, she muttered to herself all the way back to the house. *Odious man. Bully. Drat him, he's right. It isn't smart for any of us to go off by ourselves anywhere on the homestead, especially the orchard with Mr. Emory on the prod?* She set her chin and put her nose in the air. *Mr. Emory will not keep me from my work or my daily chores. I will pick our apples and pears this morning. I will not be cowed, not by Mr. Emory or Mr. Kenyon.*

Chapter Ten

Shortly past mid-day, Oren and Ephraim set the last boulder against the west side bank beneath the support. Leif scrubbed his hands clean in the cold water of the creek and wiped them on his muddy shirt. "I'm going to get cleaned up and let Zola know we're done. I think we should have our lunch at the house, on the porch. No need for her to bring it down here," Leif said to Ephraim as they clawed their way up the bank. "After we eat, we'll get these wagons across."

He retrieved his rifle from the campsite and waved to Ephraim, and set off for the house. Peeking in the kitchen window, looking for Zola, he saw no sign of her. At the well, he stripped off his muddy shirt and trousers, gave them a good slosh in the water pail, wrung them out, and laid them across the handrail before going inside the porch. In his long-johns and stocking feet, he rushed through the house to the stairs and up to his room.

Wearing a clean pair of socks, scrubbed clean, fresh shirt and trousers, hair brushed, he made his way back down to the kitchen, expecting to find Zola. The stove was cold, the table bare, and the trout lay in a pan covered with a tea towel on the back porch. The rifle wasn't in the rack.

The orchard? She'd said she'd be in the orchard.

He grabbed his rifle and leaped down the porch steps, and set off at a run to the orchard of apple, pear, and plum trees on the east side of the house and barns.

He spotted the ladder right off and a basket of apples, but of Zola he saw no sign. Stomach coiling up in a tight knot of fear, he cautiously ducked under the low-hanging branches of an apple tree. In the next row, he found another basket half full of apples. On the other side of the basket, spread out on the ground, he spied the sky blue of Zola's skirt gently fluttering, revealing her white, stocking-encased ankles.

Heart sinking to the bottom of his ribcage, he approached quietly, dreading what he would find. At first, the red scarf she wore to hold back her beautiful hair scared the hell out of him, thinking it to be blood until he realized blood didn't flutter in the breeze.

She lay, shoulders and head leaning back against the fruit-laden apple tree, eyes closed. He fell to his knees at her side, searching her face for bruises, signs of battle. Finally, it dawned on him. She wasn't wounded but sound asleep. Not dead, not hurt, bleeding, but asleep in the orchard like a lovely sprite or wood nymph—he sent up a silent prayer of relief.

The breeze played with her hair. Instead of waking her immediately, he sat back on his heels, taking in every curve and delicate feature, from her ankles to her eyebrows. Unable to resist, he leaned over and brushed her warm cheek with his lips. A sweet little sigh of pleasure emboldened him to place a kiss on her slightly opened lips. She tasted of sweet, sun-ripened apples. Her hair smelled of drying leaves and earth. He sat down beside her and shifted her body from the tree to lean against his side, his arm around her. To his delight, she snuggled in, her hand going to his chest, her legs folding and leaning against his thigh.

He cuddled her and kissed her forehead. She sighed and wiggled her body even closer. He hated to wake her, this was heaven, but wake her he must. "Zola," he said and brushed her cheek with his finger. "Zola, wake up. Wake up, Sweetheart."

"Hmmm, no," she said, all drossy, his stubborn, loveable Zola.

"Sorry, darlin', but you must. The afternoon is passing. Your brother will be home soon, and we haven't had our lunch."

"Fish," she said, wrinkling her freckled nose, eyes squeezed tightly shut.

That made him chuckle. Her eyes flew open. He froze. She blinked herself awake. "Mr. Kenyon," she said and shoved herself out of his embrace.

Cheeks bright pink, she tugged her skirt down, then adjusted the bandana on her head. "Oh, my word. How silly of me. I fell asleep. What time is it?" She made an attempt to get up and tipped forward, falling against his chest.

Leif couldn't help himself. He couldn't stop laughing. He caught her in his arms. "Unfortunately, it's time for you to wake up."

"Forrest? Is Forrest home?"

"He wasn't when I left the house."

"What are you doing here?" she asked, indignation in her tone and struggling to get to her feet—which had become entangled in her skirt.

Leif took pity on her and offered his hand to help her to stand. "We finished the bridge repair. You weren't at the house. I came looking for you. I was worried about you."

"You needn't have worried. I brought the gun with

me," she said, looking around her and behind the tree. "It's here somewhere. I filled a basket. I think I left it beside the basket."

"This basket?" he asked her, "or that basket over there next to the ladder."

"The ladder, I left it on the ground behind the ladder."

Leif found the rifle and checked the chamber, which was empty. "Did you happen to bring cartridges?"

She ducked her head. Giving her scarf another adjustment, she tucked her curls behind her ears. "You said I could use it as a club."

In a huff, he put the rifle over his shoulder. "Even as a club, it wouldn't do you much good if it's over here and you're asleep on the ground over there."

****

Ashamed of herself for needling the man, she dipped her chin to her chest and wrapped her fingers around the cartridges in her apron pocket to keep them from clacking together. She never carried the rifle loaded, not over uneven ground. It wasn't safe. Shrugging off his scold, chin up, she said, "I still have to pick the pears. Forrest and I, we'll come up after he gets home from school."

"Leave the baskets. Oren can get them in the morning," he said and took her arm, propelling her towards the house. "And tomorrow, you and I are going to take a ride up to the meadow for a shooting lesson. You need to get used to handling a gun."

Suppressing the urge to snicker, she nodded her consent. "Yes, I'm looking forward to it."

Taking long strides, his hand firmly under her elbow, they made their way through the orchard, Zola skipping to keep up.

"I want to go back up to the meadow again, look around. I was thinking of building the sawmill up there somewhere."

Coming to a sudden halt, tipping forward, Zola planted her feet in the tall sweet grass of the orchard. Rounding on him, she jerked free of his grasp. "On the meadow? You want to put your dirty, smelly, noisy mill on my meadow?"

Attempting to move her, he tugged her arm and laughed at her. "It's about the only open spot around here. And it's away from the house. There's bound to be more traffic on the road. I thought to keep it as far away from the house as possible."

He had her by the arm again. Furious, she gathered up her skirts and set off at a brisk quick march out of the orchard. This time, he had to skip to keep up. Voice raised and echoing, shouting over her shoulder, she listed all the reasons why the meadow was totally unsuitable for any kind of industrial enterprise. Every objection she posed, he countered, offering practicalities—*so annoying*.

Reaching the front porch, Zola, on purpose, to give herself a height advantage and the ability to look him squarely in the eye, stopped on the second step and turned to face him. "Tomorrow, I'll show you an alternative, and you will agree with me it is a better location, eliminating a good mile of road, a better source to water, and far less disruption of a natural habitat for the wildlife. Now, I'm done arguing with you," she said and turned her back on him.

Laughing at her, he said, "Arguing? We are discussing. I love discussing with you, Zola—very stimulating."

Her mistake, she turned around, ready to give him another set-down, only to find herself in his arms. No doubt thinking to distract her from her indignation, he planted a very firm and lengthy kiss on her opened mouth. To her everlasting disgust and dismay, she melted. However, recalling her outrage, regaining her senses, she shoved him away and caught herself before she slapped his prepossessing face.

Fists balled, out of breath, flustered, she said, "You shouldn't do that. What if someone sees us? Forrest or Ephraim? You must stop doing that…that…just stop."

Naughty smile in place, he said, his voice a purr, "We're married, Zola, newly married. It's what newlyweds do. They kiss and smooch in broad daylight."

"No," she said, shaking her head, "no, we are not…not your typical newlyweds, and you know it. We are strangers, really, Mr. Kenyon."

Putting his forehead to hers, she had nowhere to look but directly into his eyes. "We're getting to know one another. The judge said—"

Placing her hand over his mouth, she stopped him right there. "The judge said you may kiss your bride as part of the ceremony. It is traditional. He said nothing about all the time, when, and wherever."

Puckering his lips, he kissed her fingers before moving her hand to his jaw. "No, no, now, he gave me permission to kiss my bride, and I'm taking his direction to heart."

"You are ridiculous."

"I'll stop if you don't like my kisses."

Oh, what a despicable man. Of course she liked his kisses. She'd never been kissed. So horribly mortifying and ridiculous to be so vulnerable, and by the look in his eyes, he knew her weakness. Oh, he knew she loved being held and caressed, touched. But, it wasn't dignified. It was wonton. She would not surrender to his advances. Well—not yet, anyway. Gathering up all her dignity, she said, "You're taking advantage of our situation, Mr. Kenyon."

He pulled back and straightened his wide shoulders, looking pleased with himself. "Yes. Yes, I am, and I will continue. But right now, I've got wagons to move," he said with a wave of his hand.

"I'm hungry for some fresh trout," he said, leaving her to simmer in a stew of outrage and desire.

Chapter Eleven

Certainly, she could ride a horse. What a stupid question. At breakfast, the urge to pour the contents of his coffee cup over his head nearly got the better of her. But Forrest giggled, and Oren choked on his biscuit when Mr. Kenyon asked the stupid question, and their mirth stopped her from resorting to violence. The most infuriating thing about the situation, Mr. Kenyon proceeded to prattle on as if he didn't know it was a stupid question. He went right on talking about putting up a poster in town to advertise for qualified, hardworking employees to help him set up and run his filthy mill.

Teeth clenched in a forced smile, instead of pouring coffee over his head, she informed the odious Mr. Kenyon she'd be ready for her shooting lesson and their ride to scout the best place to set up his mill as soon as she cleared away breakfast.

Wallowing in the unfairness of his assumptions, Zola tossed a pair of old trousers on her bed and selected a flannel shirt from her dresser, as well as a pair of much-mended long johns. In her bloomers and chemise, she debated an old brown dress over long johns or trousers and a shirt?

Oren, pears, and apples for the mercantile loaded in the wagon, and Forrest mounted on old Billy, headed for school, had left over an hour ago. Mr. Kenyon would be coming for her any minute now. The time had come. She must choose one or the other, modesty or comfort. Comfort won. To hell with modesty, vanity, and femininity. She hoped she'd repulse him, give him the pip.

Wearing the black trousers she'd hemmed and modified to fit her waist, hair pulled back into a queue, she placed her black felt hat firmly on her head and cinched up the string tight beneath her chin.

On the way down the stairs, she thought it as well the house no longer housed a full-length mirror. She must look a fright.

****

The sorrel gelding saddled and ready, Leif told himself even if Zola wasn't a novice horsewoman, the gelding was the best choice, even tempered and not easily startled. His mare, however, fidgety and frisky, more than ready for a long ride, tugged impatiently at the reins he'd tied off to the porch rail.

Zola came out the door. He looked up, and his heart stopped. Open mouthed, blinking, he asked himself, *"Did she know those trousers amplified her rounded hips and tiny waist?*

She donned her work-worn jacket, and the buttons on her flannel shirt split open, revealing the red underwear beneath. The black hat brought out the glorious copper color of her hair and did nothing to tame the unruly curls escaping, fanning her ears, bouncing over her shoulders and down her back.

Ignoring him, she took the mare's reins. Coming out of his trance, he shook his head and handed her the gelding's reins. "You ride Romeo. He's easier to handle."

She scowled at him, huffed, and went around him, mounting the gelding in a lithe little leap from the ground to the saddle in one graceful move, affording him a view of the many angles, intriguing curves, and dips in her backside. Her bottom filled out the back of those trousers as no other bottom he'd ever seen—not big buttocks, just round and perfectly formed buttocks. Swallowing hard, he rushed to help her get her feet in the stirrups, but when her foot almost connected with his ear, he put up his hands and backed away.

Dismissed and disappointed, he mounted the mare. He had a good idea where they were headed this morning. He'd gone up to the meadow when he'd scouted the timber, but he hadn't paid much attention to what lay on the other side of the creek, and that's where Zola wanted him to put his mill. He wasn't convinced. Allowing her to lead the way, she further baffled him, urging the gelding out the homestead gate instead of turning to go up the track behind the barns.

Puzzled by the direction they were taking, he followed her across the bridge. He opened his mouth to protest but quickly shut it when Zola, after urging the gelding off the road, found a narrow deer trail leading down into a shallow ditch behind a dense thicket of willows, ivy, and brambles. To his surprise, the trail opened up on a nearly flat, small meadow.

She reined in and turned in the saddle. "If you put your mill here, or even farther up the hill, you wouldn't have to reinforce the bridge or make it wider. You'd have a southwest face with a noise barrier of a hillside and the woods for the homestead."

"I didn't look at this side of the property when I was here. Where's the property line? How far south does it go?"

"Probably a half-mile, maybe more, out there to that copse of oak, maybe a little more. The best thing about this spot, no one owns west of you."

"No one, not Emory?"

"No. His property is all on the other side of the road and goes in back of the town and stays north of the creek."

"Who does own it then?"

"I don't really know. Papa wasn't interested in it. He said this land had way too many rocks, and he wasn't about to try to farm it, and the grass is poor, not good for grazing. He was thinking sheep, maybe, someday."

"Is there a way we can get up there?" Leif asked and pointed to a basalt pillar on the side of the hill.

She urged the gelding into motion. "One of my favorite spots," she said.

"Don't you mean another one of your favorite spots?" he said, falling in line behind her. "I still want to look at the meadow."

"I know, but I think you'll come to your senses. This is the best place. No bridge, a little closer to town, and easy to put in a road."

Ignoring her, he said, "We'll set up a target there behind the outcropping, probably better than the meadow."

****

While Mr. Kenyon set up the targets, Zola walked to the edge of the basalt ledge to take in the vista before her. The meadow below, the neat double row of homes and businesses of the town, the church spire, the farms and orchards dotting the small valley at the base of the Cascade Mountains presented a picturesque tableau. The last time she'd come up here, she and her mother had sat here to enjoy a picnic.

With memories of happier days, her head full of melancholy thoughts, she didn't notice when he'd come up behind her. "I can see why this is one of your favorite spots," he said, a hand to his brow to shade his eyes from the afternoon sun. "I see what you mean about the meadow below, a road in and out would be no problem, and the trees, and this hill would definitely make a good barrier against the noise and traffic. C'mon, I've got the targets ready. And I checked out your rifle. It's in pretty good order. Someone's oiled it recently, probably Ephraim."

Irked, she pressed her lips together. Yes, she kept the rifle in good order as her mother had taught her.

Mr. Kenyon pointed to the sticks he'd positioned on a fallen log, three in a row about twenty yards away, three more ten yards farther back, and a white cloth tied and waving in the breeze from a branch above the log.

She let him go through all the safety instructions. "Let me see you load the shells."

He nodded his approval, and she waited for his next instruction but found herself unprepared for his next move. He got behind her, his arms going over her shoulders to position the rifle just so, his body pressed intimately against her backside, she could feel his belt-buckle in the small of her back.

"Relax. Try not to startle or tense up. The recoil could bruise your shoulder. Site in the rifle. Pick your target."

Stifling a nervous giggle, she inhaled and squeezed her eyes shut. Willing herself to concentrate, she released her breath, focused on the target, took her shot, and splintered the first stick. Automatically, without thinking, she held out her hand for another shell, loaded, and took out the next stick and so on, coming to the white cloth waving in the tree, which she shredded before detaching the limb at the knot.

He relieved her of the rifle, his expression inscrutable, and replaced it in its scabbard. "You are a liar. You accuse me of lying when you are a much better liar than I could ever hope to be, Miss. Pretty. How can I trust you?"

Unable to meet his gaze, she fumbled with the buttons on her jacket. Addressing her buttons, she said, "If I had told you I'm a crack shot and I've been shooting a rifle since I was old enough to carry it without falling down from the weight of it, you would've dismissed my claim as boasting, and assumed I knew nothing of how a rifle actually feels and works." Raising her chin, challenging him, she looked him square in the eye. "Of course, you couldn't wait to instruct, helpless, dumb little ole' me on how to use a big, bad manly weapon."

Ignoring his narrowed gaze and scowl, regrettably, she continued, unable to stop herself from over-justifying her silly, petty motives for lying. "My mother taught me how to handle a rifle. My father didn't think it proper a woman should know anything about guns. Forrest knows how to shoot. I think Oren taught him. He's brought home game. But mother and I, we enjoyed shooting at targets, moving and stationary. We never shot to kill anything." Pressing her lips together, she told herself to shut up.

Expression softening a bit, he removed his hat, scratched his head, replaced it, and asked an unseen entity above, "What are we gonna do? We're both liars."

"We could promise not to lie to each other," she said and kicked a rock, watching it tumble to the side of the trail.

A snort that could've passed for laughter escaped his lips. "You believe your parents had a good marriage?"

The question caught her off guard, coming out of nowhere. "What has that got to do with anything? Yes, they were devoted to one another."

"Did your mother tell your father you and she were wasting bullets on targets and tree limbs?"

"You really are annoying." She could feel sweat forming on her scalp at the base of her curls beneath her hat and swiped the darn thing back from her head, letting it hang by the strings down her back. Shaking out her hair with her fingers, she said, "My mother would've adored you. She always said there is no such thing as an absolute truth, only shades of dark and light in circumstance."

He took a short walk around in a circle and came back to her. "I like that. All right, here's the deal, if circumstances arise, and I believe it's for your protection or peace of mind, I won't lie, but I might withhold facts, or shadows, so to speak."

Hands on hips, she shook her finger at him. "You most certainly will not withhold facts from me as you did yesterday morning. All of us must be on our guard, alert."

Grasping that shaking finger, clasping it tightly within his hand, he grinned at her. "Fine, I promise to tell you of any and all threats to your safety in a timely manner before or after they occur."

Zola considered his words. He'd given himself wiggle room. She didn't like that. But she didn't have to show all of her cards either. Rocking back on her heels, choosing her words very carefully, she said, "I promise…I promise to carry a loaded rifle when I go into the orchard or take my walks up to the meadow. And I promise to stop being a stubborn fool if you will stop being a know-it-all bully."

He didn't blink but narrowed his eyes and twisted his lips to the side, drawing her closer to his body. His hand tightened around her hand. "Neither of us should promise more than we can deliver."

She slapped his chest. "You're really, really annoying."

"You'll get used to me," he said and passed her the gelding's reins. "Now, on to the meadow."

Reins in hand, she didn't move. "We'll have to go back down and cross the creek at the falls."

"Falls? There are falls?"

"Pretty Falls, they aren't much, shallow, but there's good fishing in the deep pool below the falls," she said. Ducking her head, she added under her breath, getting between the horses so he couldn't possibly hear, "As if I have a choice of getting used to, or not, getting used to you, you annoying man."

****

Crabapple trees and hawthorn lined the meadow. On the slope above, bright colors from vibrant yellow and orange to deep rust and crimson decorated the alder and maple. Emerging from the conifer forest trail onto the expansive meadow, meadow grass up to their shoulders, four doe and a six-point buck stood nearby, wide-eyed alert, jaws grinding the apples they'd gleaned from the ground and low hanging branches.

"Close your eyes," Zola said.

Leif hesitated, bit his tongue to keep from asking why, and did as ordered.

"Visualize a big, loud, messy mill in the middle of this paradise. In the spring, it bursts into a bouquet of iris, meadow sweet, camas and daisies, wild carrot. The deer are always here and the elk too. You can't put a mill here."

Leif opened his eyes and patted the mare's neck, taking a good hard look around at the geography. "No, not the right spot. It's too far from the road. Obviously, it's an old slide. The ground is unstable. It could slide again if disturbed. I see it now." He urged the mare into the open, and the deer ambled off to take cover in the deeper woods.

Zola dismounted and let the reins fall to the ground. The gelding began to graze. She plucked a white head off a wild carrot and twirled it between her fingers, her gaze to the west. "We should probably get home. It must be time for lunch."

Leif dismounted. The mare joined the gelding, nudging Leif to the side to get at the succulent grass hidden beneath the taller dry blades. "We promised truth," he said, standing close behind her. "At the risk of scaring the hell out of you, I'm going to speak my mind."

He heard her suck in her breath. Her shoulders went back, head up, she stiffened. He put his arms around her and drew her back to rest against his chest. "Today, I'm overwhelmed by my incredible good fortune. I'm a patient man. But I dream of taking you to wife in every way. To keep things equal, I hope you will take me to husband in every way, favor for favor.

She made a weak attempt to step away from him. He couldn't allow that, of course, and brought his face down to the side of her head so he could speak in her ear.

"In the spirit of finding our way to a better understanding, I'm going to share a bit of personal information with you. It's only fair, after your…shall we call it…disclosure, when you told me about your mother and how you were together."

He felt her body relax ever so slightly. He wouldn't call it encouragement, but she didn't try to get away.

"My brother has always been my friend, my partner. Two weeks ago, you became my new partner, whether I liked it or not. You, Zola, you are my partner. It is a very, very good thing. I'm grateful. No one is more surprised than me. I could never have imagined I'd have anyone in my life, a woman, who would challenge me, advise me, and like my brother, put me in check. But I want more. I want you to be my wife, my friend, and my partner, Zola."

She remained rock still. He could feel her heart beating wildly beneath the hand he had on her chest to hold her against him. "Say something, Zola."

Her voice a breathless whisper, she said, "I can't."

Going limp against him, she said, "I can't. It's too soon."

He allowed her to turn within his arms. Placing her hands on his chest to hold him at arm's length, she said, "Days, only four days living in the same house together, three, really."

"Are you afraid? Are you afraid of me?" Head down, she wouldn't look at him. He tipped her chin up with his finger. Her cheeks were bright pink, her freckles delightfully cinnamon-pink, eyelids fluttering, working hard not to look him in the eye. "C'mon, talk to me."

"I am most certainly not afraid of you. You make

me nervous."

She put her arms down to her side. "But…since we are speaking of glaring truths here, yes, I do have something to say." She stepped away from him. "Basically, you bought me along with the house, barns, and animals. All things considered, I shouldn't like you at all, but I do, and I hate myself. I feel a traitor to my parents because I…I like you too much. I've never had a friend. And you are the closest I've come to having one. It's sad—pathetic?"

Dismissively, Leif shrugged his shoulders. "No, I don't think it's pathetic. My brother is ten years older than me, and he's the only parent, friend, and brother I've ever had. I know what you're saying. I understand.

"My brother and his wife are friends, partners. When he got married, I felt betrayed for a very long time. I got over it, but there for a while, I was a real bastard. I swore I'd never marry. But here I am, married to you, and you are my partner. We're still setting the rules of this partnership, but I'm confident we can do it."

Fingers to her lips, she took a moment. Finally, she met his gaze. "My mother and father were, I think, just husband and wife, not partners or friends. They loved one another, but Father didn't consult with Mother. And as you pointed out, she didn't share everything with him. He didn't care about counting the bullets because he rarely carried a gun. He did clean it, and keep it in good order."

"I'm a greedy son-of-a-bitch, Zola. I want it all," he said and stepped closer to her, resisting the need to hold her in his arms. "Now I have a wife, I want her—*you*, not just as my partner and friend, but my lover. I want you in my bed every night. I want to kiss you in broad daylight. If you can't or won't allow yourself to give this marriage your all, I need to know. I'll back off, ignore you as much as I can."

Startled, big brown eyes flew open. "You want an answer right now, this minute? Today? "She shook her head. "This partner thing is really about the fact you want me in your bed. You want me to surrender, let you use me for your base, animal pleasure."

Leif, a brief stab of guilt holding at bay his denial, admitted to himself, yes, she'd hit it right on the head. He wanted her. He wanted her complete compliance. And he didn't want to wait, spend one more night alone in that big bed and haunted room. Releasing his breath, he said, "All right, yes, God help me. I didn't expect I would be this desperate to have you."

"Why? Why are you desperate? Is it because I'm not falling all over you?"

Damn the woman, of course, she couldn't let the subject die. She waved her arms over her head, shoving herself away from him. "Oh, this is a ridiculous conversation. It's embarrassing. The frankness is…unnerving. I'm a very down-to-earth person, I hold very few illusions, and I have absolutely no fancy dreams of any kind of bliss, but this…this is beyond pragmatic. Where's the romance?"

That made him smile and gave him a lot of hope. "I love it that you're a practical person. I saw it immediately. I think you'd laugh in my face if I tried to romance you. You know you would. I bet there have been suiters, suiters with flowers and candy plying you with compliments. I bet you were sickened rather than impressed."

She pursed her lips and shook her head. Going to her

mount, she muttered under her breath. "Soppy hog-wash, odes to my hair, my eyes. My hair is awful, and I know it." Putting one foot in the stirrup, she gave a bounce and swung herself into the saddle. "I'm hungry."

Leif handed her the reins. "You haven't answered my question."

She nudged the gelding into motion. "I'm thinking, I'm thinking."

Chapter Twelve

"I put the posters up and got the word out you're hiring," Oren said, reaching for another slice of ham. "Miss Gladys made me promise to remind you two they want to treat you to a wedding lunch. Any day but Sunday, Miss Paulette says.

"We need to let them do that and get it over with," Leif said.

"I'd hoped they'd forgotten," Zola said and offered more coffee all around.

"Those two ladies forget nothin'," said Ephraim. "They know everyone's name. Who's gonna have a baby, birthdays, and who's related to who and where they were born. There ain't no gettin' out of anythin' with those two."

"Gotta wait for a crew, so I s'pose Saturday we go have lunch with the Abbot sisters," Leif said to her.

"I think it's gonna rain," she said. "I don't want to go to town in the rain."

For reply, Leif snorted.

****

Zola spent the afternoon doing laundry, keeping busy, trying not to think about Leif Kenyon and the coming night. When Forrest got home, they finished cleaning potatoes and squash, rubbing them with vinegar, preparing them for storage in the root cellar.

Her thoughts vacillated between tingling

117

anticipation of what the night would hold and intense resentment at being forced to make a choice. She'd distilled her choices down to two: go ahead, be a proper wife, share a bed with her husband or remain aloof, impervious to all Mr. Kenyon's charms and advances. The latter, she knew very well she could not maintain for much longer. But...the *but* was this—this partnership lacked one basic ingredient...*love.* The simple matter of availability, expediency, practicality with Mr. Kenyon set her to wondering if a marriage, a good, loving marriage, could evolve from such basic components?

Her answer? Yes, certainly. Many marriages were arranged between people, strangers, who had far less in common than she had with Mr. Kenyon, and they lasted and were successful. The fact of the matter, she had no hope of more—a marriage of love and attraction. The very least she could do for herself was allow herself a bit of warmth. That's what Mr. Kenyon offered, a bit of warmth and companionship. The physical side of marriage, the consummation, was a requirement. By supper, she'd almost—*almost*—convinced herself she had a duty to join her husband in bed.

At full dark, she had supper on the table, but the men had not come to the house. Claiming starvation, Forrest had already eaten. Unable to wait, he'd gone upstairs to his room to study. Which she didn't believe for a moment. She suspected his studies consisted of the latest dime novel murder mystery. She'd spotted it under his bed when she'd changed his sheets.

Tired of waiting, she went out to the front porch to beat the dinner bell. Riderless, Mr. Kenyon's mare trotted into the yard. Ephraim caught her bridle and stroked her nose.

"Ephraim? Is she hurt?"

"No, Ma'am. She's all lathered up, though."

Holding her skirts up, sprinting across the yard, Zola asked, "Did Mr. Kenyon say where he was going? "When did he leave?"

"He left 'bout a half-hour ago, I'd say. Said he wanted to ride next to the creek."

"Get torches," Zola said and rushed through the opened gates to the yard.

Not bothering to wait for a torch—she knew her way by heart. She made her way to the opening where the thicket ended, and the tall grass of the meadow began. On the path lay a dark form, not a boulder or a log.

"Mr. Kenyon—Leif?" Emitting a small mew of despair, Zola crumpled to her knees. "Leif?" Leaning over his body, she brushed his golden hair from his brow, feeling the warmth of his skin beneath her fingers. She realized he wasn't dead, but hurt.

Ephraim rushed to her side and held his torch up to see better.

****

Leif, eyes squeezed shut against the brightness, groaned at the indignity of his situation. He laughed or tried to. Opening his eyes, grateful help had arrived, he saw the worried faces hovering over him. They looked like floating heads, faces black, swimming in a sea of hot white. A sharp, unforgiving pain in his right side sucked the wind out of him. He wanted to get up but couldn't even roll over.

"Don't move," Zola said. She sounded really angry, which made him chuckle, sending another knife of pain into his chest.

He felt her cool fingers soothing his brow. Her face

very close to his lips, she asked him, "Where do you hurt? Your chest? Your head? Shoulder? Where? Leif, can you tell me where?"

He tried to take a deep breath and failed but managed to gather up several small breaths to say, "My pride. My pride is in tatters." Foolishly, he attempted to sit up.

Next thing he knew, when he opened his eyes again, he was in his big bed, in his nightshirt, with Zola, sniffing back tears, sitting on the edge of his bed, bathing his brow, muttering to herself, chastising foolish men who rode around the countryside in the dark.

"Ha, got you in my bed at last," he said and wished he didn't have to breathe.

"Not, *in*, I'm on—*on* your bed?" she said, wringing out a towel over a bowl of water.

Shifting his weight, he thought to sit up. A blinding pain shot from his right shoulder down his spine to his right hip.

"You probably have some cracked ribs. You've got some impressive bruising on your right hip and across your chest. Your left shoulder is bruised. Ephraim says it's not broken. You've got a big goose egg over your left brow. You're probably concussed."

"And you know all this, how?" he asked, eyes watering, hissing back the pain.

"Ephraim and Oren. They bandaged your ribs. They got your clothes off, cleaned you up, and got you in your nightshirt."

A sudden, overwhelming urge to cry swept over him. Instead, Leif just got mad. "This is a damn mess. I can't be laid up like this. I've got to get the mill set up. I need to get into town, talk to the land agent, go to the bank—talk to people. Zola, this is hell."

****

Skirts hiked up to her thighs, Zola swung her leg over him and held him down by his good shoulder to get down into his face. "Getting yourself all worked up isn't going to help your recovery."

He sank back against his pillows. "Hit me across the chest—something—felt like a tree, or a limb—hit me across the chest. I had my arm out. I held it up to get under the overhanging jungle."

"What?" she said and settled back on her haunches, careful to keep her weight off his hips and ribs.

"I could see, not full dark. Delores shied. Crows flew up, spooked her. Why didn't he kill me? He had me down and out, why not finish me off?"

"Delores? Who's Delores?"

"My mare. Named her after my first love," he said and sighed.

"Oh," Zola said but didn't move.

"I was six. Delores Downing, my teacher. Broke my heart. Left me. Married a banker. I don't trust bankers."

"You're not making much sense," she said and swung her leg to the side to stretch out beside him, her arm going across his body, a hand lying on his left arm, the arm snugged to his chest and in a sling. "I have laudanum if you need it."

"No," he said and sighed, "no, you're all I need."

"I should get you something to eat."

"No, please, don't move."

"I'm cold," she said and pulled a quilt over her. "The Amish call this bundling."

"Bundling?"

"Engaged couples are allowed to sleep in the same

bed before marriage fully clothed if the blankets are between their bodies."

"Ah, bet they don't have cracked ribs and a concussion, though."

She giggled and snuggled in. He let himself drift off into sleep.

Zola woke, the body next to her radiating heat, clammy with fever. She rolled carefully off the bed and bathed his face with a cool cloth. He opened his eyes, glazed and feverish, and said, "Thirsty."

"I'm getting the laudanum," she said before offering him a sip of water from a cup. He swallowed and begged for another drink.

"No laudanum, stuff makes me sick as a dog. Headache powder? Works good."

"I don't know if we have any."

"Ask Ephraim. Takes it for his lumbago."

Her hand pressed firmly against his forehead, "Don't try to get up," she said, her tone holding a threat. "I will be right back. Do not move." She rushed out the door.

Zola found Ephraim at the kitchen table, coffee cup in hand.

"How's he doin'?" he asked her.

"A little feverish."

"Thought he might get that a'way."

"He wants headache powder. I don't know if I have any. He says laudanum makes him sick."

"Same with me," Ephraim said and shoved a small box of headache powder across the table to her. "I could sit with him for a while."

"I've been asleep. I'm fine. What time is it?"

"Don't know, but I'd guess a couple hours before

dawn."

"I'll come back down as soon as he goes back to sleep."

"Oren, and me will get breakfast up for Forrest. You take care of Mr. Kenyon and yourself."

Zola poured herself a cup of hot water to make herself a cup of tea. "He said he was hit across the chest with something. A tree limb?"

"Mr. Emory?"

"Yes, that would be my guess too. Leif doesn't understand why he didn't finish him off."

"I been sittin' here wonderin' the same thing. Delores, she scared him off maybe."

"We have to get him well, and fast, I think," Zola said to her reflection in the window above the sink.

"Yes, Ma'am."

Chapter Thirteen

You can't keep me prisoner in this room, Zola. I'm getting out of this bed today," Leif said and tossed back the covers.

"I think you should," she said, laying out a clean towel and a cake of soap. She poured out a stream of hot, steaming water from her kettle into the washbowl on top of his bureau. "Sing out if you need help," she said and closed the bedroom door behind her.

For two days and three strange but incredible nights, Zola had not left his side for more than an hour or two. But as much as he had enjoyed her attention, it was Monday morning, and he had a new crew of men to interview and address.

Impatient, careful of his bruised shoulder, battling through the breath-sucking pain in his ribcage and a king-sized headache, sweating, he donned his underclothes, trousers, and shirt, ignoring buttons undone. Frustrated by his weakness, he left the house. The yard lay unusually quiet. He'd expected to find a few strangers roaming around, at least Ephraim or Oren. Instead, it appeared abandoned.

"Oren's gone into town," Ephraim said, opening the door behind him, and coming out on the porch to stand at his side.

"Where are the men, the crew?"

"That's why he's gone to town. No one showed."

"No one?"

"No, sir, not a single soul."

"I should've gone with him."

"No sir. You let Oren nose around a little. Come with me. We got us a problem." Ephraim led him to the side of the house. In the grass, before the wood pile, lay a tree limb about six or seven inches in diameter. "I went back next mornin' to have a look around as soon as it got light, and I spotted it right off. See that rope tied there around it? The other end is tied off to a willow. Somebody set it up and then cut the rope a'purpose, used it like a sling-shot to knock you off your horse. Lucky you ducked sideways and it hit you in the chest. If you'd been sittin' straight up, it'd whacked your head right off, and you wouldn't be standin' here. My guess is he thought he'd done killed you. Lucky Delores didn't allow him time to check."

"Something's gotta be done about this, Ephraim."

"I'd say so, sir. I'd say so."

"Has Zola seen this?"

"I have," Zola said, approaching from the house and the back porch.

"Why didn't you tell me about this?" Leif said, pointing to the limb.

"When should I have told you?" Zola asked, hands on hips. "You've had a fever for two days, in pain. What could you have done other than thrash around and make yourself sicker."

"I could...I should've gone to town this morning. Damn it, Zola, It's almost noon. We said we weren't going to keep important things from each other. I needed to know about this."

She came right up to him, her head at chin level, and

raised her face and her voice, "And I needed to keep you in bed. I had to decide what was best for you."

"So, you get to decide what's best for me to know or not know, but I don't get to decide what's best for you to know or not know?"

She had the grace to tuck in her chin and her temper. "Fine, yes, I concede circumstances will always be considered. But…but it chafes. It really chafes, doesn't it?"

He laughed and doubled up in pain, holding on to his side. "Damn it, that hurts."

Zola ducked under his arm and put her hand on his back. "Lean on me. Time to go inside. We'll wait for Oren at the table. You haven't had much to eat in the last couple of days. You need to eat."

"Wagon's comin'," Ephraim said. "We'll join you directly after we get the team unhitched."

"I want a full report. Nothing left out," he said.

Zola nudged him toward the porch steps. "Oh, hush. You know everything we know. No one's hiding anything from you."

With Zola's help, they made it up the steps and into the kitchen. Breathless and sweaty, Leif sank into a kitchen chair. "God, I hate this. I've never felt so damn useless in all my life."

Zola passed him a cup of coffee and an oatmeal and raisin muffin and sat down across from him. "Maybe we should notify your brother things haven't exactly gone to plan here."

Frustration getting the better of him, the eruption came suddenly and unexpectedly violent. He pounded the table with his fist. The table shook so hard his coffee spilled in his lap. "Hell, Gunnar would come in here and take over—run roughshod over you, Ephraim, Oren, Forrest, the whole damn town. No, not going to notify my big brother. No reason to. This is my fight—our fight—and we'll take care of it." Wincing, he hugged his bad arm, eyes watering, and he gasped for air between lightning bolts of pain.

Calmly, Zola rose, plucked a tea towel off the peg next to the sink, and handed it across the table to him.

Gathering his dignity, he calmed his breathing. "Sorry, I'm sorry," he said and rubbed his shoulder and the back of his neck. "I love my brother. He raised me from a pup. I worked in his damn mill as a kid. At sixteen, I left to join the cavalry. He didn't say a word. He didn't have to. I felt his disapproval and disappointment in every scowl and grumble he uttered. I mustered out after five years, and instead of going to work in his mill, I ran for sheriff and got the job. He didn't say a word—*again*—but his silence spoke volumes. When I quit the law, we tried going partners. That woke both of us up. We do not work well together. But we could be long-distance partners, me with my way of runnin' things over here on this side of the mountain, and Gunnar way the hell on the other side."

"Emory has to be stopped," Zola said. "He killed my father. I'm sure of it."

"He sure as hell does have to be stopped," Oren said, entering the kitchen.

Zola rose to bring her pot of beef stew and a plate of sliced bread to the table. Leif started to turn towards the doorway and stopped as a stab of pain shot up his neck and out his ears.

As soon as he could breathe again, he asked, "Well, tell us, did you learn anything? Where's our crew?"

Oren pulled up a chair and sat down. "Well, sir, word's out you are dead," Oren said, then dived into the pot of stew, spooning it over a thick slice of Zola's bread.

"Dead?" Leif leaned over the table. "How did I die?"

"Seems you came home in the dark and got smacked in the head with a widow-maker, you know, a tree limb, a broken one."

Leif held onto the side of the table. "And the source of this sad news is?"

Oren shrugged his massive shoulders. "No-one seems to know 'zactly. Some said they heard it at the bank. Others thought the sheriff or his deputy said somethin' about it. The Abbot sisters were particularly disturbed. They said their cousin, the judge, gave them the news."

"And what did you say in response?" Zola asked while she poured Oren a cup of coffee, then Ephraim, who had joined them. She set the honey and butter on the table and sat down.

"Well, I told'em hog-wash, Mr. Kenyon is alive and well and rarin' to get on with settin' up his mill. We need hands, lots a hands, to get it done. I told'em you were mighty steamed nobody showed up this mornin'. I told'em if they don't get a hustle on, you're goin' to go on over to Paradise and muster up some men willin' to work for wages, so they better line up and get a move on, is what I told'em."

Oren took a breath and grinned. "I put six men to work clearing brush from the road to the south meadow before I came in through the gate. There's nine more men comin' this afternoon. We better eat quick, get ready to line'em out."

"Oren Gooding, I could kiss you," Zola said and gave the big man a pat on the shoulder.

"Good man. It's a start," Leif said. "A damn good start. We should be able to get a road to the site and stabilize the ground for the mill set-up by the end of the week."

"*We*, Mr. Kenyon?" Zola asked, palms on the table. "You have one good arm, several broken ribs, and a cracked skull. You're weak from having a fever for two days. You go to work, work too hard, and you're going to do yourself some real harm."

"Don't you worry, Miss Zola," Ephraim said, slathering butter and honey on his bread. "Oren and me 'ill see to it he don't over-do it. Mr. Kenyon's gonna tell us what he wants done, and we're gonna see it done."

"I just remembered something, Ephraim," Leif said while he sopped up the stew on his plate with his bread. "Did you find a sack of dirt near where you found me?"

"Yeah, I did. Probably saved you, kinda broke your fall."

"Where is it?"

"I think I left it near the bridge somewhere."

"Get it, Ephraim. Get that sack and put it on the porch."

"What's in it?" Ephraim asked.

"I scooped up some silt and sand from the pool below the falls."

"From the pool? Why-ever would you do that?" Zola asked

"I want to have a closer look at it. Emory wants this place. We need to find out why."

Zola huffed and shook her head at him. Ginger brows raised over her beautiful brown eyes, and her gaze scanned the occupants of her table one at a time. "Don't any of you think we should bring the law into this? We're under attack. We all know Mr. Emory is behind these…these clumsy attempts to scare us. I'm going to town, and I'm taking the tree limb, the weapon, with me, and I'm going to drag it into the sheriff's office and put it on his desk."

"Won't do any good," said Ephraim, head down, staring at his now clean plate. He rubbed his belly. "David Daniels don't do nothin' about nothin' unless there's somethin' in it for him."

Zola pushed herself away from the table. "He certainly wasn't much help when Papa died. He wouldn't even consider foul play."

"That's 'cause you wouldn't make it worth his trouble," said Oren.

That brought the fire to her eyes and a flash of pink to her cheeks. "What could I offer him? I didn't have any money. He knew I didn't." She snatched the coffee pot from the table and set it none to gently down on the stove.

Leif and Ephraim shared a look, lips tucked up tightly to the side and brows raised. When she turned back to them, the two men put their heads down.

Leif set his fork on the table beside his empty plate. "I have yet to meet this David Daniels, Sheriff of Prettydale. Why is that?"

"Spends most his time warmin' his backside in the backroom of the mercantile. Emory, the Judge, Shaw the banker, all of'em meet up there, play a hand or two of poker, swillin' Emory's homemade juice."

"Friends with Emory and the banker, that's interesting," said Leif. He shoved himself away from the table. "Well, we need to see how the men are doing. I'm going to get my plans. They're in my room."

Chapter Fourteen

Zola followed him upstairs, and standing in the doorway, hands shoved deep into the pockets of her apron, she asked, "Did I mention they're all investors in the Northern Pacific Railroad?"

Leif rolled up the papers he'd spread out on the chaise lounge in front of the big window. "You think that's what this is about?"

"Papa mentioned it once or twice. He said they were greedy weasels. He hated the carpetbaggers. That's what he called the railroad men when they came to town and filled the town with their cigar smoke and rude, loud laughter. He said Emory and Shaw were courting them, encouraging them to look for a pass that would put Prettydale on the map, grow the town—bring more carpetbaggers."

"Mr. Prine mentioned the pass. It's on the homestead property, isn't it?" Leif asked, gazing out the big window.

"There's a trail up to the lake. It cuts across the south meadow and into the foothills. Papa bought the land. But the property boundary ends several miles short on this side of the lake. The trail goes around the lake. We used to camp there. I've never been beyond the crest of the Cascades."

Leif crossed the room and stopped before her. "I've been to that lake too. Funny isn't it? We've both been there, you on your side and me on the other, and now here we are." He pressed a finger to her cheek. "Stay with me, Zola. I don't want to be on one side of a wall and you on the other. Sleep at my side. Be my wife."

She closed her eyes and tipped her head the better to feel the warmth of his hand on her cheek.

****

An hour later, dressed in trousers, a warm shirt, coat, and hat shoved down low on her head, Zola rode Leif's gelding out to the south meadow. Reining in beside his mare, she said, eyes looking straight ahead, "I'm with you. We are in this together—partners."

"If you've come out here to nag me about overdoing….you can save your breath. I'm feeling pretty good out here in the fresh air," he said, his chin out a mile.

Gazing up at him, the brim of her hat shading her eyes, she offered him a sly smile. "I know better. Wouldn't waste my time trying to talk reason to a mule. I came out here because I thought of something you need to see."

He stared at her for a long moment. Slowly, his eyes crinkled up at the corners and a sweet smile lit up his face. "I'm really happy to have you out here with me. I promise I will tell you if I get tired."

Nodding approvingly, she said, "Good, and I promise not to say I told you so when you end up back in bed with a fever."

He tipped his hat to her and set it firmly back on his head with a tap on the brim. "Fair enough. Now, what is it you want to show me?"

"Scree, lots of scree for the road in here to your mill. Up there, beneath the basalt pillar, on the south side, there's tons of scree, gravel. I want to show you the trail to the lake, and there's a cave. The cave is more of an indentation in the side of a big rock outcropping. It has bats. Do you feel good enough to go for a ride?"

They stopped to let Ephraim know where they were going. Zola led the way around the base of the hill to the south of the pillar. The well-worn trail zig-zagged up the side of the hill. The trail, littered with loose shale, basalt and granite scree, and very little vegetation, caused the horses' hooves to send small avalanches down the steep slope. At last, the trail swung between the hill and a huge granite boulder, and the ground leveled out beneath a gnarled pine that hung out over the edge of the mountain.

Zola urged the gelding a few yards away from the edge of the trail, dismounted, and tied him off to an old fallen snag. She held the mare's reins and stood back, sensing Leif wouldn't appreciate her assistance, but prepared to come to his aid should he need it. He winced, took a deep breath, and slowly lowered himself from the saddle to the ground. He stood for a few moments, one hand gripping the saddle horn, eyes closed, and head bowed.

To cover for him, giving him some time to recover, Zola tied the mare's reins off on a dead branch and brushed the non-existent dust from her hands. "The cave is uphill a little, under the trees," she said. He had managed to catch his wind, and some color had returned to his cheeks. He was looking around, taking his bearings, she supposed.

She started up the shallow incline without giving him a glance. "Watch your step. It's wet, can be a little slippery. The spring drips over the entrance. I haven't been here for ages. You'll have to duck, the entrance is low, but once you're inside, it opens up."

Following closer than she assumed, keeping up with her, not sounding out of breath at all, he said, "Finding granite here seems odd. The basalt must've flowed right over the top of it."

"I like it. It sparkles," Zola said. Standing at the entrance to the cave, she stepped aside, allowing the daylight to filter into the opening and giving Leif room to look inside.

Ducking his head, he entered and stubbed his toe on something. Bending down to dislodge the stone from its nesting place in the soft mud, he hesitated, juggling the rock one-handed. Going on a little farther, he stopped and picked up a handful of rocks. "Let's get some of these rocks and put them in our pockets."

"Why? No, they're covered in mud and slime." She shuddered but selected several stones from the cave floor anyway, but not to put them in her pocket.

"I want to take them back to the house, get a good look at them."

Zola ducked back out into the open and took a deep breath. Sometimes the cave gave her the willies, the walls dark, closing in. Leif followed her out and, taking his time, studied the entrance walls.

"The trail goes on a little farther, going around the side of the mountain, then down into a draw. It meets up with Pretty Creek, then it goes up again," she said, stuffing her jitters aside to put on a brave face.

"How far to the lake do you think?" he asked her, handing her a handful of slime-covered stones.

Wrinkling her nose, she hesitated to take them. Relenting, she opened her coat pocket, giving him leave to drop them in if that's what he wanted. "It's a three-day ride, so fifty miles, maybe more, and mostly uphill all the way." She waited in silence, watching him stuff rocks in his pockets.

She shrugged and did the same, sorting out stones that were not covered in slime or wet mud.

He looked off into the distance. "It's about, I'd guess, thirty or so miles to the lake from the railroad line on the east side of the crest. I can see why the Northern Pacific is interested in this pass. Why don't they just ask for an easement? Don't see why a deal couldn't be reached."

Zola shrugged, unable to give him an answer.

He started back down the path to their horses. "I still think there's more to it than the railroad connection. Emory is willing to kill for whatever is here. I think he's working on his own. It's hard to believe the banker or the sheriff would want to be involved in actual murder. So why? Who knows about this trail?"

Zola mounted the gelding in her usual style, a little leap and leg swing to the side and over the horse's rump. "I guess everybody. It's on an old Indian trail over the mountain. Hunters, traders, lots of folks have used this trail for years and years and years."

Leif led his mare to the snag, stood on the stump, reins between his teeth, and managed to get himself into the saddle. He adjusted his feet in the stirrups. "Emory? Does Emory know about the cave?"

"I couldn't say," Zola said. "I doubt it. It isn't on the trail. A long time ago, Forrest and I made a pact to keep it a secret. We used to play in there. And on hot days, it's a wonderfully cool place to have a picnic. I don't think Forrest has even told his school friends about it."

****

"I put it over there, under that oak," Ephraim said. "Somebody dumped it. It's gone. Even the bag."

Giving his head a good scrubbing, Oren asked the question they all wanted to ask. "Who the hell would steal a bag of dirt?"

Purely on reflex, the mean, nasty little voice inside Leif's head quickly answered Oren's question. He narrowed his eyes, studied the fence line across the road, and cursed the devil, Amos Emory. Giving the matter some thought, pacing back and forth a bit to work off some steam, tossing aside what he'd like to do to Emory, he landed on a more reasonable, hopefully, more fruitful form of retaliation. "Ephraim, here's what I want you to do. Get a burlap sack or a pail and go down to the creek below the falls and scoop out some of the gravel and silt. A bag works best. It allows the water to drain. Make sure no one sees you. I mean, no one. Don't let anyone see the bag or what's in it. Bring it up to the back porch.

"After you've done that, you and Oren put your heads together and come up with some traps. Not traps exactly, but mines, maybe. Something not to maim or wound a critter, but traps set to make a noise or a flash of light when set off to startle the hell out of whatever or whoever is skulking around. Plant them around here by the bridge and along the road near Emory's fence line and maybe a couple in back of the house along the paddock fence. I want to give our neighbor a bit of a scare.

Ephraim's dark eyes lit up, and a grin spread across his dark face. "I know where I can get some hame bells. And I'm thinkin' maybe a fireworks or two. Nothin' that would set a fire, but somethin' that'd make a bang and boom and big smoke."

Leif slapped Ephraim on the back. "That's it exactly. We'll change locations every day. This is going to be a lot of work for you and Oren. Are you sure you can do it?"

"My boy's been prankin' since he could walk. I reckon this is right up his street. He's gonna stay up nights thinkin' up gizmos. And if they're special for our neighbor, it'll be a doubly sweet effort."

"We'll have to make sure to watch the crew and Forrest," Leif said.

"Forrest might have some good ideas. Boy is pretty inventive," Ephraim said.

****

On the back porch, fingers numb with cold from washing pebbles and rocks, Zola listened to the men plotting their idiotic plan. "This has to be the silliest, most asinine thing I've ever heard. You are grown men, not children—boobie traps and noisemakers? Think, please, think for one moment how it will be when some poor deer or coyote sets off one of your...your devices? All night long, we'll be kept from our slumbers with clanging and booming—it's...no...it won't work—it just won't."

"It isn't silly," Forrest said. "I think it's brilliant. Mr. Emory's gonna get the stuffing scared right out of him. Oren says he's found the spot along the fence where he's been crossing next to the road. He's set three of his— what'cha-ma-call-its along there and two more along the paddock fence. And three more where they cleared the thicket. I bet we catch him at it tonight. He's gonna want to see what's been goin' on in the south meadow."

****

Leif had stopped listening. Sifting the silt and scree

gravel through a screen, he'd found quartz with suspicious-looking veins of black and gold. He set the stones aside and continued to sort, feigning disinterest. The bigger stones, and the rock he'd stubbed his toe on from the cave, he'd set on the floor by his feet. He'd washed them outside, intending to send them along with his other finds to Gunnar. Let him take all the samples far away from Prettydale to be assayed.

Clearly, Emory had it right. There was gold in Pretty Creek, but how much and what grade, Leif couldn't guess. He had to assume Emory now had a sack full of gravel from which to glean his own sample. He too, at this moment, could be washing and sorting. He'd get really desperate now. He'd be done playing around.

They had to get into town first thing to see the land agent about the land south and west of the south meadow. The property rights to Pretty Creek were all about the water, but what about the mineral rights? Had Mr. Pretty actually set out stakes and claimed the mineral rights? If he hadn't, then why hadn't Emory staked a claim? It would be simple enough to do. And if he hadn't, why? Why hadn't he just staked a claim if he knew about the gold in there? Something was stopping him. Had Mr. Pretty beaten him to it? But with Mr. Pretty out of the way, the claim would've been dropped.

Not for one moment did Leif think Emory would be frightened off, or be detoured, by a few noise makers. But his wild-eyed, high-strung horse might. Leif smiled to himself at the thought. But he quickly sobered. He had responsibilities, people he cared for now, and more than himself to consider. Extra precautions were called for to keep Zola and Forrest safe, and Ephraim and Oren, and the property—the homestead.

"I think I'll go to the barn, see what Oren and Ephraim have cooked up for this evening's entertainment. Getting too dark to work here anymore," he said to Zola and Forrest.

Zola wiped her cold hands on her skirt. "Time for Forrest to get cleaned up. You need a bath," she said to her brother. "You have time before we eat. The water's ready for you. I put some kettles on the back of the stove. Tub is in the pantry under the counter. Go inside. I'll be along directly."

She shoved her brother through the doorway into the kitchen but held her hand up to stop Leif from leaving the porch. "All right," she said and closed the door to the kitchen, "I saw you set aside some rocks, gravel and you've got the big one from the cave down there next to your feet."

He shook his head and opened his mouth to give her some excuse, but she wasn't having it.

"You think Emory took the bag of dirt. Why? Why would he want a bag of dirt?"

Lips clamped shut, he inhaled, wiped his wet hands on the front of his trousers, and let out his breath. "There is some gold in the gravel. I'm not sure about the bigger rocks. They are really heavy, but that doesn't mean anything. Could be another kind of ore."

Swaying slightly, holding her breath, she squeezed her eyes shut.

He put a hand on her shoulder. "To bet on the safer side, we should...*I'm*...going to assume Emory has come to the same conclusion. For whatever reason, he's suspected there was gold in the creek all along. What I'd like to know is, what gave him the idea in the first place?"

Zola groaned. Tipping forward, she put her forehead against his chest, arms limp at her side. He wrapped his arms around her. She spoke to the buttons on his coat. "Well, Mr. Emory said we were a lot of trouble, remember. He warned you."

He gave her a little shake. "You and Forrest are not trouble. Emory is trouble. There are a lot of Emory's in this world. I know, I've arrested a few, and they're all the same. I know what to do. I'm not so certain what to do about you," he said, coaxing her, his finger beneath her chin to lift her head, to make her lips available to kiss. "I know what I want to do," he said before he pressed his lips to hers.

She allowed the kiss but shoved herself away too soon. "How can you think about…about that—*us*—when Mr. Emory is out there plotting how he's going to kill you, maybe all of us?"

He tugged her back to enfold her in his embrace. "I think we shouldn't waste one more moment. We should live and love each other as hard and as fast as we can. That's what I think."

She huffed. "Of course you do," she said and stepped back. "I've got to get in there and see to it Forrest scrubs behind his ears."

"Zola," he said, reaching for her wrist, "do you hate me? I want you, but I don't want you if…if you can't at least like me…a little."

She came to a stop, arms folded across her chest, and lifted her face, eyes to the porch ceiling. "Right from the first moment I saw you, the day you came to look over the homestead, I—I thought you were beautiful—so very powerful looking."

She had her back to him. He could hardly hear what

141

she was saying.

She wiped her eyes with the back of her hand. "You bought the homestead, and I had to keep you at a distance with my words and actions, remain loyal to my family."

She turned to face him, her brown eyes awash with unshed tears. "But now, Leif Kenyon—I am absolutely—I am absolutely certain I am the luckiest woman alive. A very special angel must be looking out for me and for Forrest. You found us. Providence sent you, and I would be an ungrateful fool to reject you, reject the possibility of finding what every woman dreams of. I more than like you, Mr. Kenyon...Leif. I desperately pray you will, someday, more than *like* me—more than simply desire my body."

Tugging on her wrist, he pulled her back into his embrace. "Your prayers, and my prayers, are the same, Zola. For now, let us settle on a mutual warm regard for one another. You need time, and I'm patient. I'm no threat to your virtue, not with these damn sore ribs."

"On the contrary," she said, tipping her face up to meet his challenging gaze, "it is your vulnerability that finally brought home to me how deeply I care for you—care what happens to you. I'm yours now. You bought me, and you've won my heart. If Emory would leave us alone, I could have peace, and I would be happier than I've been in a very long time."

He put his forehead down to press against hers. "Let's not let Emory take away our joy at being thrown together."

"Can we let him take all the gold he can glean from the creek from the bridge west to the town limits? I don't care about it at all."

"I thought the same thing. But we don't even know

if there is a claim on the creek. The city fathers might have something to say about any claims. After all, it runs right through the middle of town."

Fiddling with the buttons on his coat, she asked, "Do we have to do anything about the gold? It's just going to cause a lot of trouble."

"We can't ignore it. Emory isn't going to. Do you think your father knew about the gold? Would there be any papers or anything to hint he knew?"

Stepping back and away from him, she said, "Tonight, we'll look. But I went through all the bureaus, desks, and cupboards when I sold off the furniture. I didn't find any papers."

Chapter Fifthteen

Zola swore to him she'd found no important papers anywhere. And she couldn't recall ever seeing her father or mother pouring over any papers that looked like legal documents. She'd burned the eviction notices out of defiance. They were short and succinct in their message. She surmised the bank had the deeds to the homestead in a vault. After all, the bank held the notes against the homestead.

There had to be papers, legal papers: marriage licenses, business records. Zola had shown him the account books, but they revealed nothing more than the day-to-day expense and profit of running the homestead. They didn't reveal any information on timber sales. Which he found odd. The sale of logs should've been a substantial transaction. Dotted throughout the ledgers were the sale of hogs, the acquisition of equipment, and the trade deals her father had made, but no legal documents—none. Where were they if they weren't here in the house?

After supper, Leif searched the bare walls and floorboards for irregularities, and the fireplaces for loose bricks, in every room in the house. If the bank had them, those documents belonged to Mr. Pretty's survivors—one more thing Leif added to his list of things to do tomorrow.

The bedroom door opened, and Zola, in her night

rail, chin high and barefoot, entered, hesitating before making a production of closing the door behind her. Facing him, her voice trembling, she said, "From this night forward, I am your wife in every sense of the word. And you are my husband."

Scurrying across the room to the bed, gaze trained on her goal, she slid beneath the covers, laying herself out, arms down to her side, and shut her eyes.

She'd deprived him of his breath, left him bereft of speech. The soft cotton nightgown hid very little of the curves and contours of the naked body it covered. Copper coils of hair surrounded her face, cascading over her shoulders and arms. As she'd passed, she'd left behind the faint whiff of a fragrance not unlike a warm summer rose in full bloom.

Coming to his feet, laying aside all his questions and doubts, he began to disrobe, afraid she'd change her mind if he lingered or asked stupid questions. "I promise you won't be sorry."

Eyes closed, she nodded, adjusting the covers to come up to her chin. Unfortunately, her sacrificial pose struck him funny. Unable to stop himself, he chuckled.

His little red-headed spit-fire threw back the covers, sputtering and hissing curses, and rushed for the bedroom door in high dudgeon. Which would've been very impressive and would've doused his ill-timed and rude amusement if it hadn't been for the fact her nightgown had bunched up between her sweet, tight, round little butt cheeks, exposing her strong, shapely legs clear up to her lovely white thighs.

He caught her around the waist in mid-flight, lifting her up off the floor with one arm.

"Let me go. You said I wouldn't be sorry, then you

laugh at me. No one ever takes me seriously."

"Stop, stop kicking. I'll set you down on the condition you listen to what I have to say in my defense."

She went limp, and he allowed her feet to touch the floor.

"Let go of me," she said.

And he did.

She stood very still and erect. "I'm listening," she said, head tipped to the side, jaw tight.

"You took me by surprise. You came in here and told me you'd be my wife, then you laid yourself out beneath the covers like a virgin on the altar, ready to be sacrificed to me, the evil master. I found it very dramatic, and it struck me as…as funny, is all."

Nose up, sniffing the air, she said, "Sacrificing my virginity is no laughing matter. I did not come to you without careful consideration and thought. You are the only choice I have or ever will have. This is an important step for me. Men may look forward to losing their virginity and think of it as a rite of passage into manhood. But to me, losing my one and only virginity is…is a contract, a signature of a promise to one…one person. For you to laugh at me, take it so lightly, well, it's insulting, humiliating."

He tugged her over to the bed and sat down, coaxing her to sit on his lap. She did, reluctantly, hands folded in her lap. He smoothed her lovely hair behind one ear and dropped his hand to her waist. "I know, I know, sweetheart," he said. "I am humbled and honored. I'm sorry, and yet I'm not sorry I'm the only choice you have or ever will have." His hand slipped down to her lovely thigh. She didn't seem to notice he was touching her bare skin or that her bare bottom was sitting right on his lap.

He smiled to himself. *God, this woman could drive me insane without even trying.*

"I'd rather you look at this, your giving of your virginity, not as a sacrifice but as an adventure into pleasure and satisfaction. Because of my cracked ribs, I really don't think I'll be able to carry out a very vigorous deflowering tonight. I'll try very hard to please you, of course. You can't blame me for wanting to try. The only thing you might be sacrificing tonight is your dignity," he said and reached around to adjust her nightgown over her bare bottom and her bare legs.

Twisting, she sprang to her feet, holding her nightgown around her, and scrambled back under the covers, cheeks aflame.

He slapped his thigh and rose from the bed. "You nursed me bare-chested and slept at my side for the last two nights. You actually snuggled in."

"We had the covers between us," she said.

He stepped out of his trousers and draped them over the bedside chair. "I will keep my drawers on. Not that that would save your virginity if I really wanted it. But I'll give you the illusion of me trying to restrain myself—for now." He removed his socks, no easy chore one-handed, and got under the covers with her.

"Meet me in the middle. I'll put my good arm beneath your head like this," he said. She did as directed. "And you put your arm across my chest just like you've been doing."

"Who's going to turn down the lamp?" she asked.

"Not me," he said. "I'm comfortable right here just like this."

She started to sniffle, making Leif sorry for teasing her. He got up and turned down the lamp. "Zola, you don't have to be here with me if you aren't ready. You can get up and go to your own bed, and I promise I won't be angry with you. I'll be disappointed, but I won't be angry."

"Oh, shut up," she said. "I'm scared of just how ready I am. If you don't get in this bed this minute and hold me, touch me, love me, I think I will die of cowardice. I'm not a beauty. I know that. I'm too short and plump, my hair is an awful color, and I'm covered in freckles. I'm sharp-tongued and pushy."

"You are lovely, lush, proud and intelligent, and absolutely, irritatingly forthright, which I find delightful and challenging.

"Which brings me to confess, even though you warned me, I confess to being sore and exhausted after a day of riding up and down a mountain. I overdid it. But it is my duty as your husband, and as a man besotted, that I hold you, kiss the daylights out of you, touch you all over until you are scared no more."

"I want to be with you, here, every night for the rest of my life," she said, her words filling his heart, feeding his soul.

"I will kill Emory if he hurts you again. I swear it," she said, rolling onto her side to snuggle in close to his chest, her leg folding over his thigh.

His hand covered her full breast. He closed his eyes, savoring the feel of soft, warm flesh beneath his fingers. "No, Zola. No, don't say that. Once we figure out what he's after, we can stop him from hurting me, you—everyone."

****

They must've fallen asleep. Leif hadn't meant to. He had a lot more exploring he wanted to do. There was nothing between their bodies now. It was flesh to flesh. His shoulder burned and his ribs ached, and his manhood throbbed, begging for release, but something had startled him awake.

"The paddock. Big flash of light, loud boom," Forrest shouted through their closed bedroom door.

Leif heard the boy jumping down the stairs and sprang from bed, found his trousers, and shoved his bare feet into his boots.

"What is it?" Zola asked, groggy, rising up on her elbows.

"I think we surprised a skunk in the paddock."

"Where are you going?"

"You stay here," Leif said on his way down the stairs.

"I will not," he heard her answer and shook his head, thinking he could stop her.

****

Ephraim met him in the yard. "Oren can't stop grinnin'," Ephraim said. "Reckon our neighbor ain't feelin' too frisky this mornin', not after last night. The ground all tore up like that, my guess that fine stallion of his gave him a right good tumble. I wrapped the torch and them Lucifer's we found in the tarp. Everything's in the wagon."

Leif nodded. "I stepped on this while we were inspecting the area." He removed a shiny, silver concho from his pocket. "My guess is it came from a bridle, a very fancy Spanish bridle. Wonder if Mr. Emory's thoroughbred is missing some decoration on his tack this morning?"

Chuckling to himself, Forrest came out of the barn leading Old Billy.

Zola stepped off the porch and put on her gloves.

Ephraim waved and said good morning to Zola. He followed Leif to the dray horses to check the harness. "You and her finding your way, I reckon?"

Leif tugged on the harness. Ephraim had a not-so-subtle way of getting to the heart of delicate questions. Reliving the night, Leif smiled to himself, and nodded.

Apparently, nothing more needed to be said. Ephraim nodded in kind. "I'm right glad, Mr. Kenyon. Right glad. She's a fine young woman, always was, always will be. She deserves a good match."

"I will strive to never let you, or her, down, Ephraim. Keep the men working. I'll bring home the payroll."

He helped Zola up and onto the wagon bench, and they set out. Forrest, riding alongside on his way to school, chattered all the way to town, going on and on about the big hole in the ground where Oren's fireworks had gone off. Mr. Emory had snagged the trip-wire when he approached the paddock fence. The resulting boom, flash, and bang had gone off several yards away from horse and rider, but it had effectively frightened the daylights out of their quarry.

They waved Forrest off at the gates of the schoolyard and entered the town limits, passing the first row of homes

"I see Mr. Emory is in town this morning," Leif said.

"Where?"

"If I'm not mistaken, that's his horse tied in front of the sheriff's office. I wonder how he's feeling this morning? In the confusion, I think his horse lost a concho from its fancy tack. We'll have to check. But first, where's the land office?"

"Behind the bank," Zola said. "I don't like it that he's in town. He should be home nursing his sore backside."

"No doubt he's required to report the latest event."

"Humff," is all she said.

Urging the team down the narrow side street behind the bank and the sheriff's office, Leif surveyed the logistics. "Interesting. Handy location. Offers the banker and the sheriff the ability to keep watch from their back room windows anyone going in and coming out of the land office."

He set the brake and looped the reins around the handle, hopped down, and turned to help Zola alight. She put her hands on his shoulders. "Mr. Shaw," she said under her breath.

"Where?"

"The corner window. Must be his office." Leif steadied her once she made it to the ground.

"He's gone now," she said, brushing down her skirts.

"If you see him again, wave and smile. Let him know you see him."

"Wait, he's there again." Unsmiling, she waggled her fingers at the peepers. "I saw something sparkle. Could be the window pane reflecting the morning light. I think there's someone behind him. I can't really see who it is, but I can make out a white shirt. His face is in shadow."

Leif tipped his hat to the voyeurs. "Definitely spotted something shiny there on his chest," he said and removed a basket from beneath the bench.

"A badge? Yes, a badge," Zola said. "I thought it a trick of light." She turned her head away and pretended to adjust the reticule on her wrist.

Carrying the basket in the crook of his arm, Leif took her elbow, and they started for the land office door. "This land agent, is he related to anyone here in town?"

"Well, he's a she," Zola said and stopped to brush a non-existent spot of dust from her coat sleeve. "The widow Blashcombe is the sheriff's older sister."

Leif groaned, his hand on the land office door latch. "Is everybody related in this town?"

"I'm not related to anyone except Forrest. You're not related to anyone here, and I don't think Ephraim or Oren are related to anyone here."

"Right, but everybody else…?"

"Well, yes, nearly everyone is a cousin to someone or something closer here. Especially the families of the business owners. It is a small town."

Leif opened the door for her, and the bell over the door chimed. "Good morning, Miss Pretty, oh, I beg pardon, Mrs. Kenyon, isn't it?" said the rawboned woman towering over her scales at her high counter.

"Good morning, Mrs. Blashcombe," Zola said. "Leif, this is Mrs. Mary Blashcombe, Prettydale's Land Agent, Apothecary, and Assayer. Mary, my husband, Mr. Leif Kenyon."

Leif put out his hand for the woman to shake. She gave it a firm squeeze. "Pleased to meet you," he said, working hard not to grimace.

Mary Blashcombe was homely, plain, broad-shouldered, and ample-chested. The way she wore her mousy brown hair, drawn up in a smooth gray coil on top of her square head, made her look like she was wearing a helmet.

"How may I help you this fine morning?" she asked.

"I have a few questions," Leif said, and set the basket on Mary's counter. She started to remove the brown paper that covered the contents, but he smiled and shoved it out of reach. The weight of the contents scraped her glass counter. "I'm hoping you'll be able to tell me to whom I would speak about purchasing the acreage south and west of the Pretty homestead?"

"Hmmm? That would be on the south side of the road and south of Pretty Creek and east of the town proper."

"Yes, that's right."

"I've got a map up here on the wall. As you can see, as it stands, it's open range. There was talk of the town annexing it. Word has it the railroad would like to cut across the mountains about there. There's a low pass up there," she said and tapped the map with a wooden pointer.

"I'd be interested in purchasing this piece of land here," he said, drawing an invisible square around the acres he had in mind with his finger. "Looks to me about what? Thirty acres or so? I want a buffer between the homestead and the town should it spread out."

"That's thirty-six acres, to be exact," Mary said.

"Thirty-six. Do I stake a claim on it? Pay the county? How does this work?"

"The county, you pay the county ten dollars an acre filing fee at the courthouse. Start with this application. Fill it out. You planning on farming it, using it for grazing...what?"

"No, for now, I'll leave it unfenced, available for open range. If the railroad needs a right of way, we can negotiate."

"Yes, I see, yes, of course." Mary cleared her throat.

"Is that all I can help you with?" she asked, eyeing the basket.

"We do have one more question," Zola said. "Did my father ever stake a claim along Pretty Creek?"

Eyes averted, Mary bit her lower lip before answering. "Ah, no, no, there is no claim in your father's name on Pretty Creek."

Leif drew his mouth up to the side and narrowed his gaze at the woman. "Did he stake a claim along Pretty Creek on behalf of his children or his wife?"

Mary dipped her head, muttered something unintelligible, neither a yes or no.

Leif pressed harder, voice louder, stronger, his cold eyes hard to ignore. "Did Mr. Pretty stake a claim along Pretty Creek under the name of his daughter, Zola Louise Pretty?"

"Mary?" Zola said, "Did my father stake a mineral claim on Pretty Creek in my name?"

"I told David you'd come askin' sooner or later. I told'em I'd have to answer. Damnation, yes, yes, he did. He put it in your name. He said he wanted you to have something of your own."

"Did he ever prove it? Bring in samples?" Leif asked, surprising Zola with the deadly timber to his voice.

"No, no, he never did bring in any samples," Mary said, once again dipping her head, avoiding his eyes.

"Ah, but someone did, someone brought you a sample from Pretty Creek. They didn't tell you where they got it, did they? But you guessed. Did you tell your brother? Did you tell Mr. Shaw?"

"No, no, I never. I ain't allowed to give out that kind of information. Mr. Emory said Mr. Shaw already knew about it. And well, my brother, he's in tight with Mr. Shaw, and they made me swear to tell no one. And I didn't, not a single solitary soul, I swear. I didn't even tell you. You guessed. You guessed, and I'll tell'em, I'll tell'em you guessed."

Zola spun around to face the window, tears in her eyes, sobbing. "Mr. Emory must've beat it out of him— forced, tortured my father to tell him about the claim. Papa would never fight back. Never. He would simply take the blows, turn the other cheek. Mr. Emory beat my father to death, and for what? For gold."

Turning on Mary, she screamed. "Mr. Emory beat my father to death, and your brother knows it, and he's done nothing…nothing."

Leif retrieved the basket from Mary's counter. "Give me the coordinates of the thirty-six acres." Hand on the door latch, he turned to say, "Tell Mr. Shaw and your brother and whoever else is over there in Mr. Shaw's office, we'll be around shortly to have a little talk."

****

Trembling, Zola made it outside without breaking down. Fumbling in her reticule, she found a hankie and swiped the tears from her cheek.

Leif had his hand on her back, the basket draped over his arm. "Can you keep moving? We're being watched. Are you feeling faint?"

"Faint? No. A little sick to my stomach, light-headed, and angry, so angry. I could kill with my bare hands. My father was murdered. Brutally murdered, and no one cared. All they cared about was the gold."

She slipped on her first attempt to step up on the wheel to get up on the buckboard. "I'm sorry, I should've had more than a biscuit and coffee this morning for breakfast."

Once settled on the wagon bench, she dabbed at her tears. "Daddy should've told me. Why didn't he tell me? I could've kept the homestead."

Beside her, Leif snapped the reins over the horses' rumps. "Exactly."

The force of the evil revelation came as a physical blow and sucked the air out of her lungs. "Oh, oh, God. They didn't want me to know. They wanted me to lose the homestead. Lose everything so they could take control, steal the claim, the land, and the gold. Emory, Mr. Shaw, they didn't want me to know—ever."

"That's what I think," Leif said, his voice lowering to a growl. "I came to town and ruined everything. Ruined their scheme. If they could get rid of me, they could begin again, pick up on their original plan. But now you know, you know you're a wealthy woman, Zola Louise Kenyon. If this turns out to be true, then you could probably buy this whole damn town if you chose to do so. You can go anywhere you please, live anywhere you please."

Head shaking, sniffing back her tears, she said, "Yes, and that's exactly why Papa didn't tell me right away. I probably would've wanted to go out and buy him a new horse and buggy. Send him on a world tour. Send all of us on a world tour. Build us a big house. But I think—I think he was about to tell me—tell me something important. The day before he died, he said it was time we had a long talk. I thought he wanted to talk about the homestead and the bank notes coming due. And yes, that's exactly why he wanted to talk. I see it now. Oh, I wish he'd said something. All would've been so different.

****

Jaw tight, Leif urged the team onto the main street. *Yes, everything would've been very different. I wouldn't have come to Prettydale. I wouldn't have had to marry a fierce, red-headed little spitfire, and I wouldn't have fallen in love.*

At the moment, all his plans for a successful sawmill seemed pitiful and pointless in the face of Zola's newly discovered bonanza. Of course, they didn't know how wealthy she might be, but it was certainly wealthier than he could ever provide. She could demand an annulment now. There hadn't been a consummation of the union. A bit of a snuggle and cuddle didn't, wouldn't, count.

"This is horrible," she said, her hands going to her cheeks. "What am I to do? God, this is evil. People do awful things, horrible things for gold. Mr. Emory is a prime example of what gold will do to one's mortal soul—he killed for it—he murdered. I don't want it. Leif, what am I to do?"

"I don't know. I guess we purchase the extra acreage. Then we go to the bank, and you ask for any documents the bank may be holding in regards to the homestead, or maybe I should say, *withholding* from you. I'm hoping Emory is there. I have something of his in my pocket. We don't need to mention the word gold at all—not today—not yet. We have time—you have time to think this through."

Squaring her shoulders, Zola took a deep breath and patted his thigh, sending a shock wave of lust through his body. "Yes, you're right. I need to think about this— think about what is best for everyone—the whole town."

Chapter Sixteen

Outside the courthouse, within sight of the railway station, Leif checked the time on the station clock. The next train, which would connect with a train eastbound, would leave in an hour and forty-five minutes if it was running on time. "I'll do this," he said, removing the papers from his inside coat pocket. "You go to the Emporium and buy yourself a big hat."

"Hat? What? Why? Why? I don't need a hat. For heaven's sake. A hat, of all the silly things."

Pressing his fingers against her opened mouth, he said in a hushed voice, "We need a big hat. Big enough to hold the contents of our basket. Camouflage, if you will. I'm going to catch the next train east and take our samples to my brother. We can't take them to Mary and we can't wait for the mail."

"Leaving? You're leaving?"

He pressed his fingers to her lips again. "A quick trip, sweetheart. We can't trust the telegrapher. We can't trust anyone."

"I'll go," she said. "Let me go. You need to stay here, keep working. Send a wire, and tell your brother whatever you think. I want to meet him. I need to have a little holiday. I'll deliver *the hat*. A lady with a hat box is nothing unusual. A man with a hat box? Well, that would raise eyebrows. Especially you. You're not the least bit feminine, carrying a hat box, on a train, without a lady on your arm, no, that's too silly."

Leif set his jaw. "It is too dangerous. No."

She put her hand against his cheek. "I can do this. I want to do this."

He removed her hand from his face and hoped to distract her. "We need to get a move on. We'll argue about this later. We don't have a lot of time."

Zola, stiff, a mulish pucker on her pretty lips, allowed him to lift her down from the wagon. "We're not arguing, Mr. Kenyon. We are discussing," she said and pushed him away.

He had to laugh at that. "Right you are, Mrs. Kenyon. I'll be around to pick you up. Wait for me at the Emporium."

****

Working quickly, Leif transferred the contents of the basket into the crown of the hat, an ugly, green, silk hat with a rust and black edged rose on the crown, and thought it perfect. Certainly a better use for it than seeing some poor woman wearing it on her head. He put some bark and a few pieces of wood in the basket and covered it with the brown paper, and placed the very large, green and rust plaid hat box on the wagon bench in plain sight.

Zola, on the boardwalk before the bank, adjusted her fingers within her kid gloves. Behind her, the door to the bank opened. Mr. Emory emerged, limping, using a cane, the side of his face bruised, dark circles under his eyes, and delivered Zola a murderous scowl.

Basket in hand, Leif greeted Mr. Emory. "Ah, neighbor Emory. Look at us. Tsk, tsk, tsk. We should both be more careful. I took a tumble off my horse after a tree branch attacked me in the twilight. However did you come by your hurts?"

Emory shot a wad of tobacco juice out between his closed teeth, the spray missing Leif's boots by less than an inch. "My horse spooked."

Leif put his hand on his shoulder, fingers digging in, and said, "Come back inside with us. We're going to have a talk with Mr. Shaw. Is the sheriff still inside?"

Emory growled and shook his shoulders in an attempt to shake himself free. "I got better things to do."

Leif fisted his grip on the man's coat. "Oh, come, come, Mr. Emory, I know you want to know what we're up to. Come in, get it all first hand."

Mr. Emory, under Leif's firm control, got hauled to the side to allow Zola to enter the bank before them.

"After you," he said to her with a smile.

Pale and uncertain, Zola stepped around Mr. Emory and entered the bank. By-passing the teller, she went through the swinging gate, the portal to the offices in the rear of the building.

Mr. Prine's office door stood open. Leif tipped his hat to the man who had come to his feet to ask, "How may I help you."

"We're here to speak with Mr. Shaw," Leif said. "No need to announce us. I believe he's expecting our visit."

The door to the president and owner of the bank, Thomas J. Shaw, stood closed. Leif shoved Emory out of the way to open the door for his wife. Behind the desk sat the corpulent Mr. Shaw. A man with a shiny sheriff's badge pinned to his white shirt, long legs stretched out, feet up on the corner of the desk, occupied the one and only chair in the room provided for visitors.

Pausing, Leif assessed the atmosphere in the room. Hand outstretched, he approached the sheriff. "Sheriff

Daniels, Leif Kenyon. And of course you know my wife, Zola Kenyon, formally Zola Pretty."

The man didn't budge or take Leif's hand. Leif arched his brows and said, "You'll want to offer my wife your chair, of course." Locking his gaze on the man, he shamed the sheriff into reluctantly rising. Offering Zola a mocking bow of respect, he waved her to take the chair.

Leif turned his attention to Mr. Shaw. "We haven't met. The name's Leif Kenyon, the owner of the Pretty homestead."

Mr. Shaw remained seated, a smile on his lips and a cunning, calculating gleam in his soulless, gray eyes. "Pleased to make your acquaintance at last, Mr. Kenyon. How may we serve you today?"

The sheriff had taken up a guard position at the door, which Leif noticed was once again closed. Mr. Emory, leaning against the bookcase, cleaned his fingernails with the point of his pocket knife.

Leif placed his hand on Zola's shoulder. "My wife has a few questions," he said and set the basket down at his feet.

Startled, Zola brought up her bowed head and glowered at him. He nodded, encouraging her to speak up. She came forward in her chair, hands tightly folded in her lap. "Mr. Shaw..." Her voice faltered. She cleared her throat. "Mr. Shaw, I need to know if my father gave to you, for safekeeping, any documents before his death, such as marriage licenses, birth certificates, any documents concerning the homestead, or the Pretty family?"

Mr. Shaw, lips pursed, paused but didn't blink. Arms straight, and on top of his desk, he placed his pudgy, white fingers together to form a peak, the point of that peak pointing directly at her. "I cannot recall your father making use of my vault for any reason."

Zola glared at him and came abruptly to her feet. She shook her finger in his fat face and bent over his desk. "You are lying, Mr. Shaw. I have a brother. He always couches his lies in a bit of truth. It's a word game we play." Mr. Shaw blanched, and his chair squawked under the stress of his shifting weight.

"If you have any legal papers pertaining to the homestead or my family in your vault or anywhere in this bank, I demand they be turned over to me immediately. You have no right to withhold them from me. If you refuse to give them to me, I'll, I'll go to the judge, and he'll serve you with papers, force you to give them to me."

"Threats, Mrs. Kenyon. I do not take kindly to threats," said the now red-faced Mr. Shaw.

Leif took note of the lines of sweat wending down the man's ruddy jowls, disappearing in his salt and pepper mutton chops. The banker, off guard now, Leif leaped into the fray. "We do not take kindly to being attacked," he said, indicating the black, blue, and purple bruise above his left brow. "My wife and her brother have been the subject of Mr. Emory's relentless terrorism for months and months, and you and the sheriff know it."

He slapped the concho down on the desk. "I believe this belongs to your henchmen, or I should say the tack he uses on his expensive horse."

He turned to face Mr. Emory, who had come to attention, no longer leaning casually against the bookshelf. "Your horse is right outside, Mr. Emory. Shall we see if it matches the rest of the tack. I have in the back of my wagon the torch and Lucifers you meant to use to burn my house down."

He turned to the sheriff. "It was his second attempt. Lucky for us, we anticipated he would come at us again, and we set out strategically-placed warning traps to give us time to defend ourselves."

Leif picked up the concho and put it back in his pocket. "We haven't put together all the pieces of this puzzle, but when we do, you, Mr. Shaw, Sheriff Daniels, and dear neighbor Emory, you will have to bear the consequences of your treachery. And it is treachery to plot, harass, deceive, and murder. Yes, Mr. Emory, you murdered for the sake of wealth and power, and you, Sheriff Daniels, and you, Mr. Shaw, allowed it, possibly ordered it, definitely encouraged it."

Retrieving the basket, Leif said, "We'll return with the judge for those papers."

It worried him that Mr. Shaw simply nodded, smiled, and sat back in his chair.

On the way out, Leif intended to speak with Mr. Prine, but his office appeared abandoned, and it was almost eleven o'clock.

"You were wonderful," he said to Zola, helping her up to sit on the wagon bench. "*'We'll be back with the judge,'* that was inspired and quick thinking. Now, off to the station. You drop me off, wish me luck, and scurry on over to the judge's office. He'll help you get those papers. I'll get my ticket and send off a wire to Gunnar."

Zola shoved the big hat box over and squared her shoulders. "No."

"No? No, what?"

"You go to the judge's office. I'm taking the train."

Turning the wagon toward the far end of town, he

said, "We don't have time to argue…discuss. There's more going on here than gold. I will not let you travel unattended."

Eyes forward, Zola stated her case. "If I leave you to see to the judge, guard the homestead and oversee the workers at your mill, there will be less talk and speculation. Whereas, if you leave me alone, unprotected, abandoned, on more or less our honeymoon, there will be a lot of talk and a huge amount of speculation. You will cause a great deal of suspicion."

Leif opened his mouth to rebut. She stopped him by saying, "Yes, I agree, it's not just the gold. Mr. Shaw lied to us. I can't imagine why. He knows we went to the land office. He knows I know I have a gold claim on Pretty Creek, so why withhold the documents? Let me go, Leif." She placed her hand on his thigh again, which instantly sent the blood rushing to his groin. "I've never been anywhere, never traveled. Please, let me do this?"

He pulled the wagon up in front of the depot and looked down the line of track for a telltale puff of black smoke. Setting the brake and tying the reins off, he said what he never thought he would say to any woman. "I'm afraid to let you go. I'm afraid you won't come back, or when you do come back, you won't…won't want me. You'll have all the wealth you need very soon. You say you've never traveled. Well, you could travel the globe."

Zola put her head to his shoulder and took his hand. "I belong here, at home. You are my home. If I travel, you will travel with me. Where you are is my home, my heart.

****

In the distance, the train whistle sounded, and Zola's heart skipped a couple of beats.

Leif was talking to her, but it was hard to pay attention in the face of the prospect, the anticipation of an adventure

"The Empire runs up and down the valley, so you'll stop in Salem, get off, change trains, and board the Cascadian. It'll take you over the mountains to Farewell Bend. You'll arrive early in the morning, around daybreak." He handed her a roll of bills. "Keep this somewhere, in your shoe, down your, your blouse, somewhere safe, and get yourself something to eat. Be careful, Zola. Please be very careful. I'll get your ticket for a private compartment and wire Gunnar. I don't like this."

"You-whooo, oh you-whooo, Mrs. Kenyon, Zola dear."

"Oh, no," Zola said. Shaking her head, she looked away. "I told the Abbot sisters I needed a special hat, a real fascinator, something to make a good impression on my new brother-in-law and his family. I made up a story about why you couldn't go with me. Oh, for heaven's sake. Here they come."

Breathless and giggling, the two dears started to talk at once. "We brought you a little basket of goodies for the train," said Miss Paulette over the top of her sister, who was speaking.

"Traveling can be so tedious, and station food, well, it isn't fit for dogs." Gladys chattered on about the time she and Paulette traveled to Seattle and all the perils they encountered.

Leif interrupted to say, "I need to hurry and send the wire and get the ticket." Escaping, he rushed off.

The sisters recounted several travel adventures before Miss Paulette lowered her voice, glancing first one way then the other. With her hand on Zola's wrist, the lady stated the real purpose of their mission, "You aren't running away, are you, dear?" She put up her gloved hand, stopping Zola from speaking.

Miss Gladys put her arm around her waist, "If you ever feel in need of sanctuary, know you can come to us. We'll protect you."

Miss Paulette rushed to say, "Domestic troubles can be most uncomfortable, especially for—for—an inexperienced young bride. But...but Gladys and I are not without some knowledge of...of what goes on between a man and a woman. In short, we are not ones to ignore injustice in a marriage."

Gladys said, "Especially one made under duress such as yours. Dear Mr. Kenyon looks and acts the gentleman but...one never can tell a book by its cover."

Cheeks burning, having heard enough, Zola shook her head. "Please, Miss Abbot, Paulette, Miss Gladys, both of you stop. Be assured I am not running away. I'm...I'm actually on a mission for my husband. He is needed here to oversee the crew working on his mill. He needs information his brother can provide. It's too complicated for a telegram, and we can't wait for the mail. And besides, I've never been outside Prettydale, so this is a treat for me. A treat dear Leif is willing to allow."

"I will miss her terribly," Leif said, having returned to her side with her ticket. "Will you ladies excuse us? I would like a few moments alone with my wife before I part with her."

The misses Abbot, tittering and blushing, waved them off, wishing Zola a safe and swift journey. In a hiss of steam, the train pulled into the station. "I've given the hat box to the porter," Leif said. "And I've given him a big tip to see you safe when you have to change trains this afternoon. You have a private car for both the Empire and the Cascadian coming and going."

"Please, Leif, I'm a big girl. I'll be fine. Try not to worry."

He put his forehead down to hers. "Send me a telegram as soon as you're in Gunnar's care. Oh, oh, and another thing, we'll need two samples assayed, the bigger rocks from the cave and the gravel from the creek. We may have to file a separate claim on the cave site."

The train whistle drowned out his voice. He guided her to the steps to board and stopped. Zola folded her arms around his middle, laying her head on his big solid chest, inhaling the scent of him, memorizing the feel of his warmth.

"It is true, you know. I will miss you," he said, his hands stroking her back.

"I will miss you too," she said,

He kept a hand beneath her elbow to help her manage the deep step up and into the open end of the car. "I...I love you, Zola," he said, his voice so low she might have imagined it.

The train whistle blew again, and steam enveloped them, cutting them off from the rest of the world. "Oh, Leif, I love you so much." The train began to move away from the station. "I love you," she said, this time louder, the train rolling away from her home, her heart—tears wetting her cheeks.

Chapter Seventeen

Leif couldn't believe he'd said it, said it aloud—expressed in words what he knew in his heart of hearts. Damn it, it was true. He did love her. He'd lay down his life for her. If he lost everything, it wouldn't matter if he still had Zola at his side.

The world took on a brighter hue. Shoulders squared, he marched back to the wagon at the front of the depot. The Abbot sisters were ahead, huddled in conversation with another matron. Leif approached and tipped his hat. "I beg pardon for intruding," he said.

"Mrs. Agatha Dalton, this is Mr. Kenyon," said Miss Paulette. "We were just talking about you, Mr. Kenyon, and your lovely bride, Zola. Mrs. Dalton is the wife of Ivan Dalton, who owns the feed store."

Miss Gladys said, "Agatha is our cousin on our mother's side."

Leif, impatient with the conversation, tipped his hat. "Pleasure to meet you, Mrs. Dalton. I was wondering if either you, Miss Paulette, or Miss Gladys, could tell me where I might find the judge this time of day? It's nearly noon. Perhaps he's home."

"Oh, dear me," Miss Gladys said. "The judge is gone on his circuit. He won't be back until the end of the month. Perhaps Mr. Shaw could help you or the sheriff."

"Yes, well, thank you," Leif said. "Have a good day, ladies." He tipped his hat in farewell.

Little wonder Mr. Shaw sat there, a slimy smile on his fat lips. Clearly he knew very well the threat of getting the judge and a court order held no danger at all. He knew the man was out of town. Well, we can't wait.

Seated on the wagon bench, Leif pondered his next step. Maybe Mr. Prine could shed some light on the whereabouts of the Pretty documents. Besides, he'd forgotten he needed the payroll cash. He set the team back down the street to the bank.

At the bank, the teller informed him Mr. Prine had turned in his resignation. He'd left the bank for good short of an hour ago. And Mr. Shaw had gone home for lunch. "Mr. Prine has rooms above the Emporium, might be there," the teller said after counting out the payroll cash.

Leif recounted the pile of bills and put them in his money belt. "Thank you. Can you tell me, did the sheriff and Mr. Emory also leave with Mr. Shaw?"

"I couldn't say, sir. If they did, they left by the back door. Mr. Shaw hollered he was goin' to lunch. In the last half-hour, other than my wife, I haven't seen anyone leave or come in this door other than you just now."

Standing on the boardwalk, Leif glanced up and down the street. Stymied, he contemplated his next move—should he track down Mr. Prine? What use would he be now if he no longer worked at the bank?

He climbed back up on the wagon bench, and a slight movement in the bed of the wagon caught his attention. "Shhhh." Mr. Prine peeked up at him from under the tarp. "Get me out of town quick."

"What the hell?"

Mr. Prine, lying on his side, his back to the rail of the wagon, had taken inadequate cover, his good, black

169

suit coat pulled up around his ears, and an old canvas tarp pulled up that barely covered his head.

"Don't look at me. I think I have the papers you and Mrs. Kenyon were after. Get me out of here quick."

It was hard work to keep from asking more questions, but Leif forced himself to maintain a bland expression and set the team in motion. He nodded to a few pedestrians. There was no sign of Mr. Emory or his fancy steed. They made it past the last home on the edge of town and the schoolyard and entered the wood—he started to draw up the team to the side of the road.

"Don't stop. Keep going. Mr. Emory followed you to the station," Mr. Prine said.

"How do you know this?"

"After I handed in my resignation and cleared off my desk, I went straight to my rooms above the Emporium. My one and only window looks out on Second Street. Mr. Shaw, the sheriff, and Mr. Emory stood right beneath my window in the street, talking for a moment or two. I opened my window a little. Their voices carried, and I heard Mr. Shaw tell Mr. Emory to follow you. They know you went to the station because of the Abbot sisters. The news is all over town Mrs. Kenyon boarded the train. And by now, it's all over town I've resigned my position at the bank. Mr. Shaw wants to know where Mrs. Kenyon is going. The sisters said she was going to visit your brother."

"Yes, that's right," Leif said. "But how the hell did you get hold of the documents?"

"Mr. Shaw doesn't know I have them if that's what you're worried about. Mr. Shaw wasn't lying when he said Mr. Pretty didn't give him the papers. He didn't. Mr. Emory did."

"How did Mr. Emory get hold of the documents?"

"I've been listening outside the door of Mr. Shaw's office for a while now. I don't know how Mr. Emory got the papers, but he got them."

"When was this?" Leif asked, directing the question to the hind end of the horses.

"After Mr. Pretty passed."

"How soon after?"

"I have to think—we'd served the final notice on the homestead. Miss Pretty had sold all she could—so late summer—August, I would guess. It wasn't long after when Mr. Shaw served the order to put the homestead up for auction. I've been suspicious for quite a while. I thought Mr. Shaw would hand over all the Pretty documents, if there were any, at the time of the auction, but he didn't. Mr. Emory and the sheriff visit Mr. Shaw in his office a lot, and they stay in there talking in hushed voices, once in a while bursting into laughter.

"I was listening at the door today. I've been holding on to my resignation, but today I'd heard enough. I served Mr. Shaw my resignation immediately after you and Mrs. Kenyon left. He didn't say much, the usual "very well," and waved me away. I said my farewell to Ivan, the teller, and went straight to my rooms.

"When Emory took off for the station, and the sheriff and Mr. Shaw went in the back door of the mercantile, I took my chance and left my room. I rushed back into the bank through the back door. I wanted to see for myself if there were any homestead documents in the vault. I hadn't thought it through, what I was going to do if there were.

"Out front, the teller, Ivan, and his wife were squabbling. She comes in nearly every day to harp at him for not taking his lunch. I slipped into Mr. Shaw's office, got the key out of his desk, and I opened the vault. My heart was pounding, I can tell you. I found these papers right there, in the open, on a shelf by the door, right in plain sight. Mr. Pretty's name is all over them. I grabbed them and ducked right back out the back door, and slipped into the alley. I didn't know what I was going to do. I couldn't go back to my rooms. They'd come looking for me there. If I went to the stable, someone would surely tell them if I tried to hire a nag. Then you pulled up in front and went in the bank and, well, it was sheer providence. And here I am, a fugitive, a thief on the run."

****

Jimmy, the young porter Leif had paid to keep an eye on her, escorted her to her private compartment and slid the door aside. "The water closet is two doors down. The dining room is the other way, in the next car. There's a blanket and a pillow up here." Over six feet tall and skinny, Jimmy had no trouble reaching the high ledge above her head. "I'll see to it you aren't disturbed. Might as well sit back and enjoy the scenery. It'll be maybe three hours before we pull into Salem station. You want somethin' from the dining car? We got chicken sandwiches today."

Zola shook her head. The thought of a dry chicken sandwich held very little appeal. "A pot of tea would be nice."

"Yes, ma'am, I'll be back directly."

Pulling away from the forested foothills of the Cascades where the town of Prettydale sat, the landscape opened up to the flat, furrowed fields of the Willamette Valley. Zola, at her window, stared, mesmerized by the flocks of crows and starlings swooping and diving, gleaning in waves the leftover seeds from fall harvests.

A knock on the compartment door brought her out of her trance. Jimmy had returned with her tea. She stepped aside to allow him entrance and glanced out the open door.

Mr. Emory limped by. The sound of his cane thumped hard on the metal floor.

He'd kept his head down, black hat pulled low over his meaty brow. He'd rushed by so fast, Zola couldn't swear it was Mr. Emory, but the man certainly looked like Mr. Emory, and the cane gave him away. By the time Jimmy had moved out of the way, the mysterious man had disappeared into the dining car.

Jimmy set the tray down on the bench next to the hat box. Zola sat down on the bench opposite, knees shaking. "Jimmy, did you happen to notice the man in the aisle when you came through from the dining room?"

"He was ahead of me, lookin' for his grandma," Jimmy said. "She told him she'd be in the dining room, but he didn't find her there. Thought there might be another dining car. I told him only a young lady and a couple of gentlemen were in the private compartments, no grandmas."

"Did you get a look at him, I mean his face? Did he have bruises on his face?"

"Yes, Ma'am, he did. Looked like he'd run into a fist or two for sure."

"Is there a lock on this door?"

"Yes, you can pull the shades on the door and on the windows to the aisle and the outside too."

Jimmy left her. She immediately locked the door behind him, pulled the shades to the aisle, and collapsed on the bench. Hands shaking, she poured herself a cup of tea and selected a raisin and apricot scone from the travel basket the Abbot sisters had provided.

Mr. Emory. What's he doing here? Following me, of course.

In solitude, the miles passed as well as the time, time for Zola to worry, conjure and imagine the ways in which Mr. Emory intended to terrorize her.

****

The train arrived at the Salem Station at half-past two. "When does the train going east arrive?" Zola asked Jimmy, who had come to help her disembark, taking charge of the oversized hat box.

The Salem station consisted of multiple tracks and a large roundhouse where the big locomotives could be swung around, exchanged, and redirected. At first sight, the depot building, cavernous, and the crowded platform, compared to the little Prettydale station, threw Zola into a state of confusion and panic.

"Should be here around two forty-five, or close to it. Sorry, I got to get back on board. We pull out at two-forty on the dot for Portland," he said, having to shout over the hustle and jostling crowd around them. "Mr. Kenyon gave me instructions to see you safe, so that's what I'm gonna do. Now Mr. Mills runs this station. Mr. Kenyon told me to talk to him direct. And I know Mr. Mills personal. I'm gonna hand you over to him. You come inside, take a seat next to his window right over there by the stove, and I'll go have a talk with him, let him know he needs to take good care of you—Mr. Kenyon's orders."

The little stool by the stove sat inconspicuously to the side, well out of the way. She had a clear view of the platform and the milling passengers, as did Mr. Mills from his ticket window. She scanned the crowd for a dark figure with a black hat, walking with a cane. There were a few men of that description, but all were either too tall or too thin, or too old. She began to think she'd been mistaken. It would be highly unlikely for Mr. Emory to follow her or even know she was on the train.

Jimmy returned with a cup of strong, steaming hot coffee and handed it to her. "Mr. Mills says he knows a good porter on the eastbound Cascadian who'll take very good care of you. It's been a pleasure, Ma'am."

"Thank you, Jimmy. You've been very kind."

He waved goodbye. "Maybe I'll see you on your return trip."

"Yes, yes, that would be nice."

The coffee helped to revive her, giving her time to take her bearings and calm her nerves. Silly to think she was being followed. More passengers filled the depot, and she thought it might be wise to take this time to make use of a privy that wasn't rocking side to side and in a very small closet. She left the hat box behind Mr. Mill's counter and ventured outside to find the privy.

Footsteps on the gravel path signaled someone else had come this way to make use of the conveniences. The halting gate and the sound of what could be a cane crunching in the gravel put Zola on alert. She opened the heavy, slatted door a crack and waited. The opening and closing of the privy shack next to her sent her flying as fast as her feet would carry her back to the safety of her little stool next to the stove under Mr. Mill's watchful eye.

Mr. Mills, startling her out of her fright, leaned over the edge of his counter to address her. "They serve a fine supper on the eastbound Cascadian." All she could see of Mr. Mills was his face and black cap. He had hang-dog, sad, brown eyes, and a lantern jaw. "If you choose, you can order it sent to your compartment. Give this message to the porter. His name is Curtis Staub. He'll be along momentarily. You can rely on him, Mrs. Kenyon. We'll see you safe to your destination."

Chugging into the station, coming from the east, the Cascadian pulled into the station right on time. Locomotives were turned around on the turntable in the roundhouse, cars were disconnected and reconnected, and the passengers boarded. Zola waited inside for the porter, Curtis, to come get her, fearing if she tried to board by herself, Mr. Emory would grab her. He was still close by. She knew it. She could swear he was watching her.

A stout, red-nosed, sharp-eyed porter approached her, a pleasant smile on his ruddy face. He tipped his black cap, "Curtis Staub, at your service," he said, a bit of a brogue sneaking into his speech. Mr. Mills handed off the hat box, and Curtis led her through the crowded platform and into the car and her private compartment.

"I'll be around again in an hour or so," he said, having settled the hat box on the bench and getting down the blanket and pillows. "I'll escort you to the dining car, or you can have your meal brought in here. Menus there in the magazine holder next to the door."

"Curtis, I'm curious about something," Zola said before he could leave. "You and the other porter, Jimmy, and Mr. Mills, you're being, well, very careful of me. Do all your passengers, upon request, get this kind of attention?"

Curtis chuckled, dipped his chin into his coat collar,

176

head shaking. "No, Ma'am, but when Leif Kenyon gives an order and pays in cash, we obey. He's famous, he is. Brought down the entire Dickerson bunch nearly single-handed. I helped him put the shackles on the dirty thieves. They'd robbed us three times, but Mr. Kenyon caught'em without firing a single shot. He pretty much tamed the town of Centerville all by himself. The folks there were real sorry he decided to leave. You're his missus, and that makes you real special in the estimation of all of us that work this railroad. You got a good man there. And I'm thinkin' he's done all right to have found you. Now, gonna get dark soon, lamps up here and the striker box. I'll be back shortly to check on you."

Her compartment window looked out on the platform. It was a gloomy afternoon, cold and damp, and everyone had their winter coats and hats snugged in close to necks and over their ears. She stood to light her lamp, and there he was, Mr. Emory, not more than eight feet away, standing on the platform, looking right at her. He ducked his head and nipped in behind a luggage cart the second their glances collided.

Holding her breath, she pulled the shades on the windows, including the ones to the aisle and on the door.

He is following me. The big question is, will he abduct me, hold me captive, or simply kill me? He couldn't know what I have in the hat box—could he? Does he know about the rock samples? The purpose of this trip?

And Leif—is he in danger too? We're separated now, vulnerable, both of us. It wouldn't be hard to make us disappear—meet with some horrible accident.

A weapon, I need a weapon. I won't make it easy for him. I won't. Unlike my father, I will fight back.

Do I sit here in the near darkness, wait for his attack, or do I dare go out, mingle with the other passengers in the dining car?

Choosing not to sit or cower alone, she stood, straightened the line of gold buttons on her coat, and made secure the hat pin in her little fur muff of a hat. "If he wants to attack me, he'll have to do it before an audience," she said to herself and opened the door to her compartment.

****

Poor Mr. Prine, shaken and guilt-ridden, sat at the kitchen table. A cup of coffee in hand, he picked out the nuts from the slice of Zola's raisin-apple soda bread.

"You can't very well be hauled in for stealing something we, Zola and I, were told didn't exist. If Mr. Shaw tries to say you took the papers, stole them from the vault, you can't steal something that was already stolen without implicating yourself. So, I don't think I'd worry about any kind of legal trouble from Mr. Shaw or the sheriff. But they do pose a real threat. And I think I see why," Leif said and slid the claim document across the table to Mr. Prine. "Look at the date. This claim expires in four days. Zola never proved this claim because she didn't know about it, and Shaw and the others sure as hell weren't going to tell her, or me, or anyone."

"But she's gone to your brother's and won't be back in time. And she doesn't have any proof of gold."

"She has samples with her. She's gone to the assayers in Farewell Bend. My brother is going to meet her there. She'll have proof soon enough if she gets there safely. She could get the results back to me before this expires. You said Mr. Emory followed us to the train station."

Mr. Prine nodded. "He knew where she was going. But it's doubtful he knew her purpose."

"Hmmm, he's tried to abduct her before."

"No, he never?" Mr. Prine said

"The day of the auction. I caught him outside the bank. He had her and was attempting to toss her in his carriage. She wasn't making it easy. And Forrest, he was doing his best to discourage the lout."

Mr. Prine scrubbed his head of white, thinning hair. "What's to be done? You can't go after her. It's too late. It's almost four o'clock, and she's on the train headed for the mountains."

"With any luck, yes, she is, and let us hope Mr. Emory isn't on the train but is home sucking down some of his poisonous homebrew—with any luck."

Chapter Eighteen

Forcing herself to be gregarious and sociable, Zola greeted the diners, even going so far as to beg the elderly couple she'd seen coming out of their compartment if they would mind her joining them at their table, claiming she hated to dine alone.

Concentrating on following the conversation, she commented on the weather, the good haying season, the price of hogs and beef, and children, of course. The couple had great-grandchildren. She spent a good hour and a half listening to Mrs. McGuire recite the latest naughty antics of their oldest grandchild.

When the porter cleared away their dishes, Zola, noting the cribbage board on the window ledge, inquired if anyone was interested in playing a hand or two. Fortunately, a lady, a spinster school teacher, who had also been forced to dine with strangers, took Zola up on her offer.

Supplied with a bottle of bourbon and cigars, five gentlemen at the other end of the car played a lively game of poker. Their industrious wives sat across the aisle, knitting bags open, knitting needles clacking, and yarn balls rolling.

But as the evening wore on, the teacher began to yawn, and the knitting circle broke up. Zola had to retreat to her compartment. The private compartment car was dark, save for three scones on the outside wall above the aisle.

She followed Curtis in the gloom. "I'm the only person back here. Except for the McGuires? I suppose they're fast asleep. I should use the water closet," she said, embarrassed and uncertain how to explain the danger of being alone anywhere on this train.

Curtis cleared his throat. "I'll stand guard at the door to the dining car. Take your time."

Curtis held her compartment door open for her the second she left the water closet. "We'll be stopping to take on water and fuel above Lost Pool," he said, moving past her to light her lamp. "When we get to the Santiam Roundhouse at the crest, we'll change locomotives and hook up with the eastbound Cascadian. It takes about a half-hour or so–depending on the weather. It's started to snow," he said, pulling aside the shade and looking out the window.

"I hadn't noticed," she said, her thoughts flying off in a hundred different directions. "I did notice the sound of the locomotive. It's working hard."

The hat box, it was gone.

She had to tell Curtis, but what to say, how to put it. "I hope the railroad won't charge me, but I think someone has stolen the brick foot warmers I put in the hat box."

Curtis furrowed his brows. "What's that, Ma'am?"

"I put the bricks in the hat and the hat in the box. And the hat box is gone. It's missing."

"Why would anyone take your hat box, and I won't ask why you put them bricks in your hat."

Zola took a deep breath to gather her composure and suppress her panic. "Mr. Kenyon asked you all to see me safe to my destination because of what I had concealed in the hat box. I believe I'm being followed, and I needed to know if they wanted me or what was in the box. So I transferred the contents into one of the pillowcases and deliberately left my compartment door unlocked to see if the person following me would take it, and he has. And now, I'm afraid he might try to stop me from reaching Farewell Bend. I've tricked him. This person does not like to be tricked. Forgive me. Charge me for the pillow case and the bricks."

Curtis double-checked the lock on her door. "I'll put the word out we've got a thief on board. Don't you worry, Mrs. Kenyon, we'll catch him. He shouldn't be hard to spot, he's got your hat now and the box it came in."

Zola laughed, some of the tension leaving her body.

"Lock this door," Curtis said. "We'll patrol this aisle now."

"Thank you, Curtis. Goodnight."

Zola locked the door and listened to Curtis's footsteps fading away. She turned down the lamp. With the grinding chug and growl of the locomotive in her ears, she snuggled beneath the blankets and arranged the pillows behind her head. Leaning against the outside corner of the compartment, as far away from the door as she could get, she held fast to the big rock Leif had found on the cave floor in her hand.

So Mr. Emory had raided the compartment. The bait had worked. He'd guessed the purpose of her mission and meant to stop her. The layup at the Santiam Camp would be a good time for another attack. But it was snowing hard now. They were deep in the mountains. Surely he wouldn't risk abducting her up here in the wilderness—no, better to wait—or so she hoped.

Meanwhile, she had to think. Think like Leif. Think like her husband, and outmaneuver the skunk.

The crawl up the mountains wore on her nerves, making sleep impossible. The cars tipped and careened, wheels screamed on every curve and berm. At last, the train came to a slow, hissing halt. A soft knock on her door brought her up to a sitting position. "Taking on water and fuel, Mrs. Kenyon," Curtis said, his voice barely above a whisper.

"Thank you, Curtis."

****

Pacing the kitchen, Leif cursed himself for allowing Zola to get on the train. He'd given Mr. Prine her room, assuring the man again he was in no way a fugitive—Mr. Shaw didn't have a leg to stand on. It was tempting to ride over to the Emory place to see if the man was home, drunk, not on the train with Zola.

The train would be stopping for wood and water. Then another two hours at least, depending on the weather, it would reach the roundhouse at Santiam Camp.

"It's starting to snow," Ephraim said, coming in the back door. "Saw a light on in here. Mr. Emory's not in town, no sign of his horse. I rode over to his place. It was dark, nobody home, horse isn't there. I'm needin' a cup of coffee. Any cake left?"

"She's alone on the train with a maniac, I know it. And damn it to hell, I'm here, and I can't do anything. There's nothing I can do."

"Tomorrow, me and Oren will ride along the creek and look for claim markers. Mr. Pretty must've set some."

"Yes, yes, good. Take some stakes and drive them

183

in and around the cave. You do know where that is?"

"We'll take Forrest with us. He and Oren go campin' up there all the time. They should know it by heart."

"Good. I knew I was doing the right thing getting you and Oren out here. I'd be lost without your help."

Ephraim laid a hand on his shoulder. "She's gonna be fine. Got a good head on her. By now she knows he's on the train, and she'll be ready for him. You got people lookin' out for her," he said.

"Yes, she is careful, I know that. But it seems to me she's always on the defensive—shield up—wary. That's part of it, damn it. She's not had a lot of peace in the last couple of years. I'd hoped to give her security and peace of mind. I'd hoped she could let her guard down. With Emory on the loose, she can't rest for a minute. She has to be all right. She just has to be all right."

Ephraim gulped his coffee down and cut himself a large piece of the cake, and headed for the back door. "Good night, Mr. Kenyon."

"Good night, Ephraim."

Zola on his mind and a cup of coffee in hand, Leif retired to the parlor to stare into the fire. Closing his eyes, he brought up her face before his mind's eye: her beautiful, expressive brown eyes, the freckles on her nose, and the warm, soft creamy feel of her skin beneath his fingers. And her hair, that lovely curling, coiling mane of glorious red hair, the way it fell across her shoulders and down her back—God, he missed her.

****

Zola came back from a light slumber cold, chilled to the bone. Snow whizzed by the window, howling, screaming. A faint glow of a lantern weaved back and forth beside the track, first one, then two more yellow, fuzzy lights shone, swinging in the blowing snow. The locomotive clunked, bumped, and jerked, breaking away from the cars. The lanterns floated out of sight. A soft knock on her door brought her up to full alert. "Mrs. Kenyon, are you there?"

"Yes, Curtis."

"Everything all right?"

"Yes, I'm fine."

"Haven't found your hat or the box or the bricks. Could be they got tossed overboard. Switching locomotives, we'll be a half-hour, maybe more. Storms slowing us down a bit. We head downhill from here. Should be in Farewell Bend right after daybreak."

"Thank you, Curtis."

"We'll be keepin' up the patrols."

She heard him walk away. Drawing the blankets up to her chin, tucking them in and around her, she thought of last night, lying in bed, warm in Leif's arms. Eyes closed, she imagined his eyes, blue eyes challenging her to be smart.

The storm would surely discourage one from carrying out an abduction. What if Mr. Emory's ambitions had changed? What if he had decided to be rid of her once and for all, dispose of her? Where better than up here in the middle of nowhere, in a blizzard? But would he do it before he found what he'd been looking for? Did he even know what he was looking for? Wouldn't he want to torture her first like he'd done to her father, torture her into telling him what she knew? The problem was she didn't know anything, not really.

Tense, cold and fearful time dragged on until at last, the cars lurched back, clunked, bumped, and thunked in line behind the locomotive that would take them down the mountains. The train blew its whistle and started to move in a cloud of steam, leaving the lights of the roundhouse behind.

Zola hoped Leif's brother would meet her promptly at the station if she should be so lucky to make it that far. Curtis would be with her. Yes, and maybe she would help the McGuires off the train. They were expecting to meet their daughter and grandchildren. Yes, there would be safety in numbers.

Drowsy, eyelids heavy, she drifted into a light sleep. A loud bump against the door of her compartment, followed by a grunt and thud, brought her around. Without thinking, she scrambled to stand on the bench, rock held over her head, ready to strike whoever or whatever came through the door. An ominous silence hung in the dank air, and then a brick shot through the glass in the window beside the door. A dark arm snaked through the window blind, thick fingers worked the lock.

She took a deep breath, knees weak, body trembling, and lowered the big rock swiftly down on top of Mr. Emory's dark head.

Ooofft! He crumpled to the floor. For a second, Zola thought she might have hit Curtis, but no, it was definitely Mr. Emory. She recognized his dark coat and hat.

In the aisle outside her door, Curtis lay on his face, holding his side, moaning. She leaped off the bench, stepping on Mr. Emory's shoulder to get out of the compartment and into the aisle to give aid to the porter.

Mr. Emory struggled to his knees, pulling himself up using the door. She saw the knife in his hand, glittering in the faint light of the scone. "It's time, sweetheart. Your time is now," he said, his voice a threatening snarl.

He raised his hand, knife aimed for her neck. To ward off the strike, Zola swung her arm to the side, forgetting entirely she still held the rock. Her defensive move struck Mr. Emory in his crotch. He doubled over, crumpled in a ball of agony.

Two more porters rushed through the dining car door. Mr. McGuire appeared in the doorway of his compartment. Curtis rolled to his side, blood on his hands. Zola helped him to sit, his back against the outer wall. "Where are you hurt, Curtis?"

"He missed me back," he said. "I was turnin' to knock on your door. He got me in the side, no vitals. I keep tickets in this pocket, so it's naught but a poke."

The knife? She found it beside her hip and handed it up to the young porter she'd seen serving food in the dining car. "He's still breathing." She pointed to Mr. Emory's inert form sprawled out in the doorway of her compartment. "We need to bind him somehow before he recovers."

"Mailbag, empty," Curtis said. "Denny, get the mailbag. It's there at the end of the aisle on the peg. I meant to take it back to the baggage car. I forgot."

"He might have another knife," Zola warned the young porter. "Remove his belt and shoes. And tie his hands behind his back. Once you get him in the bag, you might put the belt around the middle to be sure he can't wiggle out."

"You think like your husband, Mrs. Kenyon," said Curtis as he inched his way up the wall to stand on his feet to give Denny and Pat room to stuff Mr. Emory, still doubled over holding his crotch, into the canvas mailbag.

The locomotive, by the sound, was working more efficiently now, at last out in the rolling countryside of the Deschutes Basin. It was starting to get light, and a skiff of snow covered the sage and juniper.

****

Obsidian Hotel, Farewell Bend, Gunnar Kenyon— stop—

Pencil in hand, Leif paused, uncertain how to express his panic. Zola was on a train, in the middle of a blizzard, in the remote mountains with a madman whose prime goal was to stop her from returning to Prettydale.

Meet wife—bring sheriff, doctors—trouble on train.

Gunnar. Leif could hear his laughter when he read this damn telegram. Damn it to hell, he better not. He damn well better take it seriously. Zola—dear God— Leif prayed she would protect herself, use self-defense against the threat of death.

Helpless, absolutely useless, Leif sent the telegram and paced in front of the telegraph office at the station, waiting for a reply.

The station clock heralded the coming dawn, half-past the hour of six o'clock. The eastbound Cascadian would be pulling into the station in fifteen minutes—that is, if it had made it through the storm.

****

Zola, sipping a strong cup of coffee and enjoying a sweet roll at the table with Mr. and Mrs. McGuire in the dining car, took a deep, relieved breath. Denny had seen to Curtis and his wound, padding it and putting gauze on it to stop the bleeding. Curtis would need to see a doctor, but he insisted he was good enough to stay on the job.

The school teacher and the other passengers stopped by the table, all to offer their compliments on her bravery. The porters had removed Mr. Emory to the baggage car. He was making far too much noise, his curses bringing forth blushes.

The train arrived at Farewell Bend, and Zola apologized again for stealing the pillowcase, offering to pay. The conductor assured her they had plenty of pillowcases. They could spare one. She disembarked behind the McGuires, not giving much notice to the crowd. A cheer went up as soon as she stepped onto the platform.

A big, golden bear of a man, full beard, golden brown, wavy hair, and blue eyes, wrapped his arms around her and lifted her off her feet. "Zola Kenyon, Leif said you were a red-headed beauty—a spitfire—he said. And by God, here you are, the heroine of the day."

"Mr. Kenyon? Gunnar?" Zola said, finding it difficult to breathe.

"Yes, Leif's brother," the bear said, setting her down on her feet. "Now, the sheriff has the assassin in cuffs and chains. The doctor is seeing to poor Curtis. He'll be good as new in short order, thanks to your quick, courageous action."

"Mr. Kenyon," Zola said, overwhelmed by the crowd and Gunnar's big presence.

"Gunnar, please," he said.

"Gunnar, Leif is waiting to hear from me. Help me get away from here."

"Mrs. Kenyon," said a man, notebook in hand. "The name's Jack Larson. I'm with the Central Oregon Crier. Give us a rundown of the incident. The Crier will run the story. We need details. Who is the prisoner, and why did he attack you? What are you doing here in Farewell Bend? What's in that?" the reporter asked, indicating the white bundle she held close to her breast.

Gunnar moved her aside. "Mrs. Kenyon is here to pay a family visit. We'll have a statement for the press as soon as she's had time to recover from her ordeal."

"Yes, but we'll want the story in time for the evening run."

"You'll have it," Gunnar said. Turning his back on the man, he swept aside the crowd of people with a wave of his big arm to guide Zola toward a waiting horse-drawn sleigh.

"What's in the bundle?" Gunnar asked her once they were moving down the street.

"Rocks."

"Rocks?"

"It's complicated. How did you know? How did everyone know about the trouble on the train?"

"Leif. He sent up the distress flag in the form of a telegram, urging me to meet the train with the law and a doctor."

"I don't know how he could've known there was trouble on the train," Zola said to herself, "but I'm glad he did. But all those people cheering, why?"

"Leif is a legend here. You're the wife of the legend. I showed the sheriff the telegram, he told his deputy, and the news spread like wildfire, Leif's bride was in trouble on the morning train. The porter, Denny, hopped off the train while it was still moving. Didn't take him long to spread the tale of how Mrs. Kenyon had taken down a would-be murderer with nothing but a rock."

Zola groaned. "I had hoped to come into town unnoticed. It's important I keep my real purpose here secret. We have to be careful what we say in our wires to Leif. It's entirely probable they are being passed on to some very evil parties out to destroy everything. I'm afraid your brother purchased a lot of trouble when he purchased the homestead."

Chapter Nineteen

The telegrapher stepped away from the key to pour himself a cup of coffee, and the wire started to chatter.

"Get the hell over here." Leif pounded his fist on the counter. "Damn you, forget the coffee. Man your post."

The telegrapher muttered an apology and rushed to translate, writing the message on a scrap of paper to the side of the key. He transferred the message to the telegraph form and handed it to Leif.

Safe with Gunnar—stop—interference dispatched—stop

Leif rushed to answer, *my heart—stop—surprise October 7ᵗ—stop*

Next message from Gunnar. *Package arrived safely, no damage—stop—fire-brand glows—stop—lucky man*

The wire sounded off again, this one from Zola. *Papa remembered October 7, 21st Birthday—stop—rushing—stop—more later today—stop—you are with me—stop*

Leif didn't put it in a telegram, but he swore to himself he would never again allow Zola farther away from him than the length of his arm. The wire went silent. Leif gathered his messages and left the office, and nearly collided with the sheriff.

"Mrs. Kenyon have a safe trip, did she?"

The urge to slap the insolent sneer off the man's prepossessing face had Leif balling his fists into a cramping knot. "She did, thank you for asking," he answered. "And, the train was on time, no thanks to the weather. Well, good day, don't want to keep you. I'm sure you have telegrams to read."

****

"Mr. Kenyon."

"Gunnar."

Corrected, Zola dipped her head to start again. "Yes, Gunnar, is there somewhere we can go? I have a lot to tell you, and I don't have a lot of time."

"We've rooms at the Obsidian Hotel. It's up on the hill. You're a celebrity, but I think we will be able to lose the public at the hotel. My wife, Willa, and our twin boys, Conner and Cameron, are at the hotel. Breakfast is waiting for us in our rooms. We thought you might want a quiet place to rest after your trip."

"We aren't going to your home?"

"No, Centerville is a good thirty miles south. Leif said this was a rushed trip. We often stay in town at the hotel when I'm on business."

Gunnar helped her into the sleigh, and the crowd parted for them. Zola smiled and nodded, overwhelmed by the attention.

The Obsidian Hotel, a cut-stone building three stories high, sported a covered, pillared portico to accommodate quests, and keep them well out of any inclement weather. Zola had never seen anything so grand. Inside, placed in groupings about the lobby, breathtaking crimson, velvet, tufted chairs and sofas welcomed the visitors. Moss-green velvet drapes at the mullioned windows completed the opulent atmosphere.

Gunnar greeted the spindly, officious little desk clerk. He skipped around his counter, eager to be

193

introduced. "Charles, this is Leif's bride, Zola Kenyon. Zola, this is Charles Beatty. He's the brain that keeps this hotel running like a finely-tuned clock."

Zola shook hands with the funny little man, unable to say more than "Pleased to meet you" in between his litany of profuse compliments on her bravery, her intrepidity—it was embarrassing.

Gunnar interrupted. "Charles will see to it we aren't disturbed, won't you, Charles?"

Charles, mouth open, stopped in mid-sentence. "Yes, of course. Certainly, Mr. Kenyon."

"There's a reporter from the Star, Charles. He's eager for an interview. Don't let him up," Gunnar said, stressing the order. "On second thought, give him this." Gunner quickly wrote a note on the hotel stationary. "We'll—Mrs. Kenyon, will see him at one o'clock for an interview. That ought'a satisfy him for a few hours and give us time to decide what he needs to know."

Out of the corner of her eye, Zola caught a movement at the entrance. The reporter sidled in and moved quickly to the chair behind one of the columns that held up the ornate, embossed lobby ceiling. "You could give it to him yourself," Zola said. "He just came in. You'll find him behind the pillar in back of you."

Gunnar winked at her and approached the column. "Ah, Mr. Larson, I was about to have this delivered to you, but here you are," he said and handed the note around the column.

Mr. Larson, a sheepish grin on his face, stepped out into the open and tipped his hat to her.

"You will have your interview at one o'clock, Mr. Larson, after Mrs. Kenyon has had some time to recover from her adventures," Gunnar said, unsmiling, a warning edge in the tone of his voice. "You will come here to the desk and Charles will escort you to our rooms. Now, if you please, leave us alone. Stop following us around like a bad smell. Go pester someone else."

Hand over her mouth to stifle a giggle, Zola coughed. The brothers Kenyon were very much alike, direct, armed with a delightful yet annoying way of being rude and funny at the same time.

"One o'clock," said the reporter. Accepting surrender, he made a leisurely retreat.

Zola had never seen a marble staircase before. Their footfalls echoed—overhead, chandeliers dripped with crystal prisms. Their rooms took up the entire second floor. Gunnar and Willa had a four-room apartment to themselves. The boys had two connecting rooms. Their nanny, Dina Richards, had a room to herself. Zola was given a lovely suite with a parlor, a bedroom, and a bath with inside plumbing that consisted of a water closet, a copper tub, and boiler.

Wandering from room to room in her suite, she stopped to gaze out the big window, for the first time taking in the magnificent scenery. The rising sun cast a golden glow upon the startling white, snow-covered Cascades to the west. White clouds drifted in a sky of perfect azure over a high desert of gray-green sage and stunted juniper. She'd never seen anything so beautiful, so wide-open. She could see for miles and miles. Not at all like home, where huge fir, oak, and maple interrupted the vista. A tear trickled unchecked down her cheek. She missed home. She missed Leif. Leif was home. Before Leif, home was her parents, the land, the house and the barns, and the animals. Now home was Leif.

"I was born and raised on the plains of the Dakotas,"

Willa said. "This country still takes my breath away, and I've lived here for fifteen years now."

Willa Kenyon, her gown of deep sapphire bombazine, a creation meant to give the illusion she was not an Indian but a white woman looked out of place here amid all this Caucasian opulence. Zola thought Willa should be garbed in soft kid instead of bound up in cruel corsets and stays. Her raven-black hair, neatly fashioned in a coiled braid, formed a crown on her proud head, accentuating the woman's high cheekbones and flashing black eyes. Leif should have warned her his brother had married a full-blooded Sioux. Willa Kenyon—one more experience Zola had never encountered before.

"How could Leif bear to leave this?" Zola asked, her gaze never leaving the mountain scene.

Willa, beside her, hands folded at her nipped-in waist, said, "Gunnar casts a long shadow. Leif needed to move into his own light, expand—grow. They are both big men in so many ways. They kept getting in each other's way. I'm thinking he has found something he would never have found here if he had stayed."

"Well, he certainly hasn't had time to be bored," Zola said and turned away from the window.

"I came to get you. Breakfast is getting cold," Willa said, guiding Zola away from the window.

It surprised Zola how hungry she was. Seated at the table, she started to explain her mission. She'd stopped and started twice, uncertain where to begin. "I had to come. We think there's gold in the rock samples I brought with me. We didn't trust the land agent in Prettydale. The person who does the test samples is the sister of the sheriff."

"The same sheriff that's in cahoots with this Emory

fellow?" Gunnar asked.

Zola nodded, "Yes, the same. Leif wanted to bring the samples, but I talked him into allowing me to do it. We had the samples in a hat box, you see, and I thought it would look suspicious if Leif got on the train without me, hat box in hand."

She was rambling, and she knew it. That telegram had set off alarm bells. They didn't have enough time. It all looked hopeless. And there was too much to explain. Where to start? "But now, according to Leif's telegram, the one I just received, we only have four days to prove the claim and refile. No, now we only have three days. My birthday, my twenty-first birthday, is October 7th, that's day after tomorrow. My father filed the claim in my name. He didn't prove it. I'm sure he didn't intend to wait so long to tell me what he'd done. We don't know how, but Mr. Emory, the banker, and the sheriff knew about the claim."

She took a breath, shook her head, more or less talking to herself, she continued. "They withheld all knowledge of the claim from me. You see, my father died. The homestead was in financial difficulty. The bank forced my brother Forrest and me to auction off the homestead to repay the debt. Even after, after Leif purchased the homestead, we were terrorized by Mr. Emory. He tried to kill Leif. He didn't succeed. Leif sustained some broken ribs and a concussion, but no lasting hurts."

She sat back in her chair and closed her eyes to hold back her mounting hysteria. "They are desperate men," she said, eyes open, looking directly into Gunnar's piercing gaze. "We can't trust any of them. I believe Mr. Emory murdered my father. My father was a very passive, non-violent man. I suspect Mr. Emory attacked him. My father was beaten to death. I can't prove it. But I put nothing past Mr.Emory. When he came after me on the train, I knew he meant to kill me. It was the only way he could stop me—us–the only way. And now I understand why. He had to kill me before my birthday."

Gunnar scratched his full head of golden curls. "I still don't understand what made Leif think there was gold on the property."

She dabbed her napkin to her lips and put her hands in her lap. "Mr. Emory's continued attacks I'm sure made him suspicious. He knew the railroad was interested in the homestead because of its proximity to the pass. But he thought there had to be something more than just the land. Mr. Emory's attacks were that of a desperate man. Lief asked if there was gold in Pretty Creek. I told him I didn't think so. But he picked up a few rocks from a cave I showed him and along the stream. He scooped up some of the sediment below a little waterfall. And he had a strong suspicion there was gold in the samples we'd gathered. I still can't believe it."

"That's quite a story," said Gunnar. "We have a lot to do and not a lot of time to do it. We need a lawyer. And we need to get your bundle of rock samples to the assayer."

"I don't see how we are going to do everything. There isn't time. The reporter is out there waiting for us to make a move. He'll want to know why we are going to the assayer's."

"Don't worry about him. We'll send him on a wild-goose chase or two. It's not even ten o'clock, and we might get the assayer's report by the end of the day if we can make it worth his while. We have today. Time is against us, but we'll find a way. We'll find a way."

"Why do we need a lawyer?" Zola asked.

"He might have some suggestions on how to proceed, maybe toss a spanner in some crooked wheels."

Zola shook her head. "Even if I caught the train home in the morning, I wouldn't arrive until the next afternoon. I'd be too late to refile."

"True," said Gunnar. He came to his feet and began to pace the room. "But," he said, coming to a full stop before one of the windows in the room, "if Leif were there, in the land agent's office, say camped there, way before the banker trimmed his whiskers, and he staked the claim the second it became free, it would stay with the homestead."

"Of course," Zola said, popping up from her chair at the table. "That's so simple. I must be half-asleep to not have thought of it. Leif is the owner of the homestead, so of course, it should be in his name.

"I don't want the gold. I told him I didn't want it. Gold causes trouble. I wouldn't know what to do with it. He'll know how to handle it. He really is the most wonderful man."

In the next hour, Randal, the errand boy employed by the Obsidian Hotel, left the Kenyon apartments with a pillowcase wrapped around a pair of Gunnar's shoes and carrying a note inviting Stephen Lamont, lawyer for Kenyon Enterprises, to pay a call at the hotel and to please return shoes wrapped in the pillowcase.

As soon as Randal left, the nanny Dina Richards and the Kenyon boys set off for the park. The nanny carried her knitting basket as usual—a bit heavy today, but she managed to make it look no different than any other day.

From her hotel window, Zola watched the nanny march her charges down the street, taking purposeful strides, no one giving her any notice. She and her charges veered off the main street taking a detour. Zola had been assured their outing would take them right by the apothecary, where an assay of the samples could be made.

The lawyer Mr. Lamont and the nanny arrived back at the Kenyons' apartment door at eleven-fifteen. Nanny reported she'd cautioned the apothecary to keep the results of the tests confidential. They were to be done in a prompt and timely manner by the end of the day—two tests, one of the sediments, and one of the bigger stones. The apothecary took his payment, nodded, and when she'd left him, he'd already set to work, promising her he would do his very best.

The children were hustled off to their rooms to partake of their lunch. Mr. Lamont made himself comfortable in the easy chair away from any windows. "You know the reporter followed me here?" he said and deposited Gunnar's shoes on the floor. "He hounded me, kept after me to tell him what was in the white bag."

"What did you tell him?" Gunner asked as he poured himself and Mr. Lamont a shot of brandy.

"I told him the truth," Mr. Lamont said and took the drink. "I told him a pair of shoes as big as boats."

Gunnar burst out laughing. His laugh sounding so much like his brother's, brought tears to Zola's eyes.

The lawyer took a long sip and savored his libation before asking, "Now, why all the covert maneuvers?"

Gunnar gave the man a rundown of Zola's mission. Mr. Lamont handed Gunnar his empty glass. Gunnar refilled it. Mr. Lamont took it back and stared into the amber liquid. "You've got the right idea," he said at last. "If Leif were so inclined, he could take the claim out in the name of the homestead, incorporate you, Gunnar, Willa, Zola, your brother, Forrest, and anyone else who he felt deserved to be included. He'd have to set up a board, have meetings, make member decisions, all very democratic and equal."

"No, not me," Gunnar said. "I have my businesses, the mill, this hotel. Leif should have his. I've come to terms with his decision to leave. He was right. Incorporating is a good idea. What do you say, Zola?"

Zola didn't know what to say. She sat in shock to think Gunnar owned this grand hotel, and it was hard for her mind to move beyond that startling fact. She nodded, cleared her throat, and clasped her hands in her lap very tightly before speaking. "We have two very loyal men working for us. Leif hired them the very day he bought the homestead, and it would be wonderful to include them. I wish he were here. I need to send a wire. But we have to wait, don't we? We need the results from the apothecary. This may all prove moot. And nothing will need to be done at all."

"When it comes time to send the wires, you give them to me. We'll keep them away from the reporter if we can. I'll send them for you," Mr. Lamont said, handing off his empty glass to Gunnar. Hat in hand, he rose from his chair.

"Stay for lunch?" Willa asked.

"The wife is waiting for me. She's resting. You know how that goes. I have to check in."

"Give Carolyn our regards," Willa said. "Dina and I will come around to visit tomorrow. I remember how tedious was my own lying-in. But her time is coming near. It won't be long now. I think Dina has a baby blanket for her."

"She'd like company. And I would appreciate it. You'd make my life easier, give me some peace of mind knowing someone is with her."

Zola tuned out the conversation. She had to think. How in the world was she to write a telegram that would include all of this without giving anything away?

Late in the day, the sun hanging low over the mountains, the test results came in, delivered by Randal. Zola couldn't decide if she should laugh, cry or scream. The time had come to send the telegrams.

Chapter Twenty

Ephraim, Oren, and Forrest hadn't returned from their mission to find and set out stakes, and the day was fading fast. Another storm moving in from the north promised more snow. Leif dismissed the mill crew, making the decision to ride into town to the telegraph office to see if Zola had sent any more messages.

On his way to the station, Shaw and Daniels came out of the mercantile. He nodded and rode on. The telegram from Zola was there waiting for him.

"Thought I'd have to send the sheriff out to the homestead to deliver this," said the telegrapher.

"You have copies of this?" Leif asked.

"No," said the man.

Leif glared at him. The man was lying. He'd blinked and looked down at his desk. "You don't write the messages out on any other paper before you transfer them to the forms?"

"Well, yeah, I do, but it's just scrap paper and kind'a messy."

"I'll take the scrap paper and any other scribbles you've made concerning this telegram."

"Why?"

"Never mind why I want that paper. Now give it over, or I'll come back there and get it myself."

Grumbling, the man ripped the scrap paper from his pad and tossed it over the counter. "You'll have to recite this one from memory to your masters," Leif said and tucked the paper in his inside coat pocket as he left the office.

He stepped out of sight from the street to the side of the station to read the message, hands shaking.

School chum Lamont—stop—claim—stop—file—incorporate—stop—surprise birthday—stop—note:—stop—sending telegram per-request Abbots—stop—proof catalog—stop—color number—stop.

He had to read it several times to make any sense of it.

I don't know any Lamont. File, claim, incorporate? What the hell does that mean? Positive surprise birthday, I think I might know what that means. That means we've got a bonanza on our hands. Wait! Lamont? Stephen Lamont, Kenyon lawyer. God, she talked to a lawyer—clever girl. Incorporate? Incorporate, of course. I can file the claim and incorporate. But what the hell is this second telegram to the Abbot sisters about—numbers and catalog colors?"

He dashed back in the telegraph office. "I want the second telegram. Where is it?"

The man stammered. "I delivered it. It wasn't yours, so I had it delivered."

"Right, right, okay. I want that scrap paper too."

"No," said the man, backing up, but not before Leif grabbed him by the shirt front. "Give me the scrap of paper."

"All right, all right, hold your water," the man said and dipped down into his wastebasket and retrieved the scrap paper. "Take it and get out of my office."

Leif turned to leave and held the door open for Shaw and the sheriff.

"Little late for you to be in town, Mr. Kenyon. Hope the news isn't trouble," said Mr. Shaw, a sly gleam in his sharp gray eyes.

"Telegram from the wife. She's enjoying her stay with my brother," he said, and waved his telegram in their noses as he headed out the door—destination—the Emporium.

Miss Gladys, busy with a customer, waggled her fingers at him when he entered. Miss Paulette greeted him with a cheery, "Good afternoon, we were about to close. Funny you should come by, we were talking about you. We were wondering how you were getting along without your bride."

"I'm fine, thank you, Miss Abbot. I miss Zola, but she'll be home day after tomorrow." Leif put his hand under the little woman's elbow to steer her to the back of the store. Keeping his voice down, barely above a whisper, he asked, "The telegram from Zola, may I have it."

Miss Paulette whispered back, "Well, we did think it very strange. Couldn't make any sense of it: catalog numbers and color codes. There was no real message at all, just letters and numbers."

Leif could barely stay in his skin. He shook his head at the woman. "Yes, no sense at all, but can I have it?

"Well, of course, you may have it, dear. I put it back here on the wrapping table, I think."

"What is it, Paulette?" asked Miss Gladys.

"Mr. Kenyon would like to see the telegram from Mrs. Kenyon. I thought I left it here on the wrapping table."

The urge to roar like a lion, throw paper and boxes, had Leif gnashing his teeth. Finally, Miss Gladys unearthed the yellow telegram from beneath a pile of tissue paper.

He turned his back on the ladies, and the store, to read the message. At first glance, he had no idea what he was looking at. Gladys was right. It didn't make any sense. In the first line, a row of symbols and numbers followed the word *stream sediments,* and in the second line, a row of symbols and numbers followed the word *cavern.*

He swiped his hand down over his upturned face. He started to laugh, laugh, and laugh. Zola, bless her, had found an ingenious way to send him the results of the assayer's tests on the samples.

Neither Mr. Shaw nor the sheriff would be interested in the ladies' catalog and color numbers. Sending the information to the Abbot sisters guaranteed it would remain confidential. The little weasel telegrapher hadn't even bothered to keep it.

"Zola, Zola, how I love your mind," he said aloud. "Can't wait to show you how much I love you when you get home. Ring? The girl needs a ring for her birthday, a symbol of what she means to me. Miss Paulette, Miss Gladys, show me some of your finest rings."

****

"Leif, they're going to try and stop you," Mr. Prine said. "Mrs. Kenyon says in her telegram 'interference dispatched', but what does that mean? Even with Emory gone, Sheriff Daniels could show up anywhere, anytime."

"Do you think Mary Blashcombe is in on this?"

Mr. Prine didn't have an answer, but Ephraim had an opinion. "I don't think she wants to be, but that brother of hers…he's a hard one to say no to."

Leif spread the plat map out on the kitchen table. "Show me on the map where you found the markers Mr. Pretty set out."

"There's pitchforks on both sides of the narrow gorge about four miles up from the falls," said Oren. "There's two shovel handles stuck in the rocks, one on each side of the creek here and here, and below the falls, adzes, two of'em, one on each side kind'a hidden in the weeds, but definitely claim stakes dated and initialed."

"Damn Pa to hell," Forrest said, giving the table leg a good kick. "He knew about this, and he said nothin', nothin'."

"He thought he was protecting you," said Leif, a hand on the boy's shoulder.

"What about the cave?" Leif asked.

"We staked all around it good," said Forrest.

Giving himself a moment to think, Leif poured himself another cup of coffee. He missed Zola's coffee. Mr. Prine had taken over kitchen duties, and he did a fine job. But nothing, no one, could cook like Zola.

"We need a distraction," Mr. Prine said under his breath.

"We have time to think about it. Zola will be on the train tomorrow. It won't get in until late in the afternoon on Friday. I'll file as soon as Mary opens up."

"No, don't think that's gonna work," said Ephraim. "She lives above the shop. You can bet the sheriff and Shaw will be there to greet her as soon as she comes down to light the stove."

"It all depends if Shaw and the sheriff still believe they have the upper hand. They won't be expecting us to try and beat them to refiling."

"That's a pretty big if," Mr. Prine said.

"They've been pretty arrogant so far," Leif said. "Leaving the documents in the vault in plain sight, that was mighty stupid."

"Not really," said Mr. Prine. "No one is allowed in there except Mr. Shaw. I'd never been in there before. If I had something I needed from the vault, I had to ask him to get it."

"Ignoring Emory's misdeeds, putting the homestead up for auction, and standing Zola and Forrest up there, how cruel can you get? Arrogant and cruel. None of them worried about losing the property. They had the gold. All they had to do was keep Zola from finding out about it. And even when she did find out about it, we played into their hands again. Putting her on the train with Emory on board to make sure she wouldn't return. I don't think they know we know about the date on the claim. And they can't be sure Emory did his job if he's been 'dispatched' as Zola said. They've been following along, reading all the telegraph messages except for this last one. I took the scratch sheet away from the little worm telegrapher. I doubt he can recite word for word what the message said."

"I read those messages, and I don't know what she's talking about," said Forrest, a scowl on his face as he sliced himself another piece of apple pie.

"You do know the day after tomorrow is your sister's birthday?" Leif asked.

"Shoot, no. She ain't—hasn't said nothin' about birthdays since Pa died. She's gettin' too old for birthdays, and so am I."

"She remembered your birthday," Oren said. "I had a piece of your cake, carrot cake, I think it was. I remember that cake. You got a slingshot and a pair of socks she knit herself. Your pa had been gone only a few weeks, but your sister remembered your birthday."

"Yeah, yeah, I guess."

"Well, your pa remembered Zola's birthday, all right," Leif said. The telegram tells us the claim is *A* grade positive for gold. Gunnar's lawyer Stephen Lamont recommends we incorporate. All of us will be partners on this gold claim if I can beat out Shaw and Daniels to the filing."

"Another one of them pretty big if's," Ephraim said.

Leif prowled around the big kitchen and stopped to look out the window above the sink. Early in his career as sheriff, he'd fallen for false emergencies a couple of times, emergencies staged to keep him away while crimes were committed. Never would he have thought he'd be the one to use the device. He chuckled to himself at the irony.

"The Abbot sisters," he said. "The Abbot sisters are going to have their Emporium robbed. Mr. Prine, Shamus, you know them well?"

"We're cousins twice removed. Known them all my life. They're family."

"You go to town tonight and fill them in on everything."

"Everything?"

Leif nodded. "Everything. Friday morning, very early in the morning, their store is going to be robbed, and they are going to need the sheriff to come posthaste. Tell me they have a lien against their store."

"Oh, my, yes," Mr. Pine said. "They borrowed heavily against their trust fund. But Mr. Shaw isn't too worried about it. He collects a hefty amount of interest on the loan."

"Well, you tell the sisters not to worry about their loan. We're going to take care of it once they are members of Pretty Pride Mines Incorporated. Now, we need something to occupy Mr. Shaw. What shall it be?"

Chapter Twenty-One

"I don't know how to put this," Zola started to say. Willa walked beside her at the train depot with Gunnar ahead of them.

"You don't have to say anything, I know. I know Leif is going to hate this. But I can't stop my husband. He's too big, and I'm not just talking about his size. My husband has a huge will. He's like a tornado. You can't stop it—all you can do is get out of the way."

"I'm going to miss you," Zola said to the lady, her tears blurring Willa's beautiful face. "I hope we see a lot of each other. I'll have to come back when Mr. Emory goes on trial. I suppose. Leif will come with me then."

"Meanwhile, we'll write letters."

"Yes," Zola said and stopped to embrace her sister-in-law.

"Time to board," Gunnar said, wrapping his big arms around both of them. He kissed his wife on the lips, holding her fast for a few moments. Unable to move, embarrassed, Zola looked away. "You both must realize that, in good conscience, I can't allow Zola to make this trip over the mountain unescorted. Considering all that's happened and considering what she is now transporting, I must see her safely into my brother's care." He patted the bulges in his coat's hip pockets.

He removed his arm from around Zola, and she stepped back. His wife firmly held against his chest, his square chin resting on her shoulder, he said, "I promise, I'll make my stay a short one. And I'll do as you suggested. I'll work on curbing my habit of taking over my brother's business."

His wife laughed in his face and patted his jowls. "I will miss you. Give my love to Leif."

The train whistle sounded, and a geyser of steam enveloped the boarding passengers.

"Come, Zola, we must board now. Love to the boys," Gunnar said before he gave his wife a parting peck on the cheek.

****

Frowning, muttering to himself, Leif slapped the rolled-up Examiner down on the kitchen table. The local weekly paper's attempt to supply the residents of Prettydale with news, statewide and local, was full of terrifying news as far as Leif was concerned. "Damn, damn."

The lead article, in bold print, leaped off the double-sided, single-page rag.

October 4, 1887: Shepherdess slays Goliath with a rock. Prettydale's Mrs. Zola Kenyon, formally Zola Pretty of the Pretty homestead, on her way to visit her husband's, Leif Kenyon's, family in Farewell Bend, narrowly escaped death with nothing but a rock to defend herself against her attacker, prominent Prettydale citizen, Mr. Amos Emory.

Mr. Curtis Staub, porter on the eastbound Cascadian, who sustained a knife wound to his side during the attack, reported Mrs. Kenyon, who escaped Mr. Emory's knife attack by subduing him with her rock, swiftly came to his aid. While giving aid, Mr. Emory recovered and once again moved to strike Mrs. Kenyon a mortal blow. In a defensive move, weapon in hand, a large stone, Mrs. Kenyon struck Mr. Emory in the lower regions of his body. He fell to his knees.

Disarmed and immobilized, Mr. Emory was secured by two porters. Binding his hands, they stuffed him in a mailbag. Mr. Emory was thus transported to the authorities in Farewell Bend.

The reasons for Mr. Emory's attack upon Mrs. Kenyon with a knife remain a mystery. Mr. Emory is being held responsible for attacking Mrs. Kenyon and Curtis Staub and will be charged with two counts of attempted murder. Trial date pending. More on this story as it develops.

Ephraim read the article and chuckled to himself. "So now we know what she meant when she said in her telegram, *'interference dispatched.'* Miss Zola dispatched him good and proper, she did."

"Oren," Leif said, finally coming to a halt behind his chair at the table, "did Shamus give you any idea how the Abbot sisters intended to carry out their parts when he gave you this…this excuse for a newspaper this morning?"

Oren shook his head. "They hadn't worked all the knots out of their plans yet. But he did say the sisters were eager to participate. They also told him to tell you although they appreciated your generosity, giving them inclusion of ownership wasn't necessary. To quote Miss Paulette, 'Miss Pretty has been horribly mistreated, and we will do everything we can to see her rightful inheritance put right.'"

"I don't know how they're going to get Shaw there—at the Emporium. Or what excuse they intend to give for their presence at the store that early in the morning.

"This," said Leif, tapping the paper with his index finger, "isn't good. Shaw and Daniels will be on alert now. Even if they're not sure of what we know, they'll be watching, anticipating. Zola will be home tomorrow, and one way or another, this will be brought to a conclusion, whether for good or ill."

"Well, at least Emory is out of the way," Ephraim said.

"Dad," Oren said, "you and me are volunteer firemen, ain't we?"

Ephraim wrinkled his heavy brows, then he broke into a wide grin. "I think we needs to pay a call on the Abbot sisters and have a talk with Mr. Prine. It's gonna be a busy mornin' I'm thinkin', a robbery at the Emporium and a fire at the bank, tsk, tsk, tsk, most unfortunate."

Leif slapped Oren on the back, hope restored. "You two pay my respects to Miss Paulette and Miss Gladys. I'm beginning to think we might actually pull this off." He raised his shot glass to his co-conspirators. "To Pretty Pride Mines Incorporated and to the members of her board of directors. And to Zola, the love of my life, and the most courageous and proud woman I've ever met."

****

A copy of the Farewell Bend Crier sat on the bench next to Zola. She'd read the damn article and now worried Leif had seen it too. And worse, Sheriff Daniels and Mr. Shaw had also read it or a version of the story in the Examiner. What would they do, desperate now, and Leif was in very real danger if he tried to file a claim on Pretty Creek. Mr. Shaw, no doubt the brains behind the scheme from the beginning, wouldn't hesitate to kill Leif in cold blood should he get in the way.

The train stopped at Crystal Lake for water and wood, then continued on huffing and puffing. The train crawled up the steep mountains on its way to Santiam Roundhouse. Several feet of new snow slowed them down, and it was a little past noon when they reached the roundhouse.

"We should eat," Gunnar said, his voice breaking through her worried thoughts.

"Yes, of course. You must be hungry," she said and slid the paper farther away from her side.

"I can go days without eating, live off the fat of the land as it were, but a little bit of a thing like you needs to eat often and hearty. Worrying won't help, you know. Leif's had time to consider all the contingencies. You said yourself, these two men he's hired to look after the homestead are good men. He was a law officer in a very rough town for nearly six years, and he knows a trick or two."

"I know...but..."

"But?"

"We're so new to each other. We barely know each other. We were just getting close..."

"Food, you need food. Look, we're on the move again. We'll be out of the snow in an hour. It's downhill most of the way now.

****

In the dark, bitter cold of predawn, Leif, Oren, and Ephraim crossed the schoolyard, dismounted, and tied their mounts to the back step. Forrest slid off the back end of Oren's horse and silently landed on his feet. A dark figure came out from behind the schoolyard privy to meet them.

The four of them huddled in, voices low, "My pistol, Shamus, if you're comfortable with the plan."

"Been a while since I fired one of these things," Shamus Prine said, accepting the weapon, handling it with great respect. "Since I don't have to aim it at anything but the sky, I can do it."

Leif patted the man on the back. "Good."

"Oren and me will head off to the stable," Ephraim said.

"I don't have to warn you two to stay out of sight."

"No, Sir," said Ephraim.

"Wait for the shots," Leif said.

"Right," Ephraim said over his shoulder.

"Forrest," Leif said, his arm around the boy's shoulders.

"I know," said the boy, "stay out of sight. Climb through the windows, set the smudge pots, light them and get the hell out without making noise or getting stuck."

"Yeah, that's about it. Your sister will peel my hide if you get hurt. I don't think she'd approve of our little plan. Sorry, it's up to you to set the smudge pots. You're the only one that'll fit through the basement windows."

Leif had been given the location of the sheriff's home, two blocks from the sheriff's office. He hoped they had their timing right. The Abbot sisters lived in the big house next to the school. Their parlor lamps were lit. Leif tapped lightly on their door. Miss Paulette, in her night rail and robe, nightcap in place on her silver curls, answered the door. "We're up and waiting for the signal," she said by way of a greeting. "We'll come running. Dear Shamus has explained the plan in detail. Don't you worry, we know how to put on a performance—we did Shakespeare in finishing school."

The twittering, flighty Abbot sisters, the weak links in this plan, compelled Leif to go through it one more time. "As soon as we get the bank full of smoke, Shamus will fire the shots. You two come hot foot down the street. Shamus will set up a hue and cry, declaring he'd fired at burglars attempting to rob the Emporium. At the sound of the shots, Oren and Ephraim will begin ringing the fire bell, summoning the fire brigade, alerting Mr. Shaw of the smoke filling the bank. And by this time, with any luck, I'll be inside the land agent's office, claim in hand."

Miss Gladys, pulling her sweater up around her jowls, wagged her head at him. "Yes, yes, we're ready. It's cold. Close the door. We've got the windows open. We'll hear the shots. You best hurry, Mr. Kenyon. It's five-fifty. Mary will be getting up soon."

Leif and Forrest walked back to the road. Forrest had warned him of the big dog across the street from the Abbot home. The dog started to bark. Forrest tossed a piece of buttered biscuit over the fence at the beast to shut him up.

They reached Second Street undetected. "I'll keep watch until you get out of the basement."

Setting the pots in the basement wasn't as easy as Leif had hoped. The windows were painted shut and narrow but unlocked. Forrest had to wiggle his way in, his jacket hanging up on the casing. Leif was proud of the boy, he did his work silently and quickly, and soon smoke began to seep out into the frosty, pre-dawn air.

Forrest ducked around the corner of the bank out of sight, and Leif ran to the back of the land office. Around the back, above the back rooms, a faint light appeared.

The smell of smoke wafted low to the ground, seeping around the buildings and over the town. Two gunshots echoed upon the crisp air coming from the direction of the Emporium

Dressed in an oversized wool robe over her nightgown, boots on her feet, big Mary Blashcombe stumbled down the wooden stairs headed for the back door of her office. Leif sprang out from behind the steps and caught her, one arm going around her chest, a hand going over her mouth. It was all he could do to hold her. She was a strong woman. "It's me, Leif Kenyon, Mary. Everything is under control. I assure you, the town is not on fire, and no one has been shot."

Propelling her, he turned her toward the office door. "Let's go inside. We have business to take care of." She struggled and attempted to break free, heading for the front of the building. "Aha, ha, now we'd be in the way out there on the street."

She huffed and shook her head and relaxed in his arms. He removed his hand from her mouth.

"Mr. Kenyon, what the devil is going on? Get your hands off me," she said, shaking her shoulders to wiggle out of his arms.

Her body locked firmly under his control, he said, "Open your office, get inside." She did as instructed. Leif closed the door with his foot. "I'll let go as soon as you promise me you won't scream. I'm here to conduct business, and that's all. Let's go out front."

She huffed and shrugged him off. "Get your hands off me. I'm going, I'm going."

He let her go, following her through a maze of counters littered with beakers, scales, and stacked boxes full of chemicals, to the front office.

"I understand Zola Pretty's mineral claim expires today. I have a plat map and proof of the claims. I'm here to refile that claim and one other. Both to be under the umbrella of Pretty Pride Mines Incorporated. You'll find the names of the corporation's associates here," he said, handing off all of his papers. "If you would be so kind as to proceed with the necessary paperwork, I would be much obliged."

Raised voices out in the street caught Mary's attention. "What the hell is going on out there?"

"Never mind about all that. We have business to conduct and posthaste, if you please."

She turned on him, giving him a hard look. "What the hell have you done? You know what my brother and Shaw are up to, don't you? I told them you was a knowing one. I warned David. I tried."

Leif squared his shoulders and met her hard gaze with his own. "My question to you is this—are you willing to aid and abet?"

She huffed and sputtered. "No, I am not," she said and snatched the forms out of her file case. "Light the lamp. I can't see a damn thing. We'll have to hurry. David could come along any minute."

"I believe he has business at the Emporium, a possible robbery, I believe."

"Well, Shaw, then," Mary said, searching her counter for her inkwell.

Leif, at the window, said, "Seems there's smoke filling the bank, and Mr. Shaw appears very concerned."

Lief observed the fire brigade break down the back door of the bank. Six volunteer firemen, including Ephraim and Oren, charged through the smoke, disappearing beyond the door. And by the volume of his raised voice and curses, they proceeded to ignore Mr. Shaw's protests.

Down the street, the sheriff, surrounded by the chattering, excited Abbot sisters and the disheveled Mr. Prine, argued, pointing fingers at one another.

Mary meticulously filled out her forms, talking to herself, copying the information from Zola's telegram to the Abbot sisters to each sheet. She stopped to check her work and slid the first of the five forms to Leif. He'd added his signature to all but the last form when the front door of the office burst open.

Forrest came stumbling into the office, his arm cranked up and into his spine, Sheriff Daniels pressing a pistol to the back of his head.

"You son-of-a-bitch, Kenyon, you're a dead man. I spied this little rat grinnin', peekin' around the corner of the bank. I knew right off it was you behind this mornin's work. Emory really botched it. You should be long dead. Mary, you tear up them forms."

Mary, bless her, squared her very substantial shoulders and said with a calmness Leif admired more than he could say, "I will not. I'm done being pushed around by you, David, and that crook Thomas J. Shaw. Let the boy go."

Shamus, voice cracking, hand shaking, moved in behind the sheriff and jabbed Leif's pistol under the man's shoulder blade. "Best do as she says, Sheriff. There are two federal marshals on their way. Your boss, Mr. Shaw, is at this moment speaking with two state bank auditors. I notified them day before yesterday of possible misappropriations, and they arrived last night. The Abbot sisters, just now, received a telegram from the sheriff in Farewell Bend via a lawyer by the name of

Stephen Lamont. It seems Mr. Emory is talking. He's mentioned your name."

Daniels shoved Forrest to the floor and swiped Shamus aside to make a hasty exit but ran into a solid, dark wall of humanity. Ephraim and Oren Gooding knocked Daniels to the ground and made short work of subduing him.

It took a while to set the town back in order, but by eight o'clock, Leif and members of the Pretty Pride Mines Incorporated, with the exception of the missing Zola, walked into the hotel dining room and took a corner table. The waiter assured them breakfast would be compliments of the establishment.

"Was all that stuff about the federal marshals on the way true?" Leif asked the moment the waiter left their table.

Shamus, hand shaking, set his coffee cup aside. "Got the telegram right here." He reached down in his trouser pocket and retrieved the message. "I forgot I had the gun in my hand. The kid from the telegraph office kept interrupting us. We were trying to keep Daniels from getting to Mary's office. Daniels dashed off and grabbed Forrest. I didn't know what to do. I guess I waved the damn gun in the air or something, and the kid threw the telegram on the ground and took off running. You know, the funny thing is, I only had two bullets in your pistol. It was empty. I stopped Daniels with no bullets. It's just now starting to set in."

"I'll be damned," Leif said to himself and set back after reading the telegram. "And the auditors?"

"They're at the bank," Shamus said and took a restorative sip of his coffee, having to hold the cup with both hands. "I have a meeting with them in a half-hour."

****

Disembarking the train in Salem, having spent nearly twenty hours cooped up in a small compartment going out of her mind with worry, Zola signaled to Gunner she needed to stretch her legs and set off on the path to the privies. Emerging from the outhouse, a light, cold drizzle misting her cheeks, she took a deep breath and prayed for forbearance. She circled the depot twice, and on her third time around, coming to the corner of the building, at the platform, she stopped and stepped back out of sight. Gunnar, Mr. Mills, the station clerk, and two official gentlemen she recognized by their dark coats, hats, and the shiny silver stars on their chests as federal marshals, stood in intense conversation.

Gunner spotted her and waved her forward. "Zola, Mr. Mills you know."

She greeted Mr. Mills with a smile and a nod.

"These two men are U. S. Marshals, Zola, Marshal Ramos and Marshal Butler. They're on their way to Prettydale. Gentlemen, this is Zola Kenyon, my sister-in-law, my brother's wife."

Marshal Ramos tipped the brim of his black hat to her, an inscrutable expression on his weathered face and unreadable gaze. "Mrs. Kenyon, Marshal Butler, and I would like to speak with you. We'll be on the train with you."

"My husband, Leif, tell me, have you heard something? Is…is he…all right? Why are you going to Prettydale?"

Marshal Butler answered, "We're on our way to Prettydale to question persons named by the prisoner Amos Emory, currently being held in the jail in Farewell Bend on two counts of attempted murder. We are pleased to have met you here. This affords us an opportunity to speak with you in a private setting."

Zola thought she might have to scream or stomp her foot. Tears coming to her eyes, she took a deep, steadying breath. "I see, but you haven't heard anything about what's happening in Prettydale this morning?"

"No, Ma'am, we're only interested in the Emory case."

Zola pressed her lips together and sniffed back her tears. "I see."

Gunnar laid his arm around her shoulder. "A few more hours, and you'll be home. You'll see he's fine. The town will still be standing."

"Yes," she said, struggling to smile, "I hope. Speaking to you, on the train is, well, it's better now than when we reach Prettydale. I won't have time then. I need to be with my husband. Make sure he and my brother are all right. Mr. Emory isn't the only one who poses a danger to me and my family."

"That sounds very interesting. We'll want to hear all about it," Marshal Ramos said.

Chapter Twenty-Two

The young porter Jimmy greeted Zola, pleased to show her and her traveling companions to their compartment. Backing out, he promised a pot of tea and a plate of molasses cookies.

The train, in a cloud of steam, pulled out of the busy Salem station. Gunnar pulled down a blanket. Grateful, Zola tucked it in around her lap and legs. The marshals removed their long coats, but not their hats, and sat down on the bench opposite. Marshal Ramos lost no time to begin the interrogation. "Tell us from the beginning, please, how you come to know Mr. Emory, Mrs. Kenyon?"

"He's our neighbor. Was our neighbor for six years, or maybe seven years," she said, beginning at the beginning.

Jimmy returned with their refreshments. Zola smiled at him when Gunnar offered him a dollar tip. She resumed her story as soon as Jimmy closed the door behind him. The pot of tea and the plate of cookies were all gone by the time she got around to how she'd come to be on a train, with Mr. Emory following her.

"You have the gold the assayer extracted from the samples on you right now?" Marshal Butler asked.

"I have them," Gunnar said, patting his coat pockets.

"And you don't know if Sheriff Daniels and the Banker Shaw were able to stop Mr. Kenyon from refiling your claim, is that right?"

"Correct," Zola said, finding the entire interview irksome. "This article in the Sun doesn't help matters. I'm sure Prettydale's Examiner has run the story too. It's a small town, and Mr. Emory was a big presence. The editor of the Examiner is very diligent. He prides himself on keeping up with the latest news, especially when it concerns a local citizen."

"Your account of the attack matches Mr. Staub's. Mr. Emory, however, claims you used unnecessary force. He only meant to frighten you. He never intended to kill," Marshal Butler said, more than a hint of an accusation in his tone.

Zola instantly bristled, and squared her shoulders, chin up. "I'd seen him. He was definitely following me, stalking me, if you like. I knew he was on the train, and there could only be two reasons for his presence. Either he wanted to abduct me, rape me, then kill me, or he simply wanted to kill me—none of which appealed to me. So I prepared myself to take defensive measures. I was not going down without a fight. When I saw the knife in his hand, I didn't bother to smile and ask, *'Why dear, kind Mr. Emory, whatever do you mean by flashing that knife at me*—I'm not stupid. He'd tried to abduct me before. He'd tried to…to…molest me. He also attempted to burn down the homestead—*twice*. I had no reason to believe he meant no harm. I took the knife he held in his hand very seriously, I assure you."

Marshal Ramos shook his head and leaned towards her. "We understand that. We have to pose these questions. He's going to get a defense lawyer. You need to keep to your side of the story, no wavering or hesitation. So far, you're doing fine."

"But he is implicating the sheriff and the banker?" Gunnar asked.

Marshal Ramos sat back. "Oh, yeah. The banker especially. Seems Mr. Shaw gave the orders. Emory took his orders to eliminate the obstacles to their obtaining the gold and the homestead property literally."

****

At twelve minutes past four o'clock, the southbound train, the Empire, pulled into the Prettydale station, almost a half-hour late. Leif could hardly remember to breathe. The Abbot sisters, Ephraim, Oren, and Forrest were there too, but he couldn't think about anything other than seeing Zola, getting her safe and in his arms.

Inside the train, a green coat passed by the car window. Leif followed it to the end of the car and stepped forward. Zola appeared on the deck between cars, and the moment their gazes locked, she tipped forward into his arms, clasping him around the neck, babbling, repeating his name over and over.

Her tears warm on his neck, he strived to soothe her. "Shhhhh, Zola. You're home. You're home."

Her lips moving against his skin, she said, "Yes, I'm home." Eyes closed, she sought his lips. They both began to giggle, and he allowed her to slip down to stand on her own two feet. Leif opened his eyes, and there was Gunnar grinning at him like a big dumb fool. "What the hell are you doing here?"

"I'm here giving escort to your precious cargo," he said, golden brows raised, a challenging gleam in his blue eyes.

Leif opened his mouth to respond, but Shamus cut off all thoughts, running up, winded, waving his arms. "Shaw, he's boarding. Brown coat, hat, satchel. Stop him."

The two U S Marshals took over. Leif didn't know where they'd come from, but he recognized the stars on their chests and their uniform of black coats and hats.

"Shaw? That's the banker?" the darker of the two marshals asked Shamus.

"Yes, sir," Shamus said, also recognizing authority. He visibly gathered his composure, took a deep breath, and squared his shoulders. "I was at the bank in the middle of helping the auditors. Mr. Shaw went to his office for the vault key. He didn't come back, so I went to look for him, and the vault door was open, and so was the back door. I caught a glimpse of him running down the street in this direction. I didn't know he could run. He's—he's, ah, ah, portly. He's on the train, I'm sure. Brown coat and hat and a brown satchel."

The marshals split up, and signaling each other, they entered the passenger car from both ends.

Leif introduced Gunnar to Ephraim and Oren and moved Zola and Forrest behind him. It didn't take long before the sounds of an altercation inside the train reached their ears. Someone, a lady, screamed. A few curse words, snorts, and grunts, and the satchel came flying out the end of the car. Leather straps broke, the satchel spilled open, and a pair of black satin pajamas fluttered in the cold afternoon breeze. Beneath socks and underwear, bundles of bills, a lot of bundles, slid out onto the platform.

"Those are one-hundred silver dollar certificates in those wrappers," Shamus said, reverence in his voice.

The U. S. Marshals removed Mr. Thomas J. Shaw, red in the face, sweating, none too gently from the train, shoving him past gaping boarding passengers. The whistle blew, announcing the end of the show.

A moment of silence ensued. "I'll go along," Shamus said. "I ran out on the auditors. Mrs. Kenyon, it is really good to have you home safe and sound." He started to follow the marshals but turned back to Leif. "Emory owed a lot of money. A lot. His place is entailed to the hilt. I had no idea how bad. The auditors are talking about putting it up for auction. Might not be a bad investment," he said, wily salt and pepper brows arched.

"What did he mean by that?" asked Zola, tugging on Leif's coat front. "What's been happening here? Auditors at the bank—Mr. Shaw? Where's Sheriff Daniels? What happened? Did you file the claims in time?"

"I have a lot of questions too," Leif said. His hand on her back, he moved her toward the depot. "The sun is going down. We need to get you home.

"Gunnar, wipe that grin off your big face.

"Oren, please bring the buggy around to the front of the depot."

"Zola, dear," said Miss Paulette, skipping to keep up. "You have a lot to talk about tonight."

"We are so relieved you're home safe," said Miss Gladys on Leif's other side.

"Yes, indeed. All is well, and justice is going to be served," said Miss Paulette.

"If those bank auditors have any sense, they'll put dear cousin Shamus in charge," Miss Gladys said.

"Thank the Lord we have horrible cousin David locked up where he belongs," Miss Paulette said. "He's been horrible to Mary."

"Just horrible," Miss Gladys said

"We need to get home, Sister," Miss Paulette said.

"Yes, yes, I could use a strong cup of your tea," Miss Gladys said.

"With a strong dollop of Papa's West Indies Goods," said Miss Paulette.

"And lots of thick cream and honey. What a day, what a day we've had. We shall sleep well tonight now we have our world set to rights." The two trotted down the street, chattering and planning what they were going to have with their tea.

Zola planted her feet, refusing to move one more inch. She gathered Forrest to her side and said, "For heaven's sake, Leif, stop herding us around. Now." She took a breath and smiled at Gunnar. "This is my brother Forrest. Forrest, this is Gunnar Kenyon, Leif's brother."

Gunnar offered his hand to the boy, grinning like an idiot, in Leif's opinion. "I'll want to hear your version of everything that happened today," Gunnar said with a wink. "My brother, if I know him, is about to give us a watered-down, diluted account."

Leif shook his head, his hand beneath Zola's elbow to get her moving again. "Don't listen to him," he said to Forrest. "He'll turn you into one of his spies. My brother isn't happy unless he's in everyone's business."

"I'm not asking the boy to pick sides," Gunnar said, following Leif to the buggy. "I want to see the big picture from another perspective, nothing wrong with that. You leave out the interesting details, drama—tension. I swear I'm not here to interfere. I promised Willa."

"Ha," Leif said over his shoulder.

****

Gunnar and Leif bickered and picked at each other all the way out of town, reminding Zola of herself and Forrest, making it impossible to get any of her questions answered.

"Ephraim," Leif said, calling the man to ride alongside the buggy. "You and Oren go on ahead, light the fires and start heating water for Mrs. Kenyon. She'll want a bath."

"Oh, do I now? I wasn't aware I stink," she said and jerked away from him.

"Oh, damn it to hell, you don't stink. You smell wonderful, like clover and honey. I just thought you might like a long soak after traveling all day."

"I've said it before, and I'll say it again, Leif Kenyon, you are bossy. You're not happy unless you're ordering someone around."

On her other side, Gunnar chuckled. "And you," she said to him, "You're no better. The reason you two don't get along is you both want to be boss. It's a case of too many kings and not enough serfs. But—but yes, a long soak would be wonderful, very thoughtful, thank you.

"Have you been gone from home all day?" she asked Leif.

"Yes, we rode into town about an hour before daylight." She nodded at his cryptic answer and decided he needed a sharper prod. "Oh, for heaven's sake, what happened? Were you able to file the claim? Did you get the wire I sent to the Abbot sisters with the results of the assay?"

Nodding, he laughed at her. "Yes, yes, and yes, I did. I have the papers right here in my inside coat pocket. They are duly recorded and notarized. You, Forrest, Oren, Ephraim, Shamus, Paulette, Gladys, and myself, are now owners of Pretty Pride Mines Incorporated."

"Mines? We have plural mines?"

"Well, actually, two claims. They aren't mines, not

yet anyway. Any gold taken out of the creek and any gold extracted from the cave will be divided among members of the corporation. We'll all sit down soon and discuss how we want to work this. Tonight all I want to do is get you home. Damn it, Zola, Emory tried to murder you— cut you, stab you to death. I can't get the image of it out of my head. I've been going insane here."

She bounced on the seat to face him. "You? You were going insane? Yesterday and all day today, I thought I would go mad. How was I to know Daniels wouldn't follow through—kill you—and Forrest, to get what he and Shaw were after. I think we know now they murdered my father. Murder once, twice, no difference to men like Daniels and Shaw and Emory. Emory certainly intended to kill me. I'm certain of it. Follows to reason they'd planned on getting rid of you too, and Forrest, anyone who got in their way—keep you from filing the claim. Gunnar will tell you, I could hardly eat. You can't get up and walk around on a train. You have to sit and sit and sit and stare out the window. At least you could move around, do something." Her voice cracked, and much to her chagrin, she sobbed and couldn't stop.

Leif pulled up on the reins to stop the buggy. "I'm sorry, sweetheart," he said and gathered her into an embrace, stroking her back. "I'm a cold, bossy bastard. Once I get you home, and you've had a good hot soak and something to eat, I'll give you the details, all of it," he said, looking straight into his brother's eyes. "For now, know this, no one was hurt, we have our home, and the future is looking very bright, very, very bright."

Gunnar snickered, then burst out laughing.

"What do you find so amusing, brother?" Leif

asked.

Gunnar pressed his lips together but couldn't stop chuckling, shoulders shaking. "I'm...I'm just so damn tickled you're happily married at long last, little brother. Never thought I'd see the day you'd admit to being a cold, bossy bastard. As one cold, bossy bastard to another, I tell you it happens to us all if we're lucky."

His answer brought Zola's histrionics to a halt. Thinking of Willa and how she and Gunnar worked together within their marriage, her sense of the ridiculous kicked in, and she began to giggle, tears streaming down her cheeks.

It took Leif a second or two longer to forgive the insult. He flicked the rein. Eventually, seeing the irony, he burst in a shout of laughter that echoed up and down the road.

Chapter Twenty-Three

"I thought you'd gone to bed," Leif said.

"I went out to the barn," Gunnar said. "Been talking to Ephraim and Oren."

"Grilling my hired hands, were you?"

"I found you left out the part about Forrest being shoved through the land agent's door at gunpoint by a deranged killer. Do you really think the boy is going to keep that part a secret for very long? It's the most exciting part."

"I gave him twenty dollars. We decided there was no cause to inflict any more stress on his sister. It is all over, in the past. No harm came to any of us."

Gunnar lowered himself into the chair nearest the fire in the parlor and held out his hands to warm them. "Ah, I see. Being thoughtful again. It's going to backfire on you. She'll find out sooner or later."

"Well, later then. Not right now. We both need some time for the dust to settle."

"I wish you luck." Gunnar leaned back in his chair and stared into the flames. "I wasn't sleepy. Missing Willa, I took a walk outside and ended up in the barn. I thought you'd gone to bed. Which leads me to ask, what the hell are you doing down here? Shouldn't you be upstairs making love to your intrepid little spit-fire?"

Groaning, Leif rose to pace, ending at the parlor window. "With everything she's been through, I thought

I'd leave her alone for a while—let her fall asleep. I didn't want to impose any more demands."

"Liar."

"Yeah," Leif said and returned to the settee. "We, Zola and me—we haven't—we're not really—we haven't gotten…

"You know, Zola said practically the very same thing, using the very same disjointed words," Gunnar said. He lurched forward and slapped Leif on the knee. "For Christ's sake, Leif. Go up there, take your woman in your arms and get it done. You both want it. The longer you wait, the wider the gap will grow between you."

"What if she's asleep?"

"She's not. I saw her shadow moving against the shade. She's up there waiting for you and you're sittin' down here like an idiot. My God, the woman leaped off the train, without giving it any thought, right into your arms. She trusts you. She knew you'd be there to catch her. That should tell you all you need to know."

Leif got to his feet. "I'm grateful to you for seeing her safely back to me. Thank you."

Gunnar nodded. "I'll be around for a few days. I want to see how the mill's coming along, take a look around. I like what I see so far. You chose well, very well indeed, little brother."

"Good night," Leif said.

****

The bath was wonderful. Supper, however, left a lot to be desired—two hot cakes and a rasher of ham now sat on her nervous stomach like lead. Twice Zola started for the door, having come to the conclusion she'd have to go downstairs and drag her husband to bed. Each time, she'd dropped her hand at the doorknob, doubts eating her alive—he didn't want to come to her bed. He'd decided to leave her alone. He'd given up on ever bedding her. He was visiting with his brother. They had a lot to talk about, and she wouldn't, couldn't interrupt.

The idea he was leaving her alone on purpose saddened and infuriated her, and once again she headed for the door. When it opened, and he stood there, uncertainty written on his face, she knew he'd been feeling everything she'd been feeling, and somehow they had to get past it.

"I'm sorry," they both said at the same time.

"What are you sorry for?" Leif asked her and softly closed the door behind him.

"I don't know," she said. "I'm sorry I don't know what I'm supposed to do or how to do it."

He didn't say anything but went to his side of the bed, removed his boots, and unbuttoned his shirt. "I'm sorry for making you feel uncertain," he said as he unbuttoned his trousers and let them drop on the floor. "When you got off the train, you didn't hesitate. You came right to me. I want you to feel that way always, Zola. Never hesitate, or apologize for coming to me, wanting me, needing me."

"All right then, I think we should stop this," she said.

"This? Stop what?"

"All of this dancing around," she said and shimmed out of her nightgown. Blushing, she stood before him naked. "This is me, freckles, red hair, and all. I want you, Leif Kenyon, in every way a woman wants a man. Do you want me?"

"Zola, My God, you are the most glorious, beautiful creation I've ever seen."

He swallowed hard and came around the bed, scooped her up in his arms, laid her out on the bed, and began to plant nibbling kisses all over her body, driving her wild with tingling sensations, sensations Zola had never known before or dreamed possible. His fingers probed, caressed, and massaged. She ached, arched and at last let go of every doubt, every fear. When he finally moved on top of her, entering her, connecting their bodies, she held on, riding waves of unimagined wonder.

****

Zola snuggled against him, her hand on his bare chest, and muttered something about freckles. Reveling in the moment, he closed his eyes against the faint light of the new day in the window and ignored the smell of coffee and sausage drifting up from downstairs.

"Is it morning?" Zola asked, turning her head into his chest.

"It is. We talked about a lot of things last night, but we forgot something?"

Zola kissed his chin. "I can't imagine what. Seems to me we covered all the details and then some."

He laid a leg over her thighs, a hand going between her legs. "You had a birthday yesterday, and no one said a word."

"You gave me the most beautiful birthday gift I've ever had," she said, reaching down, urging him to give her more.

****

"You know, we should get up," she said, finally able to breathe normally again.

"Hmmm, I suppose," he said and rolled off her to his back. "First, there is the matter of your birthday. I haven't forgotten, although you did your best to distract me."

She set the covers aside. "Best birthday I've ever had, I tell you. But I'm hungry, and a girl can take only so much giving and accepting."

Leif retrieved a small enameled box from his side table and snaked his arm around her waist to stop her from leaving the bed. "A birthday gift for you."

"A gift? An actual present? Leif, oh, oh, thank you."

"Not really a gift, more of a symbol of my promise to you. I love you, Zola, only you."

Hands shaking, she held the box in the palms of her hands, her breath caught in her chest. "Leif. I love you. I never thought I would have anything so sweet—what have you done?"

"Open the box."

A leafy, dark vine winded its way around the circumference of the gold band. Tourmaline stones, in rainbow hues of rose, to pink, to deep green, glittered and winked among the vine and leaves.

"The vine is me," he said. "I'm the vine, clinging to every facet of you, holding you, growing with you. Thriving as I have never thrived before. You complete me, Zola," he said, placing the ring on the third finger of her left hand. "I was told, by Miss Paulette, to give one a tourmaline is to give them hope, and it just so happens your birthstone is tourmaline. You have hope, Zola. No matter what happens now, you and I have hope."

Below, someone knocked on the front door. "Who could that be?" Grumbling, Leif flung the covers aside.

"We should get up anyway," Zola said. "I think we've missed breakfast. I wonder who cooked. I hope not Forrest. He makes such a mess."

Leif shook his head. "I know, but this was so nice. I

don't want to get up. I can't think of one thing I have to do that would be more important than staying right here with you all day."

She kissed him, her fingers playing with his ears. "We could do it again tomorrow and tomorrow."

"Maybe we could come up here in the middle of the day?"

"Maybe," she said, quickly getting away from him, getting away from the temptation to never leave.

"Shamus Prine is here," Gunner said outside their door. "He's a bit excited about something."

"Shit," Leif said under his breath. "We'll be down in a minute," he said to the door.

****

Leif dressed first and found Gunnar and Shamus at the kitchen table with Forrest.

"I must apologize for intruding," said Shamus. "You and Mrs. Kenyon deserve some quiet and time to regroup from all your turmoil. I waited as long as I dare, but you should know David Daniels hung himself last night in his jail cell. He left a note confessing everything."

"Everything?" asked Zola from the kitchen doorway.

Shamus came to his feet. "Good morning, Mrs. Kenyon."

"Please, I'm Zola to you, and you shall be Shamus to me," she said and gave the man a brief hug. "Sheriff Daniels, you were saying—he took his own life, and he left a note?"

Leif poured Zola and himself a cup of really black coffee—Ephraim's, he suspected—adding a healthy amount of cream and sugar to the brew in each cup. He put the coffee on the table and pulled out a chair for Zola.

She thanked him and sat down. Shamus sat back down in his chair, then hesitated before saying, "He confessed everything."

All the blood drained from Zola's face, and she began to tremble. Leif pushed her coffee toward her and put his hand on her shoulder. "Everything," she said. "Mr. Emory beat my father to death, didn't he? That's what Daniels confessed."

Shamus nodded, "I'm so sorry, my dear. The three of them, Shaw, Daniels, and Emory, stole money from the depositors and invested heavily in the stock exchange. The bank is barely solvent. It will take a very long time to regain trust. Poor Mary Blashcombe, she's been made responsible for paying off her brother's debts. The silver certificates Mr. Shaw had stashed away in his satchel almost covers his debts. But Mr. Emory, he'll pay with everything he once owned. Which brings me to one of the reasons why I came out here this morning. The homestead is Emory's nearest neighbor. His livestock has been abandoned for nearly a week. His horse was being stabled in town, but the livery wouldn't keep it any longer with no payment coming, so I had him brought back out to the Emory place. It's there now. I've been made temporary manager of the bank. Would Forrest be willing to take on the chore of seeing the Emory stock fed and watered until new owners can be found?

"I'd like to offer the place up for sale first. Auctions don't see much of a profit margin. And the Emory place, I was just over there, is, well, it's opulent by Prettydale standards. Not a lot of folks around here could afford it or even need that big of a place."

"Can I?" Forrest asked Zola. "I'll go right now. Can I go start right now? I'll keep up with my schoolwork, I promise. The horse, the Tennessee walker, I'd like to take care of that horse."

Zola opened her mouth to speak, tears coursing down her pale cheeks.

"You go ahead, Forrest," Leif said for her. "We'll come over after a while, and take a look around."

"Well, I best get back to the bank. I've got a lot to do," Shamus said. "You should think about making an offer on the Emory place." He nodded to Leif. "I'll come up with a price if you're interested. We'll talk about it." He dipped his head to retrieve his hat from the back of his chair.

"Yes, we'll have a look around," Leif said as he rose to shake the man's hand. "It's not a bad idea. I have a couple of thoughts about the bank, too. Now we've got the mines, we might put it back into the community, give folks around here a bank they can count on to help them through rough times."

Zola rose from her chair, wiped her cheeks, and blew her nose with her kerchief. "Thank you for coming all the way out here to deliver the news, Shamus. It was kind of you," she said to the man. "Are the marshals still in town?"

"Oh, no, I almost forgot," Shamus said and set his hat on his head. "They hauled Mr. Shaw away this morning. Put him on the first train going north. He's headed for a federal prison to await trial. They had Daniels' confession. It matched up with Emory's confession. It doesn't look good for Shaw."

"I hate this nightmare, it never ends," she said.

Forrest grabbed his coat and hat.

"Have you eaten?" Zola asked him.

"Sure, hours and hours ago. I'm goin'. See you over

there. I'll be in the barn."

Zola braced herself on the kitchen counter, arms straight and shoulders hunched. "I've never been farther than the gate of the Emory place," she said, her gaze following Forrest across the paddock.

Leif wrapped his arms around her. "It's over. Shaw is gone, Emory is gone, Daniels is gone, and we are free of the past. We have nothing to stop us from having a happy life." He turned her around and tipped her face up to meet his gaze. "Believe me, from this day forward, we are going to have nothing but joy and peace."

She shook her head at him. "That's impossible. You can't promise me that. And I don't expect a perfect existence—that would be boring."

"Stop looking back," he said. "You couldn't have changed anything. And I, for one, am not sorry circumstances, as horrible and despicable as they were, brought me to you. Please, don't be miserable. I can't stand it. You were so happy, content this morning."

Taking his face between her hands, she planted a good strong kiss on his lips. "You are right. I'm being ungrateful. Papa would be ashamed of me. I must go forward now, grateful for the good things, grateful for you, and the joy of the good people around me. I've never had friends. Because of you, I now have good friends. And Forrest, he's becoming a good man. I think I have you to thank for that. You came along at just the right time. I'm proud of him."

Chapter Twenty-Four

Zola joined them on their ride. Gunnar raised his eyebrows but said nothing when she appeared in her cord trousers, coat, and slouch hat over her braided red hair. Leif hid his grin and turned his head away when she put her foot in the stirrup and hopped up into the saddle, swinging her leg over the horse's rump with no assistance. She led the way, crossing the bridge first.

Gunnar pulled his mount up alongside Leif. "I think you and I are in a lot of trouble."

"And why do you say that?"

"We both have hitched our wagons to very strong women. We must be very careful to never stumble or fall behind."

Leif nodded in agreement. "Wouldn't have it any other way."

First, they toured the mill site. Gunnar surprised Leif, agreeing with him on location, interested in where the railroad might lay tracks south of the mill. Zola pointed out the location of the trail that led up to the lake and the general direction of the cave. They rode along the creek to the waterfall and crossed the stream to the meadow. Turning back through the orchard, they headed over to the Emory place, tying their horses off at the barn.

Zola, quiet, finally said, "It feels like we're trespassing. I half expect Emory to come out of the house, gun cocked."

Forrest, pitching hay into stalls, stopped what he was doing. "The horses were out of water, and the stalls were full of dung. I'm almost done," he told them. "I still have to feed the chickens and collect the eggs."

"Put your pitchfork down. Let's go inside the house. Your sister needs to see the inside. It's very grand."

"It's very grand outside," she said.

"It certainly is," Gunnar said. "What, are there, four or five gables? And how many rooms?"

"I think there are four bedrooms upstairs and a full bath. And a front and back parlor, another water closet off the kitchen and a formal dining room, and a full pantry downstairs," said Leif. "I had a chance to give it a quick once over when Mr. Emory made restitution offering beds and bedding in lieu of payment for his destruction of Zola's garden."

"I found Grandma's painting," Forrest said, stabbing the fork in the wagon of hay parked immediately inside the barn.

"The painting of the windmills?" Zola asked. "Where? Is it out here in the barn? Mr. Emory bought it when he bought the other furnishings," she said to Leif. "I didn't want to sell it. I'd meant to take it down before the sale began, but I got so busy. Mr. Emory took it off the wall without asking. I'd left the room. One of the other buyers asked a question about the cook-stove in the kitchen. I left him alone. He wanted it real bad, said it was beautiful—reminded him of his roots. He offered a really big price for it. I was desperate."

"Well, he didn't think that much of it," Forrest said. "It's around here, behind the barn in an old shed. The frame is busted. He tore the canvas off."

The shed, not much more than a lean-to made up of

old fence rails and shingles, looked more like a scrap heap. Leif opened the slatted door, and Zola stepped over a coil of fence wire and moved a dented bucket aside. The picture frame lay in splinters, the old canvass drooped in a drunken fold. Leif gathered up the frame and took it outside to get a better look at it.

"I think we can repair this," he said. "The canvas is in good shape. Needs a new frame, but I can take care of that easy enough."

A yellowed and stained vellum envelope had fluttered to the dirt floor when Leif removed the frame and canvas. Zola turned the envelope over to find her name, in her father's swooping hand written across the front. *For our beloved daughter Zola Louise, twenty-one years today. October seventh, 1887. Thank you for the gifts of immense pride and abundant joy, more precious than gold.*

There were words on the back of the envelope, water stained and smeared, she had to hold the envelope toward the light to read. *Always remember: A good name is to be chosen above great riches and loving favor above silver and gold.*

Trembling, she handed Leif her find. "Mr. Emory? Papa would've uttered his special prayer in his dying breath. It's there, written in Grandmother's hand on the painting. He said it before and after every meal, at the beginning and end of every day. It's an inaccurate quote from the Bible, but Papa didn't care, his mother had given it to him, and he'd made it his own.

"The claim papers, this is where they were. This is where Mr. Emory found them. He saw the prayer on the painting—the envelope—it might have fallen out when he took the painting down from the wall. I don't know, but he knew what he had. He'd come looking for them, and with Papa's clue, he found them."

****

The homestead Savings and Loan held a grand opening on the first Monday of November, exactly one month since Zola's birthday. The owner of the bank, Pretty Pride Mines Incorporated, unanimously voted she be given the honor of christening the new bank and unveiling the brass plaque over the door. *"A good name is to be chosen above great riches and loving favor above silver and gold."*

Leif, to avoid the crowd on the boardwalk, took up a vantage point in the street. A tug on his sleeve brought his attention to the boy waving a telegram in his face. The railroad line's telegrapher, upon the new sheriff's— Oren Gooding's—recommendation, had been replaced with a more reliable, ethical operator. Now all messages arrived secure and private.

Leif fished a nickel out of his pocket and gave it to the boy. *Stop—expect invasion—stop—Christmas week—stop—Gunnar—stop*

"Who's that from?" Zola asked as she came down the bank steps and into the crowd.

"Gunnar," Leif said and handed her the telegram.

"Christmas? No, oh no. We aren't even moved in yet. I'll need to clean before we move in. I'm not going to move in on top of that awful man's dirt. I want the still off the property before the mining engineers' meeting. They'll probably be staying with us at the house. Forrest…and Forrest insists on riding the…the beast of a horse to and from school. We need to do something about that. And he wants a dog."

Leif put his arm around her shoulders. "Yeah, he

told me one of his friends had a new litter of collie pups. I told him we'd talk. I've never had a dog. I wouldn't mind a couple dogs. And Ephraim and Oren dismantled the still yesterday. I can use some of the parts at the mill. I asked them to go ahead and get a crew together, go through the house, wash windows, scrub floors, clear the cupboards and closets. They start tomorrow. By the end of the week, all we'll have to do is move our beds over. You need to decide what you want to do with the furnishings already in the house. I know some of it belongs to your family. The Abbot sisters said they'd try and sell the plates and flatware in their store. We have six weeks before Christmas. We'll be all settled in our new home way before then."

"It's so big. The house, it's huge. It's going to cost a fortune to furnish. I suppose it would be prudent to keep some of the things. They've hardly been used, after all. All those rooms, I don't know what to do with them."

"We'll fill up the rooms in no time," he said and pressed his lips to her forehead.

"It's too soon to be thinking about that," she said, her voice a whisper, glancing furtively around to see if anyone was looking their way. "We can't be sure."

"Oh, I'm sure," he said, his hand moving to her waist.

"Don't," she said, laying her hand over his. "Someone might see. I don't want to get the Abbot sisters all excited. They love sticking their noses in, you know that. They haven't stopped planning how we should decorate the big parlor. Paulette showed me the most god-awful drapery material—green with red, white and yellow cockatoos, and palm fronds…" She shuddered. "Gladys assured me the big front room could carry it off."

Shamus, smiling, moving through the crowd, stopping to shake hands, made his way toward them. "I wanted to give you these," he said and passed Leif a blue packet stuffed with documents. "These are your final closing papers on the property. I've drawn up the lease you asked for. Ephraim and Oren will have the homestead for one dollar, due October first, for the rest of their lives. The lease stays in effect for any and all heirs of the Gooding family. I notarized all the papers."

Leif extended his hand. "Thank you for seeing to all of this. You're a busy man these days."

"I'm doing things my way. I'm sleeping nights, my stomach doesn't hurt, and I catch myself smiling all the time. Scares the hell out of me. I don't recognize myself."

Laughing, Zola took his hand. "Please come out to the homestead tonight for supper. Oren is barbequing one of the hams. Gladys and Paulette are coming too."

****

In the homestead Parlor

Their dinner guests gone, Forrest in his room, Zola and Leif sat on the settee, Leif's arm around her. "I think I'm dreaming," she said, staring at the old painting hanging above the mantle. "I never knew my Grandmother Charlotte. She died on board ship when they left Holland. Papa said I looked like her. She had red hair and freckles, and she was built close to the earth like me, Papa said. But looking at her painting, I feel I know her. You made a beautiful frame for it."

"I like the stormy sky," Leif said. "I can almost smell the rain coming, hear the wind catching the sails on the mill." He paused. "Are you going to be sorry to leave the homestead—this house?"

"I thought I would be, but no, I don't think I will. I'm really happy Ephraim and Oren will have a good place of their very own. We'll share the properties, and we'll prosper together. I feel really good about that, and I think Papa and Mama would be very happy too."

"But the bigger house, is it too much for you? Can you be happy there?"

"I'm happy where you are. If we had to move into a cave, I would be happy. Well, not really, but I would do it because I know you would do your best to make me comfortable and safe. I would be lying if I told you I hate the big house. It's beautifully laid out. I'm starting to get really excited about decorating the rooms. Gladys and Paulette's enthusiasm is infectious."

"Speaking of enthusiasm," Leif said, nibbling the nape of her neck, "I have a mad desire to take you to bed and decorate your lovely tummy with kisses."

"I would not want to be the one to get in the way of your creative aspirations. So to bed, we must go," she said. "I have some aspirations of my own to explore."

"Hmmm, exploration is always encouraged," Leif said and took her hand to lead her up the stairs.

"I love you," she said at their door.

"I love you," he said and softly closed the door behind them.

A word about the author...

Born in Burlington, Iowa, the youngest of six children, all of us spaced three to four years apart, which meant that I had an older brother who was twenty when I was born. Moved with my parents, and an older sister, to Oregon when I was ten years old. Grew up in the Willamette Valley, attended a vocational school, clerk stenographer course, which was enlightening but not useful. Married high school sweetheart. Had two children.

I've worn many hats: store clerk, meat wrapper, kite factory production line, pumped gas, then I discovered water exercise because of debilitating arthritis and became an instructor. I enjoyed that for eighteen satisfying years. I still do water exercise for my own enjoyment and wellbeing but no longer instruct. I began writing my own stories about the time my husband went on swing shift. I was a big fan of the Georgian period, Georgette Heyer being my favorite author. Back then you had to type the manuscript on paper and send it off through the post. Came close to being published a couple of times. Then the years passed and I started to write Oregon historical fiction. I create characters who become my family. I'm home when I tell their stories, I laugh, I cry, I fume and fuss, I cheer for them, and I'm proud to be near them.

We've moved a lot, lived in: California, Idaho, Washington, Oregon Coast, Central Oregon, but we always return to the Willamette Valley. Every time we've moved we roam and learn the history and the past around us, including the geographical past, as well as discovering the impact of the human occupants. Those details I strive to add to my stories. I want the reader to see, smell, be immersed in the time and place, and join the community in which my characters live. I write stories I love to read.

Thank you for purchasing
this publication of The Wild Rose Press, Inc.

For questions or more information
contact us at
info@thewildrosepress.com.

The Wild Rose Press, Inc.
www.thewildrosepress.com